ICED

FELIX FRANCIS
ICED

A DICK FRANCIS NOVEL

DISCARD

CROOKED LANE

NEW YORK

Published in the United States by Crooked Lane Books, an imprint of The Quick Brown Fox & Company LLC.

Crooked Lane Books and its logo are trademarks of The Quick Brown Fox & Company LLC.

Library of Congress Catalog-in-Publication data available upon request.

ISBN (hardcover): 978-1-63910-292-1
ISBN (ebook): 978-1-63910-293-8

Cover design by Nick Castle
Cover images by Arcangel
Map design by Frederick Schröder

Printed in the United States.

www.crookedlanebooks.com

Crooked Lane Books
34 West 27th St., 10th Floor
New York, NY 10001

First US Edition: July 2022
First published in the UK in 2021 by Simon & Schuster UK

10 9 8 7 6 5 4 3 2 1

With my grateful thanks to:

The St Moritz Tobogganing Club, especially its
President, James B. Sunley, to White Turf for
their hospitality, to the various racehorse
trainers that I spoke to and who would prefer
to remain nameless (you know who you are!)

. . . and, of course, to Debbie.

In May 2019, at Ascot Racecourse, an auction was held in aid of the Carers Trust. Susi Ashcroft and Brenda Fenton both bought the right to be included as fictional characters within this book. My thanks go to them, not only for their generosity to the Carers Trust, but also to me for not complaining!

I love them both really.

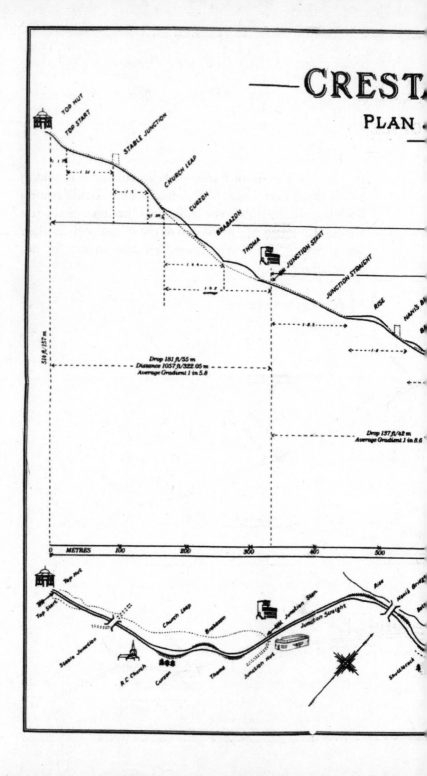

RUN —
ROFILE

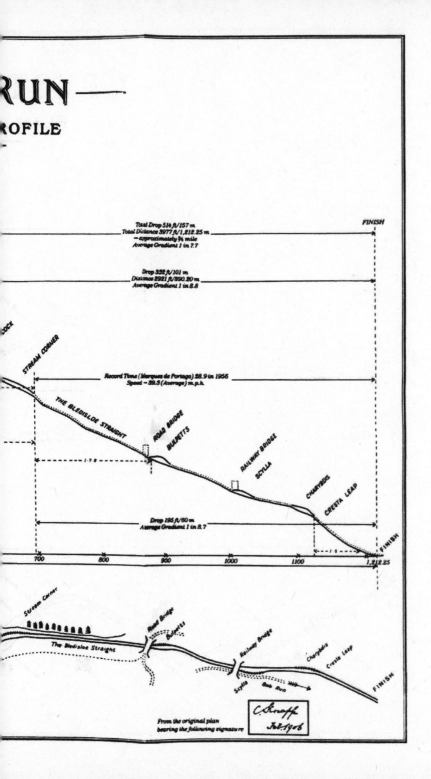

Total Drop 514 ft./157 m
Total Distance 3977 ft./1,212.25 m
— approximately ¾ mile
Average Gradient 1 in 7.7

Drop 332 ft./101 m
Distance 2921 ft./890.30 m
Average Gradient 1 in 8.8

FINISH

Record Time (Marquez de Portago) 28.9 in 1956
Speed = 89.3 (Average) m.p.h.

STREAM CORNER

THE BLEDISLOE STRAIGHT

ROAD BRIDGE
BULPETTS

RAILWAY BRIDGE
SCYLLA

CHARYBDIS

CRESTA LEAP

1 · 7 8

Drop 195 ft./60 m
Average Gradient 1 in 8.7

1 · 5

FINISH

700   800   900   1000   1100   1,212.25

Stream Corner

The Bledisloe Straight

Road Bridge
Bulpetts

Railway Bridge

Charybdis

Cresta Leap

Scylla   Bob Run

FINISH

From the original plan
bearing the following signature

C. Schaff
Feb. 1906

1

I KNOW I'M IN trouble on the run down towards Shuttle-cock, but I am laughing—I don't care.

I am once again riding in a Grand National, the first time in nearly eight years, but this isn't the four-and-a-half-mile steeplechase over the thirty fences of Aintree Racecourse. This Grand National is a different type of race altogether—a nerve-jangling, teeth-rattling, buttock-clenching, roller-coaster ride down a three-quarter-mile-long ice chute—the Cresta Run in the Swiss town of St Moritz.

As I enter Junction Straight I pull myself further forward on my toboggan. Not some sit-up-on wooden-slatted affair for the occasional snowy slopes in your local park, this toboggan is thirty-five kilograms of precision-made steel and carbon fibre, with razor-sharp runners and grab-handles to hang on by.

Moving my weight forward gives me more speed, and speed is the king. The difference between winning and losing is measured in milliseconds.

Speed. Speed. Speed.

Only speed will let you win—provided, of course you don't have too much, and crash.

All I can hear is the rushing wind and the constant clatter of the runners on the ice as I hurtle, face down, along the straight at sixty miles per hour, ever gaining that elusive speed on the steep slope. I stare ahead, searching for familiar landmarks, but my vision is blurred by the vibration. I have never been this fast before at this stage of the run.

I feel rather than see the sharp change in direction as Junction Straight runs into the right-handed Rise where the track even lifts slightly, causing the G-force to squeeze my body onto the sled.

I flash under Nani's Bridge and through the kink right at Battledore.

Next is the infamous Shuttlecock curve, where so many have fallen there is even a special club for them all, and the big question in my mind is: *Am I going too fast to make the turn?*

I slide my body back on the toboggan, allowing me some degree of steering by pressing the tail of the inside runner harder onto the ice. But do I also rake?

On my feet I wear special boots with three jagged metal spikes protruding from the toes—a bit like Rosa Klebb with her poison toe blade in *From Russia With Love*, only more so. These are my rakes—the only means I have of slowing me down.

Do I slam the points down onto the ice? Or do I take the chance that I will fly out of the track at Shuttlecock?

Unlike an Olympic bobsleigh run where the outside walls of the turns are concave, helping to keep the sleigh in the track, many of those on the Cresta are convex, which has the opposite effect. A curling stone released at the top of a bob run will make it to the bottom, but on the Cresta it will slide out at the first corner. Hence, it takes great skill to stay in, and is also deemed to be safer for the out-of-control rider, with so-called 'soft' areas of straw and loose snow provided on the outside in an attempt to reduce any injury.

I compromise.

I lower my left foot slightly to slow me a fraction and to help with the big ninety-degree left-hand turn.

As Shuttlecock begins to tighten, I can feel my legs being thrown out to the right into fresh air, so I lean my weight more to the left. I have fallen here before, in previous runs, and I am determined it will not happen again.

Not now. Not in this race.

Not in this blue riband event that I have strived so hard to be a part of.

I lean more to my left, almost further than I dare, and hang on to my toboggan for all I am worth.

And I am laughing again.

This is what is meant by living.

And the Cresta Run has helped save my life—there is no doubt about it.

*   *   *

I was born the year my father, Jim Pussett, was first crowned champion steeplechase jockey, a feat he would repeat six more times before I reached the age of twelve. And it would have been more without a dreadful leg break that kept him out of the saddle for nearly two full years.

He was my hero, and everyone else's too.

When he came back from the injury to win the title again on the last day of the jump season with a treble at Sandown, it was said that grown men cried.

I know I did.

And I cried again, four months later, when he died in a car crash on the way to ride at Newton Abbot races in south Devon.

I was with him in his brand-new, top-of-the-range silver Jaguar sports car on a wet afternoon in August when the vehicle in front of us lost control and careered to the right into the central barrier on the M5 south of Taunton. Just as in his riding, when a horse in front fell, my father took evasive action, swerving his Jaguar left, but I can only imagine that he didn't see the van on his inside. Perhaps it had been in his rear-view mirror's blind spot, or maybe the rain had reduced the visibility.

I shouted a warning from the front passenger seat but it was too late, far too late.

The collision with the van was relatively slight but it was enough to spin us round through 180 degrees so we were now facing the oncoming traffic in the slow lane—not that anything was going slowly.

I could see clearly as the fully loaded brick lorry charged straight towards me, its headlights blazing like angry eyes and with smoke belching forth from its locked-up tyres.

In the very last instant before the impact, my father spun the steering wheel so that the lorry hit broadside on the driver's door rather than directly front-on on my side.

This action by my dad probably prevented me from being killed there and then, but it almost certainly sealed his own fate.

The brick lorry tore into the aluminium side of the Jaguar, ripping through the metal with ease. There was an agonising scream from my father, cut short almost as quickly as it began, and then an awful scraping noise as what was left of the car was rolled onto its side and pushed along the road surface for what seemed like a very long way.

When all finally went quiet, I remember being quite surprised that I was not only conscious but appeared to be totally unharmed.

Nothing hurt anywhere but, even so, I was unable to move.

There were two reasons why I couldn't get out. First, the door on my side was now lying flat on the ground, and secondly, my father was sitting in my lap, the impact and gravity combined having thrown him across from the driver's seat into the passenger one.

I called out to him but there was no reply.

Even at the age of twelve, I was well acquainted with death.

My grandparents on my mother's side were sheep farmers on the North York Moors and, almost as soon as I could walk, I had been helping with the lambing each Easter holiday. The death of a newborn lamb, or a ewe giving birth, may have been a rarity, but over the years I had seen many. As my hard-hearted grandfather always said, it was an irritation but not something to cry over. He, of course, was more concerned with the erosion of his income.

And then, there had been the dogs.

Not just the sheepdogs on the farm but our own family pet dogs, plus cats, hamsters and guinea pigs—they had all come and gone with regularity. Not that I hadn't grieved over them. I had, with fervour.

However, I had reached the age of twelve without ever encountering the death of any human being that I knew, and definitely not one as close to me as my own father.

Nevertheless, I knew he was dead.

There was something strange about the angle that his head lay on my chest, and his eyes were open and unblinking.

I remained quite calm and even spoke gently to him, thanking him for taking the impact on his side and explaining to his non-hearing ears that it wouldn't be long before help came.

But it took a whole hour for the emergency services to arrive and extract us from the tangled mass of aluminium, all that remained of the Jaguar.

Two burly firemen finally removed the buckled driver's door with mechanical cutters and climbed inside. Then they lifted my father off me.

I was reluctant to let him go, and I clung to him desperately until the firemen forced him from my grasp.

That passing hour was probably the closest I had felt to my father in all my life. He had always been so busy— rising early to ride horses at morning exercise, then off to the races, before returning home, at best exhausted, at worst battered and bruised. At least six days a week, every week of the year, in the all-consuming passion to be the best, to be the champion.

Some nights he didn't come home at all and I quickly learned that hospitals were to be a major part of my young life as I was regularly deposited with friends or neighbours, so that my mother could drive dutifully to the closest A & E to where he'd been riding in order to pick up the pieces.

She had always hated watching him ride from the grandstands, and her joy at his many victories never outweighed the dread of seeing an ambulance stop next to his prostrate form on the turf. Indeed, she hadn't been to the races for years, not since the day when he'd had a terrible fall at Newbury, ending up in a local hospital with countless skull fractures and a face so swollen that she'd been unable to distinguish which one of the six patients in the ward was actually her husband.

After that, she stopped even watching him ride on the television and used to busy herself instead in the garden of our house in Lambourn, forever pruning the already overpruned rose bushes.

Maybe it was ironic that what finally robbed her of her spouse was not a steeplechase racing fall as she had always feared, but a road traffic accident from which everyone else emerged unharmed.

In spite of my protestations to the paramedics that I was absolutely fine, I was fitted with a stiff surgical collar, strapped to a scoop stretcher and airlifted by helicopter to the paediatric trauma centre at Bristol Children's Hospital.

I wanted to stay with my father but my pleas to do so fell on deaf ears—looking after the living was their priority—but it was that moment of separation that, for many years, I found most difficult to accept.

It felt as if I had abandoned him, and no amount of rational argument would convince me otherwise. Not for a long time, anyway.

CT scans, concussion tests and X-rays at the hospital told everyone else what I already knew, that I was totally uninjured. I demanded to be taken back to my father but, of course, that wasn't going to happen. Instead, I was placed in a room with a child psychologist who tried to keep me distracted with word games.

'I know my father's dead,' I said to her, refusing to play along, 'but I still want to be with him.'

Only much later, with the arrival of my tearful mother to collect me, did the enormity of the situation dawn on me—my daddy wasn't coming home, not on that day nor on any other day.

Hence my tears flowed incessantly through that night and for many nights to come.

One's heroes shouldn't die. And especially not like that.

* * *

Shuttlecock doesn't claim me, not this time.

My toboggan fishtails but I am still aboard and streaking through Stream Corner and on to the Bledisloe Straight. Now just the road bridge and the railway bridge to flash under, three slight bends and the Cresta Leap to negotiate, and then on down to the finish.

Easy-peasy.

But nothing is easy-peasy at eighty miles per hour with no proper brakes and no seatbelt.

Eighty miles per hour.

That was the speed my father had been driving at when the car in front had hit the barrier.

Suddenly, I am back there on the M5, watching the brick lorry coming inexorably towards me with its headlights blazing, the expression of terror on the driver's face still etched deep into my memory.

I shake my head.

Not now! *Not now!*

I am all too aware what is happening to me. This is the regular prelude to a debilitating panic attack when some inner voice in my head tells me that I'm not worthy to be alive when my father is dead.

'No,' I shout, 'this will not happen. This will not happen *now!*'

I begin to gasp for air, as if I am being smothered, and I can feel the palpitations starting in my chest. My palms become sweaty and I am in danger of losing my grip on the toboggan handles. I shake my head from side to side, trying to will the wicked demon back into its box.

'Not now,' I repeat, forcing myself to concentrate on the ice ahead.

I am merely a passenger as I zip under the bridges and on towards the finish.

And then, all of a sudden, I am over the line and running into the yellow foam mats that stop me careering down into the main square of Celerina, the village at the bottom of the run—and the route to the hospital where, indeed, many a failed Cresta ride has finished before now.

But I am not one of those needing emergency surgery, not today.

I lie on the mat, exhausted, still fighting for my breath.

'Hello, hello,' announces Tower loudly through the Tannoy speaker above my head. 'Miles Pussett, down in five-two point two-four seconds. That puts him in third place.'

Somehow, the announcement brings me back from the brink and the palpitations subside. My breathing begins again and life returns to normal.

But did Tower say *Hello, hello*?

That call is reserved only for a rider's personal-best time.

Fifty-two point two-four seconds *is* my personal-best time—and third in the Grand National, no less. But that was only the first run of three.

I jump up and collect my toboggan ready for the ride back up to the top to do it all again.

I laugh once more.

Bring it on.

CHAPTER

2

M Y FATHER'S DEATH understandably had a profound effect on all his friends, but especially on my mother and me, their only child.

His funeral ten days later in the Minster Church of St Michael in Lambourn was attended by all the great and the good of the racing world.

Even the royal family sent representatives.

Loudspeakers were set up to relay the service to the many hundreds gathered outside for whom there was no room in the ancient Norman structure, and the route from our house to the church was lined with men with bowed heads and women holding quietened children. TV news cameras covered the arrival of the congregation, the oak coffin and the family.

Everyone wept.

Racing itself had come to a standstill, with both the day's meetings cancelled out of respect.

My mother, however, was stoic in her loss, smiling wanly at friends and strangers alike. It was almost as if her torment and uncertainty were now over—she would no longer have to sit at home while he rode half a ton of horse-flesh at breakneck speeds over huge fences, wondering if he would be coming home tonight.

Now she knew—he wouldn't be.

I, however, felt like a fraud.

Dressed in a new white shirt and dark suit from the local Marks and Spencer children's department, I was sure everyone was staring at me with the same thoughts: *If he hadn't been in the car, his father would have survived. It's all his fault.*

I certainly believed it.

If only I hadn't insisted on going with him to Newton Abbot on that last weekend of the summer holidays, he would still be alive.

If only I hadn't badgered him to stop at the services south of Bristol so I could have an ice cream, we would have been well past the point where the car in front hit the central barrier.

If only I hadn't been in the Jaguar with him, he could have let the brick lorry hit the passenger side, and he would have walked away unharmed.

If only . . .

It was actually during his funeral service that my young mind concluded that the best tribute I could give to my father was to become him, to be the next generation of Pussett jockeys, and to be the champion, just as he had been.

* * *

My father always told people that 'Young Miles could ride before he could walk', and my earliest memories certainly involved ponies, mostly other people's, which my parents allowed to graze on the paddock behind the house for no rent in exchange for me being able to ride them.

By the time I was ten, during the school holidays and at weekends, I was regularly riding a pony at the back of the strings of racehorses as they wound their way up for exercise on the Berkshire Downs above Lambourn.

No one seemed to object, not even the team of men tending the turf gallops, but I was the son of the champion jockey so, even if they did mind, they kept quiet. And, after all, Lester Piggott was riding fully grown Thorough-breds when aged ten, and he won his first race at Haydock Park at just twelve.

Lester was obsessive about his riding, continually starv-ing his five-foot-eight-inch frame to remain thirty pounds lighter than its natural weight. And now I too became obsessive, riding whenever and wherever I could. And, when there was no pony available, I would run up onto the Downs to get myself fit, pushing myself harder and harder, even when my lungs and legs complained of the pain.

School became a huge inconvenience to my plans.

'Nothing I can learn in a classroom will be any use to me as a jockey,' I would say to my mother, pleading unsuccessfully to be allowed to skip my lessons to go rid-ing instead.

After classes, I would hang out at the racing stables next door to our house, doing all the menial tasks that no one else wanted, like scrubbing the floors or washing the tack.

Every day, I would ask our neighbour if I could ride one of his horses the following morning and, every day, he would smile and say, 'Soon, lad. When you're a little older and stronger.'

So I had spread my wings further afield and started asking other trainers in Lambourn if I could ride their horses. Even those in Upper Lambourn were not immune from my pleadings as I pedalled my way up there on my bicycle.

Just when I thought I was about to win one of them over, my mother announced, out of the blue, that she had accepted an offer from someone to buy our house and we were moving.

'Where to?' I asked with unease.

'Yorkshire,' she replied. 'To be nearer to my parents.'

How could I leave Lambourn and go to Yorkshire?

Lambourn was the centre of the universe for British steeplechasing, and all I knew of Yorkshire was my grandfather's farm in the middle of nowhere high on the moors. And sheep—lots of sheep.

I was in despair.

'I'm sure there must be some trainers there,' my mother said, so I used one of the new computers at my school to search for racing stables in Yorkshire and, sure enough, there were lots of them, especially around two towns called Malton and Middleham.

I immediately looked them up in my mother's road atlas to see if either was anywhere close to my grandparents' farm.

Middleham was much further west, close to the Yorkshire Dales National Park, but Malton was only ten miles away. So I begged my mother to look for a house in Malton.

In the end it wasn't my pleading that made the difference but access to an education for me. It felt as if, for the first time in my life, school was on my side as we moved into a rented two-up-two-down terraced house in Malton, on Princess Road.

I started at the local secondary school in October of the year I was fourteen, and instantly asked all my new classmates if any of them had a racehorse trainer in the family.

I was desperate to find a horse to ride, as the sale of the Lambourn house, together with the paddock behind it, meant that I no longer had any ponies available on which to hone my jockey skills.

It was through a school, however, that I got my break— a riding school.

One of the girls in my maths class was the daughter of the owner and she said that they had horses that needed to be exercised. 'Apart from classes, we also do pony trekking on the moors in the summer, but we have to look after the horses all year round. I'm sure my mum would welcome some extra help.'

So, after school, I pitched up in my best riding kit and was given a docile Dartmoor pony to ride around the indoor arena to assess my ability.

'Sit up straight,' shouted the girl's mother as I crouched over the pony's withers in the style of Lester Piggott.

It was as much as I could do to get the damn animal to trot, let alone canter or gallop, but at least I didn't fall off and was quickly upgraded to a full-sized horse, albeit a pensioned-off half-bred gelding aged fifteen that was as stubborn as a mule. But I didn't disgrace myself on that either and soon I found myself up on something more lively.

'OK, you'll do,' said the mother after an hour. 'Come as often as you like throughout the winter. But you'll have to work though, mucking out and cleaning. I'm not a bloody charity.'

And so started the happiest couple of years of my young life.

The girl and I became inseparable, and I even enjoyed going to school just to be with her. We rode together every day after lessons, and all the time at weekends, and I grew to adore the moors, lying on the heather with my new-found love in the summer while our mounts stood by, searching for grass among the twiggy stems.

But all the time, I made no secret of my aching desire to move on from exercising hacks and hunters to riding in races, specifically steeplechase races, and my chance came when the owner of one of the horses at livery at the riding school said he'd seen me riding, and would I like to ride his horse in a local point-to-point?

Would I? I almost tore his hand off shaking it.

But riding in a point-to-point, even in the novice riders' race, wasn't as simple as I imagined.

For a start, I had to be sixteen, and that birthday was still a few months away. Then I needed to get my doctor to complete medical forms and have my riding assessed by a qualified jockey coach. And I also had to be a member of the local hunt that was staging the racing.

It all took money, and my mother was not keen to give me any, not least because she really didn't want another member of her family riding in races over fences. She hadn't been able to watch my father and she made it absolutely clear that she wasn't going to watch me either.

So I did menial tasks all over the town, anything and everything to earn a few pounds. I washed cars or windows until my hands were red and sore. I mowed lawn after lawn, and even white-lined the local football pitch for a handful of change. I walked dogs and fed pets when their owners were away on holiday. In the spring, I may have been forced to spend my days at school but I spent my nights at my grandfather's farm helping with the lambing. All for some pocket money that went into my 'Becoming a Jockey' fund.

Fortunately the owner of the horse sponsored me with the local hunt and I was invited to ride with the hounds.

What excitement!

Jumping hedges and ditches at high speed was all I wanted to do. For me, actually chasing foxes was of secondary importance and I was secretly delighted when they got away, as they mostly did. Foxes are clearly not described as cunning for nothing.

Finally I was ready—old enough, passed medically fit and considered sufficiently competent by both the hunt and the jockey coach.

I received my Rider Qualification Certificate from the racing authorities in early January and the big day was set for a Sunday in February at Duncombe Park point-to-point races, some fifteen miles northwest of Malton.

The horse's owner agreed to collect me from home at nine o'clock in the morning but I was ready by seven. I'd hardly slept a wink, such was my nervous energy. My mother, meanwhile, refused even to get up to say goodbye.

The day was wet with gentle rain falling on already saturated ground.

'This will make the car parking interesting,' said the owner as we sped along.

'In what way?' I asked nervously.

'The racecourse at Duncombe Park is not like those you would have gone to with your father when he was riding. For a start, the course isn't there for most of the year. Moveable fences, a few rails and some flags are set up only for this one day on the parkland close to the stately home. There are no grandstands, just a few marquees and a temporary scaffolding tower for the judge, stewards and commentator to watch from. And everyone likes to park on the grass as close as possible to the beer tent, especially if it's raining.'

'How's the horse getting there?' I asked.

'A trainer friend has lent me his small horsebox. He's driving it over and also bringing one of his staff to act as our groom. I just hope they don't get stuck in the mud.'

I'd never been to a point-to-point meeting before. I knew that they were run by the local hunts and that they were for amateurs only, both riders and trainers, but I hadn't realised that they were quite so basic. But it did not dull my excitement. I was going to ride in my first race over fences and, of course, I thought I had a good chance of winning.

I had been riding the horse now for several months, helping to train him, and he was by far the fastest animal I'd ever been on, infinitely more speedy then any of the others I exercised at the riding stables. I'd also been jumping him over some schooling fences that belonged to one of the trainers in Malton.

So we were ready.

By the time we turned into Duncombe Park I was almost unable to remain seated on the passenger seat of the owner's car, such was my excitement. I felt like I was bouncing up and down already.

My race was the fifth on the card of seven but, nevertheless, we had arrived a good two hours before the first.

'I want you to walk around the course with me,' the owner said, 'so you know the way and the best line to take into each fence, and where to avoid because the ground is particularly soft.'

So we donned raincoats and wellies and set off round the track, which was laid out on the side of a hill.

'Remember, the course is not railed except at the fences and round the corners, so you must keep all red flags on your right and the white ones on your left. Then you won't go the wrong way.'

Red flags on the right, white on the left. I repeated it to myself over and over until I was sure I'd remember.

'Your race is over three miles so you'll go round the course two and a half times,' said the owner. 'You'll jump eighteen fences in all, two of them open ditches, so don't go too fast too early. It's a long climb to the finish here and if you tire your horse too soon, he'll not have the puff to make it. Just slot in behind the leaders and let them drag you round the first circuit expending as little energy as possible.'

'OK,' I said, trying to take in all he was saying.

As we began trudging up the steep hill the rain finally ceased and a watery sun came out. We stopped next to the fence on the uphill run.

'Now listen carefully. You don't jump the first two in the home straight on the last circuit so this one here is the last fence and then there's a long uphill run-in to the winning post. Be particularly careful to get yourself right.

Remember, both you and the horse will be very tired by this stage so don't ask him to stand off and give you a big jump. He won't be able to do it and he'll either put in an extra stride that you're not expecting or he'll land right on top of it. Either way you'll come crashing down.'

I hadn't thought about falling.

The owner walked on from the last fence and dug his heel into the turf. I did likewise.

'It's much softer on the inside of the run-in so try and stay out wide in a tight finish.'

I nodded. He must also think I had a chance.

'But, most importantly,' he said, smiling, 'enjoy yourself. I watched your father ride for years. A great jockey. Won plenty of money on him too. I'm very excited that his son is having his first ride in a race on my horse.'

That made two of us, then.

'I'll try not to let you down,' I said, and he smiled.

But I did.

3

'MILES PUSSETT TO the box,' announces Tower through the speakers.

The 'box' is the starting position for the Cresta Run and I drag my toboggan onto the ice with my heart rate rising in anticipation, the hairs on the back of my neck standing up as adrenalin courses through my veins.

Will I ever get used to this excitement? I hope not.

Should I try and go faster on my second run or do I take it safe and steady? Am I content to come third, or even within the top ten? Or do I want to be first?

'There's no point in racing if you don't intend to win,' my father had always said.

Four of the 21 starters have fallen in the first run, and one more has already joined that number from the early riders in the second.

You have to be in it to win it, so I plan to push hard but not so hard that I don't make it to the final run.

I hear the bell ring and the wooden barrier is lifted by the starter. Time to get going.

'Keep calm,' I tell myself. 'Keep calm. You can do this.'

Keeping calm, or rather my inability to do so, had always been my problem.

As it had been on my first race day at Duncombe Park.

*   *   *

I was almost overcome with excitement as I watched the first two races. For the second, I stood behind the rail right next to one of the fences.

I'd been close up to racing horses before, when I'd been to watch my father ride, but somehow this was different with me about to be one of those in the saddle.

I could feel the approach of the field even before I could see them, their hooves striking the turf causing the ground to tremble beneath my boots. Then they were upon me, crashing through the top few inches of birch with noise and colour against the leaden sky. How I had longed to be one of those dashing young men in their bright silks, and now I would be.

During the third, I went with the owner to the administration tent to declare our horse for the fifth race—one reserved, somewhat strangely in my view, for either novice or veteran riders.

I proudly produced my Rider Qualification Certificate and my Medical Records Book for the Declarations Clerk who was sitting at a table.

'New, are you?' he said, flicking through the pristine medical book.

'Yes,' I replied. 'This is my first ride.'

'Then take it easy at the start, lad. The ground's pretty heavy today.'

'Yes, sir,' I said.

He placed my certificate and book in a box already containing many others.

'I keep these for now.' He looked up at me and smiled. 'You get them back afterwards.'

'Thank you, sir.'

The owner did the rest of the declaration while I went to change.

The jockeys' changing room was simply a big tent with some wooden chairs placed round the edge and some slatted duckboards laid on a tarpaulin for the floor. Many of the chairs already had clothes on them so I selected an empty one in the far corner.

The riders from the third race came back into the tent, their fronts so covered in mud that it was impossible to tell that they were wearing different-coloured silks until they turned round.

'I thought I had you there, you bastard,' one of them said while slapping another rider on the back.

'In your dreams,' came the reply with a grin, his teeth shining white in a mud-splattered face.

'I'd have had both of you if that bloody nag of mine hadn't hit the second last,' said a third, pulling his filthy colours over his head. 'I'll take you next time, you mark my words.'

The first two looked at each other and laughed.

It was my first experience of changing-room banter. And I loved it. Not that it did anything to relieve my nerves, and it wasn't helped by the third rider who spotted me in the corner.

'Bugger me,' he said. 'We've got a schoolboy among us. You lost or something, lad?'

'Leave the kid alone,' said the winner sternly. He walked over towards me. 'Don't mind him. He's a prat.'

'Thanks,' I said.

'First ride?'

I nodded.

'We all started somewhere. Enjoy yourself, but keep out of the way.'

He turned away.

'But I intend to win,' I said, echoing my father.

He turned back and stared at me. 'You do that.'

I started to dress in my racing gear, my hands shaking so much that I had difficulty zipping up my borrowed body protector, to say nothing about the buttons on the front of the owner's black-and-white-checked silks. Finally, I successfully tied my stock round my neck, put rubber bands on my sleeves to stop the wind blowing them open, and picked up my riding helmet and whip.

I was ready. Time to weigh out.

The owner was waiting for me outside the changing room with the saddle I would use, a large heavy hunting affair. As was the case in the majority of point-to-point steeplechases, all the horses in my race were to carry twelve stone, that was 168 pounds. My sixteen-year-old body weighed a little over nine, so I had no need to have a light-weight postage-stamp model like my father had used. But, even with the heavy saddle, I still needed many sheets of lead slotted into a weight cloth to bring the total up to the required amount. The weight cloth would sit over the horse's withers, under the saddle.

I stood on the scale and the needle rotated round the dial and stopped.

'Miles Pussett, twelve stone,' said the Clerk of the Scales, ticking off my name on his list. He looked up at me. 'Pussett? Any relation to Jim?'

'He was my dad,' I replied.

He nodded.

'You'll do fine,' said the clerk.

For the very first time, I felt the heavy burden of expectation.

The owner took the saddle, pad, weight and number cloths from me and disappeared off to saddle the horse, while I waited nervously in the changing tent until it was time to go out to the parade ring.

Such was my nervousness that I had to rush to the toilet. Then I was nervous that I would be underweight as a result.

I waited in the changing area, pacing around with a mixture of hope and excitement, combined with a touch of fear.

'Jockeys out,' came the call at last, and I exited the tent with seven other novices or veterans. Surprisingly, it wasn't easy for me to determine which was which as some of the novices looked older than a couple of the veterans, a 'novice rider' being determined by the number of previous wins rather than his age.

I walked into the parade ring with my feet feeling that they were somehow detached from my body.

'Good luck, Miles,' called a familiar voice on my right.

I turned and there was the daughter of the owner of the riding school standing behind the rail waving at me.

I smiled at her.

Now there was an extra spring in my step. In the absence of my mother, it felt good to have someone there to support me, and especially my girlfriend.

'You look happy,' said the owner as I walked up.

'I am,' I said. 'But I'm nervous too.'

'Not a bad thing,' he said as we watched his horse being led by. 'Looks good, doesn't he?' He was beaming with pleasure.

'Yes, sir,' I said. 'Never better.'

Someone rang a bell and it was time to mount.

'Just remember,' said the owner as he tossed me up onto the horse's back, 'not too fast to begin with. Let the others lead you round the first circuit. Kick on up the hill second time round and keep away from the inside after the last.'

'Yes, sir,' I replied.

'See you in the winner's enclosure. I'm off to see the bookies.'

I instantly became even more nervous than I already was. The owner clearly did believe we would win. I just hoped he wouldn't wager too much.

The groom led the horse out onto the track and I turned him to canter down to the start.

Everything that could possibly go wrong now crowded into my brain: Would the horse run away with me? Would the saddle slip or the reins break? Would I fall off at the first fence? Would the horse put his feet into the open ditch? And, most worryingly of all, would I make a complete arse of myself?

'Stop it,' I said to myself. 'Just do what you're used to. All will be fine.'

We circled at the start as the starter's assistant tightened the girths of all the runners. And then we were ready.

My heart was pounding as the starter raised his flag.

'Walk in,' he shouted.

I looked about me at my fellow jockeys and suddenly realised with horror that I didn't have my goggles in position as they all had. I had been so focused on the coming race that I hadn't concentrated enough on the basics. And, having seen the faces of those who had ridden earlier, I knew that goggles were essential to keep the mud out of my eyes.

I raised my hands to pull the goggles up from round my neck just at the very moment the starter dropped his flag. Everything happened so fast, much faster than I was expecting, and my horse was left flat-footed as the others sped away.

How could I have been so foolish?

I had carelessly given the rest of the field a good ten lengths' start. So much for my instructions to slot in behind the leaders and let them drag me round the first circuit.

I snapped my goggles into place, kicked my mount hard and set off in pursuit.

'Calm down,' I said out loud to myself. 'This race is three miles long. There is plenty of time.'

But the urge to close the gap quickly is a hard one to resist for both horse and jockey, and we were back on the tails of the bunch by the second fence. And only then did I start to enjoy myself.

Galloping along and jumping the fences was exhilarating in the extreme and I found that I was laughing with delight. But I wasn't laughing for long.

The horse immediately ahead of me hit the top of the open ditch and stumbled on landing, sprawling nose first onto the turf in a mass of flailing legs, both equine and human, right where I was heading.

Fearing the worst, I closed my eyes—but, thankfully, my horse didn't. He landed and then immediately took off again like a show jumper, leaping clean over the prostrate forms on the ground. I just about managed to stay aboard by gripping the saddle with my knees and throwing a hand up in typical 'hailing a cab' style. But it caused me to lose even more ground on the others.

Another of the runners went down at the next fence and I swerved to my right to avoid any trouble.

By the time we passed the enclosures with one circuit still to go, the six of us standing were spread out in line astern with me back in fifth, some fifteen lengths or more behind the leader.

I decided that, in order to have any chance of winning, I needed to be much closer and kicked on down the hill, throwing caution to the wind at the downhill fence by standing off and asking my mount for a big leap. He obliged and we passed one horse while actually in the air.

'Good boy,' I shouted in his ear, and kicked him again.

We passed the third-placed horse at the base of the final climb and came close to being second but, with just the last fence left to jump, the fuel tank was suddenly empty. Just as the owner had predicted, if we went too fast too soon, we would run out of puff—and we had.

The horse jumped the fence almost at the walk, coming to a complete standstill on landing, and it was as much as I could do to get him moving again up the hill and over the finish line. It was not so much his exhaustion that was the problem, more like mine. But those behind us were in no better shape, having already pulled up. The heavy going had taken its toll.

So we finished third. In truth, it was a bad third. Third—and last.

The groom met me at the gate and led the horse into the unsaddling enclosure where the owner was waiting for us. I was worried he'd be cross and that any chance of me riding for him again would have evaporated.

'Well done, lad,' he said with a wan smile. 'At least you got round.'

I slid down off the horse's back and was so drained that, try as I might, I couldn't undo the girths. The rules clearly state that all jockeys must remove their own saddles. Only in the case of accidents, illness or other exceptional circumstances were they allowed help to do so.

I wondered if being totally exhausted was considered an exceptional circumstance.

The owner could see the problem and stepped forward, undoing the girth buckles with ease. I felt like a fool as I dragged the heavy hunting saddle from the horse's back, almost sitting straight down on the mud due to my jelly-like legs.

'Don't forget to weigh in,' said the owner. 'Then get changed. I'll wait for you in the car.'

I couldn't judge if he was angry with me or just wanted to get out of the rain that had now returned with a vengeance.

I staggered into the weighing tent with the saddle and sat on the scales. Any concerns I might have had that I'd be underweight were unfounded as the needle rotated round to twelve stone, one pound. The extra was probably due to the mud I'd accumulated on the front of my clothes.

'Fine,' said the clerk. I was within the allowable limit.

I went into the changing tent and sat down heavily on a chair, almost too tired even to feel depressed by my inadequate performance. I had thought that I was quite fit but there was clearly work to be done in that department.

I cleaned the mud off me as best I could in the wash area, dressed, collected my rider's certificate and medical book from the Declarations Clerk, and then carried my kit and the saddle out to the owner's car. At last some strength was returning to my legs.

'I'm so sorry,' I said miserably into the silence on the journey home.

'What for?'

'For making such a mess of it,' I said.

'Don't worry. Everyone has to learn somehow, and third's not too bad for your first ever race. At least you didn't fall off.'

'But you thought I'd win.'

'I did hope you might,' said the owner, 'but I didn't really expect it.'

'Did you lose an awful lot of money?'

'Not at all,' he said. 'In fact, I made some. I backed you each-way at long odds and the place money more than covered my win loss.' He tapped his jacket pocket and smiled at me. 'And you'll win on him next time out.'

'Next time?' I said.

'I think we should enter him at Charm Park in three weeks' time. Don't you?'

4

Shuttlecock doesn't get me on the second run either, but I do pay a price for being a little over-cautious.

'Miles Pussett down in five-three point one-six seconds,' announces Tower.

No 'Hello, hello' call on this occasion because my time is almost a whole second slower than my first attempt, but I'm still in the Grand National, albeit having dropped to fifth place overall.

I drag my toboggan off the ice and carry it over to the vehicle that will take me back to the top. It is called the *camion*, Swiss-German for truck.

Fifth will do for the moment, although any chance of overtaking the leading runners is slim. But, somehow, I don't care too much.

There had been a time in my life when being only fifth in anything would have sent me into a deeply depressive state, but seven years and many hundreds of hours of psychotherapy later, I have changed my outlook on life.

Now, simply being alive is like winning, and I take great joy from that alone. And I have the Cresta Run to thank for making it so.

* * *

Charm Park, near Scarborough, was a very different point-to-point compared to Duncombe. This course was on the level throughout, and turned left-handed rather than right. And a spell of relatively fine weather, plus some well-draining ground, had made the conditions underfoot hugely different as well.

Again, the owner and I arrived well before the first race to walk the course, a wide grass strip left untouched round the perimeter of a large rectangular ploughed field.

'Nineteen fences this time and a relatively short run-in after the last,' the owner said. 'Watch out for the sharp turns at the corners. It's all too easy to run wide and lose ground.'

I nodded. It felt completely different this time. Sure, I was still excited, but I was also more measured, and more determined.

'And don't be afraid of making all the running. The ground today is quite firm compared to Duncombe Park and I know our boy stays on well in these conditions. If he's good enough, he'll win from the front and you can run the finish out of the rest of them. Just don't get carried away and go too fast too soon like you did last time.'

'OK,' I said, rather shamefaced. This time I'd be ready.

For three weeks, I had been working not only on the fitness of the horse, but also on my own.

When not at school or riding, I had been running up onto the moors or working out in a makeshift gym—our over-the-road neighbour's garage fitted out with a pull-up bar and a set of dumb-bells. I had even neglected my girl-friend, and not least because I had heard her sniggering with some other friends about my debacle at Duncombe.

I had also been over and over the happenings of that first race in my head, analysing where, when and why things had gone wrong. As a result, I was far more aware of my surroundings on this occasion, and resolved that I

would be one step ahead of events rather than simply react-
ing to them.

So, when I walked out of the changing tent to the
parade ring, I had an air of self-assurance and a real belief
that we would win.

And we did.

When the starter dropped his flag, I was ready with
everything in place, including my goggles. I jumped off in
the middle of the pack of ten runners but I took the lead
going to the third and never looked back. I jumped the
remaining sixteen fences alone, did not run wide at the
corners, and won by ten lengths easing up.

My first winner.

How exciting was that?

The owner was all smiles when I returned to the
unsaddling enclosure.

'Splendid,' he said, clapping his hands together and
then patting me on the leg. 'Absolutely splendid.'

I slid off the horse, unbuckled the girths without any
problem, and went to weigh in.

'Well done,' said one of the other jockeys in the changing tent. He was the one who'd come to my aid at Duncombe. 'You said then that you intended to win, and now
you have. See you around.'

He put out his hand and I shook it.

'Yeah,' I replied. 'You will.'

And he did see me around because the owner ran the
horse three more times before the end of the point-to-point
season and we won them all.

My girlfriend wasn't sniggering now.

*   *   *

'Miles Pussett to the box.'

I carry my toboggan into position for my final run of
the Cresta Grand National.

It is do or die time, although dying is not actually on my agenda for today. Not any more.

The bell rings and the barrier is lifted. Time to go.

Just like in a point-to-point steeplechase, a good start is needed. My spiked shoes grip the ice as I run forward, pushing my sled ahead with my right hand. At the very last moment, just when it feels like the sled is about to go without me, I dive onto its surface and we are away.

The top section is where the run is at its steepest and I am soon hurtling along. Over Church Leap where the ice seems to fall away beneath me, such is the acute angle of the gradient, and then the rapid left-right-left of Curzon, Brabazon and Thoma, and on to Junction Straight where I shift my weight forward for more speed.

I flash past the St Moritz Tobogganing clubhouse with the massed spectators on the terrace a mere blur in my peripheral vision.

Next is Rise and Battledore, then the mighty Shuttlecock.

Do I rake?

Is it better to be careful and finish among the also-rans or to take a chance and go for glory? It is the same question that steeplechase jockeys have to ask themselves when in contention on a tired horse coming to the last fence. And the best of them would always say the latter.

Ruby Walsh was twelve times Irish Champion Jockey and won more races at the Cheltenham Festival than any other rider. He is one of the greatest, if not the very best ever, to ride in steeplechases. Yet he also had more falls at the last fence than anyone else. For him, it was much more acceptable to go crashing down while trying to win than end up safely being second—and to hell with the consequences, and the injuries.

It is that 'win at all costs' attitude that makes the great great.

I decide to go for glory over safety and keep my rakes up through Rise. I shift my weight back and left, ready for Shuttlecock, and I almost make the turn—but not quite. Not this time.

I rise up the outer wall and lean further to my left, but I have a fraction too much speed and suddenly, as the bend tightens, I am gone, somersaulting over and over into the straw and snow, and then painfully into the big red crash mats, all the while trying to keep out of the way of my heavy, tumbling toboggan. It is always the toboggan that does the most damage and it can kill you if it hits you in the head or neck.

I lie on the ground for a moment, slightly winded by the impact, assessing whether I have any serious injury, other than that to my pride.

Nothing appears to hurt much so I jump up and wave my arms vigorously above my head towards the control tower situated on the top of the clubhouse—the recognised signal that medical assistance is not required.

'Pussett is up,' Tower intones dryly over the Tannoy. 'And apparently unharmed.'

Damn it!

But I suppose I am lucky. There is a life-size montage of X-rays in the club bar showing the mass of metalwork that has been inserted into all parts of the human anatomy as a result of breaks sustained in falls on the Cresta. It is shown to all potential riders just before they are required to sign a liability disclaimer stating that they understand the risks and will not hold the club responsible for any injuries, or worse.

The Cresta Run was first created in the winter of 1884–5 by guests at the nearby Kulm Hotel, who formed an 'outdoor amusements committee'. Since then five men have lost their lives riding its ice, albeit far fewer than jockey fatalities in steeplechases over the same period.

Thankfully, the use of full-face crash helmets, protective joint pads and the introduction of back protectors similar to those used in horseracing mean that serious injuries are rare. Far more common are minor cuts and bruises, with the occasional lost finger after it has become lodged between the toboggan runners and the ice. As they say in the club bar, 'It can usually be sewn back on but it won't be any good again for picking your nose.'

It is often stated that the St Moritz Tobogganing Club is the last true bastion of amateurism in modern international sport and this, together with its members' *c'est la vie* attitude to mortal danger, is what attracted me to it in the first place—plus the adrenalin rush, of course.

*   *   *

After that heady spring of my seventeenth year, with four point-to-point winners on my CV, I was quickly invited to ride work for one of the Malton licensed trainers.

It was not yet the full jockey title I craved for, but it was a huge step in the right direction.

'We'll get on with the application for your amateur permit,' the trainer said. 'Then we'll see.'

And so, after six months of riding out and working in the stable yard, I was entered for my first ride in a race under the official Rules of Racing, a two-and-a-half-mile hurdle contest on a Saturday afternoon at Catterick. A race exclusively for amateur riders.

I tried to think of it as just another race, following on from my point-to-points, but there was one major difference that changed everything.

This particular contest was a handicap, so the horses had to carry differing weights, dependent on their official rating—the higher a horse was rated, the more it carried. Theoretically, handicaps should give every horse an equal chance of winning, although it never results in a mass dead heat as some run better than their rating and others worse. And, irrespective of their rating, all of the horses in the race were to carry less than the twelve stone of a point-to-pointer.

My horse was not particularly well rated and hence was handicapped to carry just ten stone three pounds but, as a novice rider with no wins to my credit, I received an additional seven-pound allowance, which meant my horse would actually carry only nine-stone-ten, or 136 pounds.

A week before my race, I stood on the bathroom scales at home and was horrified to see the dial rotate round to nine and a half stone. Much to my chagrin, I was growing taller every day, and all the work I was still doing in our neighbour's garage to improve my stamina had clearly also bulked up my muscles.

That left just three pounds for all my clothes, boots, saddle, saddle-pad, girths and stirrup irons. It was not enough.

For the first time, but certainly not the last, I wasted—the jockey's term for quickly losing weight.

I borrowed a plastic sweatsuit from one of the stable staff and, wearing two sets of woollen long johns plus two long-sleeved thermal vests underneath, I went for a stiff run up onto the moor every morning before school for that whole week. In addition, and much to my mother's annoyance, I refused most of the food put before me on the kitchen table each evening.

Gradually the weight came off and, by the morning of the race, I was just nine-stone-three, stripped. That now left a seven-pound leeway for everything else that must be weighed. I could cope with that if I used my father's old lightweight saddle. But not eating enough food didn't do much for my energy levels and left me feeling listless and tired. So much so that, when I went to Catterick races on the day with the trainer in his car, it was as much as I could do not to fall asleep during the journey.

It was my very first battle against weight in a war that I would have to wage relentlessly for the next five years.

At least I didn't disgrace myself in the race, finishing a close fourth behind the winning favourite, and the trainer seemed quite pleased with my performance. So much so that he entered me for another hurdle race at Newcastle the following month.

My career as a jump jockey was finally under way. Now all I had to do was become the champion.

5

'H ARD LUCK. YOU nearly made it round Shuttlecock. I really thought you might win the whole thing.'

I am back in the Cresta clubhouse bar after my fall, socialising with some of the other club members prior to us going for the traditional post-Grand National lunch and prize-giving on the terrace of the Kulm Hotel.

In spite of my helmet, the snow and ice had been forced up into my face during my fall and I have a split lip. But I've had worse, much worse, on a racetrack.

'Maybe next year,' I say.

It's been a long time since I was prepared to think of anything far beyond my next meal, let alone a whole year away.

* * *

At Newcastle, I had my first racing fall when my mount tripped over the third flight of hurdles and went down nose first onto the turf, taking me with him.

I rubbed the bruise on my left shoulder and felt like a proper jump jockey.

'Never mind,' said the trainer. 'You're both fine so we'll try again soon. In the meantime, you can help with teaching the novices to jump.'

It was another small but significant step on my career ladder.

'I want to leave school,' I said to my mother that night. 'What good are A levels to a jockey? I'm old enough to leave, and I want to concentrate on my riding.'

'Over my dead body,' she replied. 'You need an education to get a proper job.'

'Being a jockey *is* a proper job,' I retorted.

It was the full extent of our usual conversation, often repeated, mostly at maximum volume.

And, in the end, I did leave school over her dead body.

Life for my mother had not been easy in the years since the death of my father. He had made a very good living as a jockey but his extravagant lifestyle and his penchant for expensive fast cars, together with his long injury lay-off and some speculative hotel investments that had gone wrong, had all made a huge hole in the family finances.

After he died, my mother discovered that he had also taken out a second mortgage on their house and there was precious little equity remaining for her after its sale. So she had left all her friends behind in Lambourn to move somewhere cheaper, as well as to be nearer to her parents and her elder brother, who was slowly taking over the running of the family farm from his father.

Soon after we moved, Mum had found work as an ingredients mixer in a local food factory, making ready-meals for the super-markets. In spite of her long hours, it didn't pay well enough for us to afford the basics, let alone any luxuries. The rent on the house was our main expense and gradually, and unbeknown to me, at the time, she was falling into arrears with our landlord.

Some nights, I would lie in bed and hear her sobbing, the thin wall between our bedrooms doing little to dampen her cries. But, in my seventeen-year-old foolishness, I would not go and comfort her. I simply and irrationally concluded that, if she hadn't been so stubborn about me leaving school to become a professional jockey, I'd have been able to help.

So it was all her own fault.

Perhaps she was good at hiding the depth of her unhappiness or, maybe, as a teenage boy far more interested in horses than in people, I just didn't see the disaster that was looming.

One Friday I came home, excited, as always, that school was over for another week. I let myself into the house using my front-door key. Mum worked until seven most nights but she tried to finish a little earlier on Fridays. Then, she would always bring home two ready-meals from the factory for us to 'taste'. I didn't ask if this was official company policy or if she had simply purloined them by hiding them in her voluminous handbag. I expect the latter, as they were usually missing the outer printed sleeve that would have told me what they actually contained. But that would have spoiled the 'guess the ingredients' game my mother always insisted we played.

This particular Friday, however, I was surprised to see her overcoat already hanging on the hook near the front door. And it was only four o'clock.

I called out to her but there was no reply.

How strange, I thought. Surely she hadn't gone to work without her coat. Not in February. It was near freezing outside and she had to walk the half-mile to and from the factory.

I called her again, but still no reply.

I shrugged my shoulders and went up to my bedroom to change out of my school uniform into my working clothes, before going to help with evening stables at the yard.

As I climbed the stairs, I noticed that the light was on in my mother's bedroom.

That was strange too. She was most meticulous at always turning off everything electrical when it was not needed, to save money. She even switched the TV off at the mains, claiming that stand-by mode was simply a conspiracy by the power companies to increase their profits.

I'd left for school at seven, well before it was light, making a detour, as always, to the racing stables to watch the first lot going out. Even if I couldn't actually ride on a school day, I still wanted to be involved.

Mum usually left home at seven forty-five, ready for her eight o'clock shift at the factory. She must have left the light on by mistake.

I went into her room to turn it off.

She lay on her bed, face down, still wearing her dressing gown as I had seen her that morning. But nothing else was the same, and never would be again.

I called out to her without any response.

Her left arm was stretched out over the side of the bed with her hand resting, palm down, on the bedside table. I reached down to touch it, still thinking I could wake her. Only when I found that her hand was cold and her arm so stiff that, when I lifted it, her whole body moved as well, did I realise she was dead.

I jumped back and cried out.

I panicked, not able, or wanting, to grasp the magnitude of what was happening. I ran down the stairs, turning round and round in the hallway, not sure what to do or which way to go.

Eventually, I ran out of the house.

'Help!' I shouted at the top of my voice. 'Somebody please help me.'

The man from over the road, the one who let me use his garage as a gym, came to my aid, rushing outside as I stood in the centre of the street waving my arms about.

After that, the rest of the day was something of a blur.

An ambulance was called, then the police and a doctor, and finally, much later, a blacked-out van belonging to the undertaker, to collect the body. My uncle arrived with the police and tried hard to take me with him back to the farm where my grandparents were waiting. But I refused to go while my mother was still in the house and, short of actually carrying me out, he had no choice but to wait.

Two burly men in sober dark suits finally took my mother away in what I can only describe as a tied-up canvas sheet with bamboo stays and multiple grab handles down each side, the stairs having been too narrow and too steep to use a conventional stretcher.

I stood by the front door as they carried her out, feet first, to their van.

My mother and I had not always seen eye to eye, especially over my chosen career, but I had loved her nonetheless, and she me. But I found it difficult to weep, or even feel anything at all. It was as if all my emotions had been numbed.

And now, just seven months short of becoming a legal adult, I was an orphan.

So where did I go? Into a children's home?

In the short term, I went to live with my uncle and grandparents at the family farm, a place full of grief, shock and silence.

The question that we all wanted to know the answer to, but were afraid to ask, was: How did my mother die?

Was it a heart attack? Or a stroke? Or maybe a pulmonary embolism or an aneurism? No. It was none of those. Toxicology tests would eventually show conclusively that the culprit had been an overdose of sleeping pills.

Mum had killed herself. On purpose. She had left no parting note, but suicide was the only logical conclusion.

It transpired that she had been to her doctor the previous week to complain that she was having difficulty getting to sleep. He had recommended she take one 15mg

Temazepam tablet each evening, half an hour before going to bed, and had prescribed a four-week course.

From the results of the tests, and the empty pill packets found next to the bed, it would seem that she had taken all twenty-eight at once, on the morning of the day she died. And to be certain of the outcome, she had washed them down with half a bottle of cheap white wine and three vodka miniatures.

Temazepam and alcohol—a truly deadly combination.

Now the question everyone was asking, including me, was: Why?

This had clearly not been a cry for help, in the hope and belief of being found in time, and surviving. That many tablets, plus the booze on top, and at a time when she knew I would be at school for hours to come, could only have produced one outcome.

My mother was nothing if not determined.

But she had also been determined that I should not become a steeplechase jockey, and I had defied her.

Did that make me responsible for her death? Was I to blame, once again, for the death of a parent? Had I effectively killed them both?

That last question was one that was to haunt me for years.

* * *

Lunch on the terrace of the Kulm Hotel is a major highlight of Grand National Day on the Cresta. It is a time for fun, food and plenty of drink, plus a hefty dose of good-natured competitive banter between friends and rivals, at least those that have survived the ice once more, and are not laid-up in hospital.

Today the weather is clear, crisp and cold, with the sun shining brightly from an azure-blue sky. The vista is magnificent. St Moritz is surrounded on all sides by the snow-capped sharp peaks of the Swiss Alps, and laid out to the south of the town centre is the lake, fully frozen over now but a centre for sailing and water sports in the summer.

So thick becomes the ice on the lake throughout the winter that a full-blown racecourse is laid out on it, where on three successive Sundays in February, horses gallop at a race meeting known as White Turf.

The final Sunday of the three is tomorrow.

I stand on the hotel terrace in the sunshine, sipping on a Diet Coke and staring out over the race preparations taking place on the lake.

I feel a hand rest on my shoulder.

'Bet you wish you were riding there tomorrow,' says a fellow member of the club, another Brit and someone who, having owned horses himself in the past, is well aware of my horse-racing background.

I shake my head. 'I gave up all that malarkey long ago.'

'But you'll surely be going to watch?'

I shake my head again. 'I've left that life behind me now. It's time to move on.'

I might wish to be done with horseracing, but I am soon to discover that horseracing isn't done with me. Not by a long chalk.

CHAPTER

6

I FINALLY BECAME A professional jockey two months before my eighteenth birthday. To be precise, I was granted a conditional licence, a trainee, employed by and under the supervision of a local racehorse trainer.

I left school at the end of the term after my mother died, having successfully convinced my grandparents that any further study was a waste of precious riding time. In truth, it had been an easy task. Both my grandparents had left school at fifteen to work on their respective parents' farms, and they were both of the opinion that they had done well enough without any qualifications, so why shouldn't I?

Only much later in life would I realise that they were wrong and my mother had been right all along. But such is the determination of the young to get on with their lives that sensible planning for the future doesn't really enter their consciousness. At least, it didn't for me. I was just impatient to start riding as a professional—that was all the planning I thought I needed.

And I was going to be the champion, right?

Over the next few months I completed my pre-licence skills assessment, including a mandatory two-week residential course at the British Racing School in Newmarket. While there, I passed my medical and fitness tests as well as being instructed on such matters as technical ability, tactical awareness, financial acumen, lifestyle expectations and dealing with the media, combined with studies of nutrition and health, both mine and that of the horse.

So now I was ready to start work as a conditional jockey.

The move from being a schoolboy to a full-time employee was quite a shock to my system, especially with the early starts—first lot went out at 5.30 AM in the heat of the summer, which meant I had to leave the farm on my bike before 4.30.

In addition to riding I was now also tasked with looking after three or four of the horses in the yard—grooming, mucking out, feeding and watering—as well as cleaning the tack and the stable yard in general. Every night, my back would ache from the carrying of heavy bedding bales and muck sacks.

It felt like slavery.

But there were compensations.

Riding the horses each day at exercise was my passion, all the more so as I developed a strong bond of mutual affection with them. And, if going to the races was like the icing on my birthday cake, actually riding in one was the candles.

There were far more races reserved for conditional jockeys than for amateurs, plus a conditional was permitted to ride in any race other than those specifically restricted to amateurs. Point-to-points, therefore, were now off limits, much to the disappointment of the owner who had given me my first opportunities between the flags.

'I'll just have to back you riding on a proper racecourse,' he said with a smile when I told him.

And his first opportunity to bet on me as a professional came in a two-mile-five-furlong handicap steeplechase for conditional riders at Cartmel Racecourse at the end of August.

Cartmel is one of the smaller racecourses in Britain, being only a fraction over a mile-long circuit, but it boasts the longest run-in from the last fence to the finish line, almost twice that of the Grand National, and it attracts huge crowds to its nine summer race days, with a funfair in the centre of the track, and everyone in holiday mode.

I arrived early with my trainer and we walked the course together.

'Remember, it's a very short loop so this race is two and a half times around,' he said seriously. 'So don't think you're finishing a circuit too soon. I've seen that often done before here.'

'But the finish chute is cut across the centre,' I replied. 'Isn't it taped off until the right time?'

'It is, but I've still seen several jockeys think they're about to finish when they find the tape is still in place and there's another complete circuit to go.' He laughed. 'Even Dick Francis did it here once in a three-mile chase.'

We walked every inch of the half-mile run-in and planned our strategy.

'I think you have a fair chance,' said the trainer. 'He's pretty well handicapped in this company and he likes firm going.' He tried to dig his heel into the turf but barely made a mark. 'Maybe not as firm as this, though. Don't they water?'

It had been an exceptionally dry summer, especially in the usually rain-soaked Lake District just a few miles down the road, and there was talk of water shortages and hosepipe bans.

'Keep up with the leaders,' he said. 'This is a very sharp track and it's notoriously difficult to come back if you get too far behind. Make sure you are close-up at the last and don't push too hard on the run-in until you make the last turn. Some will go too soon and you'll catch them if you're clever.'

I nodded and took myself off to change.

I revelled in being in the jockeys' room as a professional, noting that my name in the race card was down as 'M. Pussett' without the 'Mr' in front, as in my amateur days.

A few of the older jocks came over to wish me luck.

'Rode often against your dad when I was younger,' one of them said. 'Nice enough chap, but a total effing bastard on a horse.' He laughed and I took it as a compliment.

Some of my fellow conditionals, however, were not as generous.

'Just keep out of my bloody way, Pussett,' one said with a scowl, spraying me in the face with spittle as he pronounced the P.

'Don't expect any favours just because of who your dad was,' said another in an unfriendly tone.

I didn't expect favours. But I also didn't expect it to be so raw with them.

Where was that legendary camaraderie of the jockeys' changing room I'd heard about, where a shared danger brought even fierce competitors close together in mutual respect? Not here, clearly. We were all young bucks trying to make our start in the cut-throat world of an ultra-competitive sport, to establish ourselves as the next Tony McCoy or Ruby Walsh, or maybe the next Jim Pussett, and there was clear resentment that my rivals thought I had a head start with the name.

And they were no more magnanimous when the time came to leave the changing room to go out to the parade ring to mount.

Someone tried to trip me as I walked out of the weighing-room door.

Maybe it was an accident . . . or maybe not. Either way, I stumbled and nearly had a fall before I'd even reached my horse. But it taught me an important lesson in racing—ask for no quarter and, what's more, don't give one.

The contest itself was mostly uneventful.

I didn't win, not because I did anything wrong, but simply because one of the other horses was too fast. I finished second, two lengths away, and the owner and trainer seemed happy enough. However, there was one incident going down the back-stretch for the second time that sticks in my memory.

I was riding close to the rail, trying to take the shortest route. As instructed, I was up with the leading pair that were running side by side about a length in front. The first fence on the back is the water jump, followed by three plain fences close together. As I approached the first of these I heard a call from a jockey behind.

'Give me some bloody room,' he shouted.

I glanced over my shoulder and saw that it was the one who had spat in my face, and he was trying to come up on my inside.

No chance, I thought.

If anything, I moved even tighter to the rail. If he wanted to pass me, he'd have to do it round my outside.

There was an anguished cry along with a string of expletives as he had to take a pull, and this unbalanced his horse such that it hit the top of the fence and went down onto the turf, nose first.

I smiled. Served him right.

I, too, could be a total effing bastard on a horse.

* * *

Grand National lunch at the Kulm Hotel is always a noisy affair and today is no exception.

Competitors, family, friends, fellow club members and all forms of assorted other hangers-on sit at long, jam-packed tables on the terrace, drinking beer or wine, telling and retelling tales of past exploits on the ice, all at full volume.

Some of their stories are even true.

Trophies are awarded to the winners and then there is the annual Grand National Firework, when those who have fallen in the race, myself included, are required to stand together and mime in the manner of an exploding firework. There is also a real one fired up and over the lake to a great height before it explodes with a huge boom that echoes around the valley, followed by cheers and applause from the revellers.

It is this uncomplicated fellowship and brotherhood of the Cresta family that I find so attractive after the aggressive cut and thrust of professional sport.

The lunch finally breaks up and, while some move into the Sunny Bar to continue drinking, I decide it is time to make my excuses and leave. Plus, the prices in the hotel bars are beyond my meagre budget anyway.

Riding the Cresta may be an amateur activity but that doesn't mean it's cheap.

For the past five winters I have come to St Moritz in mid-January and remained for as long as I can afford, riding the ice as many times as possible. One year, I ended up in hospital on my second day with a broken collarbone after an excursion off the track at Shuttlecock, but I stayed on anyway and, with the aid of some adhesive strapping, I was back on the ice just three weeks later.

Unlike in horseracing, there is no need for a doctor to pass you medically fit to ride the Cresta. You simply have to self-certify that, in your own opinion, you are well enough. So I had.

I walk up from the terrace, through the hotel lobby, towards the front door.

'Good God, Miles, you're a face from the past,' calls a female voice to my left.

I turn to find a pretty petite woman with shoulder-length blonde hair standing at reception. Susi Ashcroft, racehorse owner, lover of dance and the arts, socialite and doyen of London's charity set. One of the ladies who lunch.

'Hi, Susi,' I reply. 'What brings you here?'

'I'm just checking in. I have a runner in the big race tomorrow.'

'What? At White Turf? On the ice?'

She nods. 'Jerry thinks we have a chance of winning.'

Jerry would be Jerry Dickinson, racehorse trainer from Lambourn, for whom I was once contracted as a stable jockey, often riding Susi's horses. In my experience, Jerry always told his owners that their horses had a chance of winning, he just didn't tell them how big that chance was. After all, if you buy a lottery ticket, your odds against winning are forty-five million to one. Statistically, you are nearly five times more likely to be struck by lightning, and three times more likely to have identical quadruplets. But, technically, you do still have *a chance*. And people do win, even if everyone else is then so jealous that they hate them.

'Is Jerry over here too?' I ask.

'Sure is.'

'And Sabrina?' I ask. Sabrina is Jerry's wife.

'No. Jerry's come on his own. Sabrina's at home, holding the fort.'

Of course she is, but I'm still disappointed. Sabrina had been my Good Samaritan, who stopped to help while everyone else passed me by on the other side. Without her numerous interventions when I was at my lowest, I would have surely emulated my mother and killed myself.

'Jerry has two runners in the race,' Susi says. 'I just hope the other one doesn't beat us.' There is a touch of desperation in her tone, as if she thinks that that is quite likely.

'Maybe they'll dead heat,' I say tactfully. 'Then they can both win.'

She laughs. 'I don't really expect to win the race, although it would be nice. I just don't want to be beaten by Brenda.'

'Brenda?'

'Brenda Fenton. Spends a fortune on horses. Jerry's other runner is hers.'

'Is she staying here too?' I ask, looking around.

'No, thank God. She's at the Badrutt's Palace down the road. She thinks it's grander and more in keeping with her own perceived status.' Susi raises her eyes to the high, ornate ceiling. 'The Badrutt's *is* more expensive but, from the pictures online, I don't think it's so nice. Silly woman.'

There is clearly not much love lost between the two.

'And Jerry? Where's he staying?'

She seems surprised that I should ask. 'I've no idea. Somewhere cheap if I know Jerry.'

Somewhere cheap is where I am staying, too. On my first visit I'd discovered a quiet bed-and-breakfast *Gasthaus* in a back street on the edge of town, where a room cost far less for a whole week than for just one night at the Kulm or the Badrutt's Palace.

'Look,' she says excitedly. 'We've all been invited to a drinks party this evening put on by the White Turf sponsors for the international visitors. Why don't you come along?'

I laugh. 'I don't think so.'

'Oh, do come. My husband, Michael, was meant to be here with me but he's decided to attend a military history convention instead. You can come with me as my date.' She laughs. 'That will get the tongues wagging. There'll also be a few others there from England, people who know you.'

That's what I'm worried about. For the past six years or so I have been trying to keep a low profile and that's how I would like it to continue. It is better that way for my mental health.

'I have other plans,' I say. I don't, but she wouldn't know that.

'Then cancel them. You must come. In fact, I insist on it.'

I remember now that Susi always did do a lot of insisting.

'Where is it?' I ask, and immediately regret having done so.

'Next door at the Country Club. I'll meet you here in the hotel lobby at six o'clock. We'll go together.'

Before I have a chance to object, she skips off towards the open lift, giving me a big smile and a wave as the doors close.

Damn it!

Going to a drinks party with a load of former racing acquaintances is not high on my list of fun ideas for a Saturday evening. In fact, it's at the bottom.

But, after what Susi said, I *am* quite intrigued to meet Brenda Fenton.

I decide that I'll pop along for just long enough to do that—without realising it will change my life for ever.

CHAPTER

7

M Y FIRST MONTHS as a professional steeplechase
jockey could be described as steady rather than
spectacular.

I followed up my second place at Cartmel with another
runner-up slot in a hurdle race at Wetherby, and then one
more over the Scottish border at Kelso.

I was eager to go one better, and my chance came in
early November when I was engaged by another Malton
trainer to ride the favourite in a conditional jockeys' three-
mile chase at Hexham, after his own trainee was injured in
a fall on the gallops the day before the race.

I knew he'd only asked me because of who my
father had been. Thirty years before they had been
young jockeys together and he was doing the son of an
old friend a favour.

Once again, I felt the heavy hand of expectation on my
shoulders. It tightened the muscles in my back and neck,
and I woke early on the morning of the race with a headache, which persisted throughout the day in spite of me
taking painkillers with my meagre breakfast of just one
small banana.

Managing my weight was becoming a real problem.

However little I ate, the reading on the bathroom scales remained stubbornly fixed at nine-stone-three. And I was frustrated that I still seemed to be getting taller, even though all the websites I visited stated that boys should have stopped growing by the age of seventeen.

The lightest weight that can be given to a horse in a jump race in Great Britain is ten stone: that's 63.5 kilograms. However, as a conditional jockey, I received a weight allowance to compensate for my inexperience. The allowance could be as much as ten pounds, depending on the race, which meant I might be required to ride at nine-stone-four, just one pound above my actual body weight, and that had to include my clothes and boots, and, of course, the saddle, the girths and the stirrup irons, even if most of those are now made of carbon fibre instead of actual iron.

So far I had got away with it, as the horses I had ridden had not been given the lowest possible weight, but that was now all about to change at Hexham. Thankfully, my allowance for this particular race was only seven pounds, but that still meant I had to weigh out at nine-stone-seven.

Apart from the banana for breakfast, I'd had nothing to eat since the moment I'd been offered the ride. It was crazy. I was starving myself to do the weight when I absolutely needed to eat something to give me enough energy to ride. Between completing my duties at the stables and leaving for the races with the trainer, I went for a run in the plastic sweatsuit to try and shift a pound or two of fluid, and I wasn't sure if I'd made the weight until I actually stood on the scales in front of the official.

'Pussett. Nine stone, seven pounds,' said the clerk, making a note in his ledger.

'Thank you, sir,' I replied with a sigh of relief. I gave my featherweight saddle to the trainer who had been watching, and then went back into the changing room to wait.

What I needed, I reckoned, were what were known as 'cheating boots'—paper-thin footwear worn by some jockeys to weigh out but then changed for a more substantial pair for the race itself.

It was strictly against the rules, mind.

One had to wear and use exactly what was weighed, or face disqualification. But I'd heard of one senior jockey who'd once weighed out without his saddle in order to make a particularly light weight. He'd told the clerk it was under the number cloth, but it wasn't. I wondered if that was why they changed the rules so that the number cloth is no longer weighed.

Then there were stories of jockeys, in the old 'sit down on the scales' days, who would leave one foot on the floor. Hence the new 'stand on a four-inch-high platform' scales, which made that impossible.

As it was, I was wearing nothing at all under my thin nylon britches and coloured silks, other than the mandatory back protector for which there was a weight allowance. Not even socks, underpants or a stock collar round my neck. I put them on now and hoped that the clerk of the scales wouldn't notice. Then I ate a high-calorie nutrition bar and drank a glass of water, trusting that I wouldn't weigh too much as a consequence when the race was over.

Jockeys have always had battles with weight, and it is far worse for the flat-racing apprentices. The minimum riding weight for them could be down as low as seven-stone-seven—the same as for a flyweight boxer—and they are trying to control something weighing half a ton—ten times as much as the jockey.

Half a ton of inbred, unhinged and manic muscle, tendon and bone, trained to perfection to run at its limit, with inefficient steering, worse brakes, and a mind of its own that is often not in sync with that of the flyweight on its back, who may just be hanging on for dear life.

But how I loved it.

*   *   *

Hexham justifiably claims to be the most scenic race-course in Britain, with spectacular vistas from the enclosures across the course towards the already snow-covered Pennine Hills, the backbone of England.

For my part, I was too nervous to take in the view, instead sitting quietly in the changing room contemplating the task ahead.

Finally the call came. 'Jockeys out.'

The nutrition bar had given me a burst of energy and I positively skipped down the weighing-room steps to join the owner and trainer in the parade ring.

'Good luck,' said the owner, to whom I touched the peak of my cap in the manner I had seen more experienced jockeys do. He was a kind-looking man in a tweed suit, brown brogues and a trilby, and I could tell he was also very nervous. 'Please win,' he said to me earnestly. 'I think the handicapper has been very generous to us in this race.'

So does everyone else, I thought. That's why we were the favourite.

I wondered how much he had staked on his horse to win. He had the hangdog look of someone who was in far too deep for his own health, and had clearly wagered the shirt off his back.

More weighty expectation on my shoulders.

The trainer was more composed and also more specific with his instructions. 'Remember what I told you when we walked the course earlier,' he said. 'From that severe dip at the end of the back straight, there's a really stiff climb up to the last fence and then it's fairly flat to the line, so don't make the mistake of starting your finishing run too soon. I've seen lots of others do that here and run out of gas by the time they get to the last. Also, take it relatively easy at the start to conserve energy for later, but without allowing yourself to get too far back from the leaders.'

It sounded so simple.

'And, most importantly,' he went on, 'don't take the wrong course.'

'No, sir,' I said.

Hexham Racecourse is unique in British racing for having a completely separate piece of track for the last fence and run-in, running parallel with, but some distance outside and above, the main steeplechase circuit. It could easily catch out the unwary jockey.

As one of the highest racecourses in the country, Hexham is also famous for the strong winds that blow straight off the moors, and this day was no exception.

In spite of it being only early November, the icy blast cut through my thin silks like a sharp knife. So I was grateful to finally be given a leg-up onto a warm horse before I began to shiver uncontrollably.

There were nine runners in the race. We circled round at the three-mile start having our girths tightened, and then we were off.

As instructed, I settled in behind the others, but no one was keen to make the early running as we had all clearly been given the same instructions. It was almost funny as we popped over the first plain fence at only a canter. My horse didn't like it and he was struggling against the bridle, wasting precious energy, both his and mine.

In the average steeplechase, it is generally accepted that an extra pound in weight carried equates to approximately a length worse in performance over the whole race. So, if two horses of exactly equal ability race, with one carrying one pound more, the one carrying less will win by one length; two pounds, two lengths, and so on. But it is not an exact science, with the weight advantage having more of an effect over longer distances, and in heavier ground.

In this race, over the more-than-average distance of three miles, the weight-to-length advantage I had over the other runners should be more, but not if we just cantered along for the first half a mile or so, making the race effectively shorter.

Hence, I decided to push on, even if it meant taking the lead, and not least because the second fence in this three-mile chase was an open ditch, and I would need greater momentum to cross it. I just hoped that the trainer, watching from the grandstand, wouldn't believe I had simply disregarded his instructions for no good reason.

By the third, I was three or four lengths in front and making a good pace without over-draining my mount. One of the finer things about Hexham Racecourse are the copper beech hedges that form the wings to every fence. These, together with a sensible shaping of the birch, make the fences so inviting to jump, and my horse was clearly enjoying himself.

He was, without doubt, the best horse I had ever ridden and, when I got things slightly wrong coming to the water jump, he simply took control and ignored my plan to have him put in an extra stride, instead clearing the obstacle in a mighty leap that took us even further away from our pursuers.

Going down the back straight for the second time I let him take a breather, and two of the others came up alongside. One even headed us by a neck but I continued to hug the inside rail, meaning they had to go farther round the outside to get past me.

However, immediately after the dip, one of the two went for home, sprinting away and jumping the second-last obstacle with a lead of two or three lengths.

I sat and waited patiently, just as the trainer had instructed, coasting up the hill to the final jump before asking my mount for his supreme effort.

I did not take the wrong course, nor did my horse run out of gas.

I was still four lengths behind at the last fence. The other challengers had fallen back and I could see that the one horse ahead of me was wavering from side to side with exhaustion. Might I still win?

Handicap horse races are just not fair.

The poor animal in front was carrying twenty pounds more than mine, and surging so fast up that hill with all that extra weight had sapped his energy and drained his spirit. The jockey was doing his best but it was not enough.

Just yards short of the finish line, I swept past him as if he was going backwards, to snatch the victory.

The crowd cheered the favourite home, and I was applauded back to the unsaddling enclosure to be met by a beaming owner who hadn't, after all, lost his shirt.

'Champion,' he said. 'Champion.' He repeated it over and over again, the huge relief obvious in his demeanour. He slapped me on the back as I removed the saddle. 'But bloody hell, boy, you nearly gave me a heart attack. I really thought you'd left it too late.'

I didn't enlighten him that I'd thought the same.

'What part of "take it easy from the start" didn't you understand?' asked the trainer seriously. Then he smiled. 'But you did the right thing to make the running. Well done, lad, well ridden. Congratulations on your first winner as a professional jockey.'

My first winner as a professional jockey. Just how good did that sound?

A few journalists from the northern newspapers were on hand and they were eager to ask me questions or get a quote as I walked towards the weighing room. In fact,

I had quite a scrum chasing me, each of them pushing a mini tape recorder towards my face.

'Did you mean to leave your run so late?' one asked.

'Did you learn that technique from your dad?' shouted another.

'It's in his genes,' quipped a third. 'Chip off the old block.'

I suddenly longed so much that the old block himself had been there to see it. I pushed past the throng to weigh in and change, hoping they hadn't spotted the tears welling in my eyes.

8

S USI ASHCROFT IS already waiting for me in the lobby
of the Kulm Hotel when I arrive wearing the smartest
clothes I can muster—no suit, but I do have a blazer and
a tie.

It is Saturday evening and all the town hostelries are
doing good après-ski business with customers still in bright
multi-coloured padded jackets, ski boots and woolly hats,
spilling out across the pavements.

How I wish I could stay with them rather than going
to this party. But I was brought up by my mother to be
polite, especially to a woman, and I decided I couldn't just
not turn up and leave Susi waiting for me forlornly on her
own.

'Ah, there you are, Miles. Where have you been?'

'You said to meet you here at six,' I reply in my best
pained voice.

'Did I? But the party starts at six. The concierge said
he can't find your room number. Claims he's never heard
of you.'

'That's because I'm not staying here.'

'Why on earth not? Surely you're not with Brenda at
Badrutt's Palace?'

'Not there either. I'm staying down in the town.' I decide not to give too many details. Susi doesn't do budgets.

'Well, you're here now. Come on, let's go.'

Susi picks up her coat from a chair, a knee-length white fur coat with black specks, and I hold it for her as she puts it on over her little black dress and bright diamond necklace.

'Nice coat.'

'Thank you.' She smiles. 'It's lynx. Thank goodness Switzerland is one place you can still wear real fur and not get shouted at. I'd never wear this at home, not these days.'

I cynically wonder if the fur and the diamonds are all about trying to outdo Brenda.

We go out of the lobby and the hotel courtesy car is there, waiting with the driver holding open the door for Susi.

'But it's only next door,' I say. 'A hundred yards at most.'

'I'm not walking anywhere in these heels. Get in.'

The driver seems unperturbed that his journey is so short and within a few seconds we are drawing up at the entrance to the Country Club, where there is a line of people outside waiting to go in, some of whom I recognise from racing and a few from the tobogganing club who have obviously been invited, including the man I had spoken with earlier on the Kulm Hotel terrace.

'There's Brenda,' Susi says with irritation. 'Talking to Jerry.'

I look over to where my former employer is standing in line chatting with a lady and a couple of young men as they wait to go in.

Brenda is obviously playing the same game as Susi. She has on a full-length fur coat that reaches almost to the ground.

'Is that a mink she's wearing?' I ask.

'Probably sable, knowing her.'

'Is that better than mink?' I am not very *au fait* with the niceties of fur coats. I'm not even sure I know what type of animal a sable is.

'It's the most expensive fur of them all,' Susi says, clearly not liking to be upstaged. 'Brenda loves her clothes. She used to be an artist illustrating fashion in those old-fashioned newspaper adverts.'

'Is there a Mr Fenton?'

'There used to be, years ago. Made an absolute fortune from property and owning most of London's casinos and bingo halls. Brenda is his merry widow and she's now spending it. Those young men she's with are her twin grandsons. They're a right dodgy pair too, I can tell you.'

The driver gets out and opens the door for Susi.

'Not yet,' she snaps at him. 'Wait for them to go in first.'

So we sit in the car for a few minutes more, until the line has diminished and all is clear.

Finally, Susi says it's OK and we climb out.

The party is taking place on the first floor of a traditional Swiss ice pavilion that dates from 1905, from when the winter-sport business was in its infancy.

Hanging from the ceiling are old bobsleds and toboggans, and the walls are adorned with scores of framed photographs chronicling the history of the place.

And what a history.

The pavilion overlooks a natural ice rink where, in both 1928 and 1948, the opening ceremonies of two separate Winter Olympic Games took place, and on which many of the gold medals were won and lost.

But tonight, all the action is inside.

The regular restaurant tables have been moved aside and the space is occupied by a hundred and fifty or so guests, mostly sipping champagne and nibbling on canapés, although I choose a sparkling water from the offered tray.

Jerry Dickinson is one of the first to notice my arrival, and he makes a beeline straight across the room towards me. He has put on a few pounds since I last saw him and he has to squeeze his increased bulk through the throng.

'Bloody hell, Miles!' he exclaims when he finally makes it. 'What the fuck are you doing here?'

It is a typical Jerry welcome.

I haven't seen him for almost seven years—and we didn't part on the best of terms. Hence, I am not quite sure how he feels towards me now.

'Like everyone else, I'm here for the champagne,' I reply, even though I'm not actually drinking it.

'I mean in St Moritz,' he says with slight irritation.

'I spend several weeks here every winter.'

I instantly regret telling him that.

'Doing what?' he asks in astonishment.

'Oh, various things,' I say. 'It's good for my health.'

There is something that stops me telling him that I am here to ride the ice of the Cresta Run. My life is totally different now and, somehow, I want to keep it secret from those who still inhabit my former one.

He clearly thinks I'm crazy, which is not far from the truth. Last time he saw me I *was* crazy—undeniably certifiable.

*   *   *

It had been Jerry Dickinson who had enticed me to leave Malton and go back south, to return to my childhood home of Lambourn, in the year in which I turned twenty-one.

That winner at Hexham in early November, while not exactly kick-starting my career as a professional jockey, certainly gave it a boost and I was soon being offered rides by other trainers, as well as riding more of those sent to post by my actual employer.

By Christmas I had more than three dozen races under my belt, and I'd won five of them. When the jump season finished in late April, I'd ridden 13 winners from nearly a hundred rides and I was beginning to make a bit of a name for myself among the local racegoers, so much so that I was becoming recognised around the town.

'Ey up, lad!' said the man who ran the newsagents when I popped in to buy a copy of the *Racing Post* that mentioned me in an article. 'You're a reet good 'un, you are. Made some brass on yer last Wednesday at Wetherby, so 'ave that on me.'

I smiled at him. 'Thanks.'

And my flag continued to fly high as the new season progressed through the summer and autumn such that I was being offered more and more rides. But all of them were at the northern tracks and mostly for other Malton trainers.

I needed to extend my field further than that if I was to become a champion jockey, and it was a ride I was offered at Cheltenham the following spring that gave me the perfect opportunity to attract the attention of the trainers in the south.

Named in honour of the most successful jump trainer of all time, who saddled more than four thousand winners in a career that saw him become leading trainer of the year on no fewer than fifteen occasions, the Martin Pipe Conditional Jockeys' Handicap Hurdle was the very last of the twenty-eight races of the annual Cheltenham steeplechasing festival.

Held at 5.30 PM on the fourth and final day, when some of the seventy thousand spectators were already making their way out to the car parks in a futile attempt to avoid the inevitable traffic jams, it was the highlight of the meeting for me.

I was engaged to ride the same horse that I had won on at Wetherby just after Christmas and the fact that we had both made the journey all the way to Gloucestershire from North Yorkshire had not gone unnoticed by those remaining to watch. Hence, and in spite of going up in the weights due to that win, we were the second favourite in the betting.

The maximum permitted number of twenty-four runners lined up at the two-and-a-half-mile start in the gathering gloom of a cloudy late afternoon in mid-March. Some of the crowd may have already departed but most had remained—the grandstands were packed, and there was scarcely any available standing space on the members' lawn.

'This is it,' I said to myself. 'Your chance to shine in front of those that matter.'

The horse's owner and trainer had stood together in the parade ring, both of them hopping from foot to foot with nerves. Having a fancied runner at the Cheltenham Festival was a far cry from a midweek race at a sparsely populated northern track in December, and this was a big deal for them too.

Both the horse and I were all set to go when the starter dropped his flag, and we were away at a good pace as we ran towards the first of nine flights of hurdles.

I had come first to Cheltenham as a babe in arms at a time when my mother was still attending race meetings. Almost as soon as I could walk, I had accompanied my father round the course on his many visits, and I knew every blade of grass. So, in spite of this being my first ride here, it felt like home, and I was relaxed and comfortable as the field negotiated the initial loop and the first three flights of hurdles up to and past the packed enclosures for the first time.

By the time we reached the end of the back straight, I knew we were going to win. As we passed the highest point of the course and swung left-handed down the hill, I had what in racing parlance is known as a 'double handful', the true origin of which is as obscure as the saying itself. Suffice to say that it meant that my horse was going exceptionally well, full of running and still on a tight rein, while those around me were beginning to labour.

I kicked on hard down the slope and we flew the second last, gaining lengths in the air over our rivals.

We jumped the last hurdle well clear of the field and, although my horse began to tie up slightly with tiredness on the climb to the finish line, he won easily by six lengths.

I remember standing tall in the stirrups and saluting the crowd as they cheered our success. Looking back, I believe that that particular moment was the happiest I have ever been, either before or since.

* * *

'Can I introduce Brenda Fenton?' Jerry says, bringing me back from my daydreaming. 'Brenda, this is Miles Pussett.'

Brenda is flanked on either side by her attentive grandsons, who I take to be in their early twenties—identical. I dutifully shake her hand and decide that she must be in her eighties, but age has been kind to her. She's also wearing large diamond earrings and I wonder somewhat unkindly if, rather than to compete with Susi Ashcroft, they are there to distract the eye from an aging face.

'Pussett?' she says in a no-nonsense tone. 'Are you related to that jockey?'

Jerry laughs. 'He is that jockey.'

'No, he's not,' Brenda says, turning to him, unamused. 'The Pussett I know of is dead. I'm eighty-nine, you know. I go back a long way.'

'Ah, you mean Jim Pussett,' I say. 'He was my father. But I was a jockey too.'

'So, what do you do now?' Brenda asks, almost accusingly.

'Oh, this and that. I run a holiday business.'

She looks at me quizzically but I don't elaborate, so she quickly loses interest in me and goes in search of more riveting conversation elsewhere.

My 'holiday business' is actually renting out deck chairs on one of the beaches of the Isle of Wight. I also have a sideline selling windbreaks and the wooden mallets needed to bash their poles into the sand. It may not be glamorous and, in truth, it's not particularly lucrative, but it does keep me busy and provides just enough income during the few busy summer months to allow me to spend some of the winter ones in St Moritz.

It is also relatively stress-free and that helps to keep me sane.

OK, so I've met Brenda, Susi is happily talking to others, and Jerry is chatting to the former racehorse owner who is also a fellow member of the tobogganing club. It's time for me to go. I can't think why I agreed to come in the first place.

But escape is not that easy.

Word is spreading that I'm here and, as Susi had said, there are a few from England at the party—people that I once knew quite well, and some who know me rather too well, even now.

'So, Pussett, how are you keeping?' asks one of those, coming up to me as I'm trying to make my way to the exit.

David Maitland-Butler is another racehorse trainer for whom I rode a couple of times, and one of those who had been fully aware of my problems as things went amiss in my head.

The Honourable Colonel David Maitland-Butler, OBE, to give him his full title, son of a lord and ex-commanding officer of the Coldstream Guards, who only became a racehorse trainer in his late forties, after retirement from the army.

'Fine, thank you, Colonel.'

'Are you fully recovered from your mental troubles?' he asks bluntly.

'Much improved, thank you.'

I try hard not to show any emotion in my voice. I might have once worn my heart on my sleeve but nowadays I keep a tight control on my feelings.

I have learned that it is usually easier that way.

And I am not sure that one is ever 'fully recovered' when it comes to mental illness. You just have to live the best you can—from day to day and week to week—clinging on to reality by your fingernails, not letting go even for a split second, or else your life will collapse around you like a house of cards.

'Do you have a runner here tomorrow?' I ask, changing the subject.

'I certainly do. In the big race. And I'm not here just for the view. I intend to take home the trophy.'

No one could ever accuse Colonel Maitland-Butler of lacking confidence in his own ability. Not that anyone would, especially to his face. At least, not without receiving some abuse in return. He has a well-deserved reputation for being a bit of a bully towards his staff, his owners and their horses, treating them all as if they were raw recruits to his regiment. But it seems to work. He has twice recently been leading jump trainer in the UK and his yard is always overflowing with equine talent. Maybe his owners don't mind being bullied or perhaps they are prepared to put up with it to win.

'How is it,' I ask him, 'that both you and Jerry Dickinson, known mostly for jump racing, have horses running here on the flat?'

'Primarily because of the time of year. The majority of those flat horses running at home on the all-weather in February are aged two or three, but the race here is for horses four and over. Many are older than that. Mine's a five-year-old gelding. It's good experience for a young hurdler who can no longer run in bumpers.'

I remember that *bumper* is the nickname for a National Hunt flat race, run under jumping rules for young horses who are yet to graduate to racing over hurdles. The term stems from the early days when only amateurs could ride in them and they were thought to bump along in the saddle in a rather ungainly manner.

The Colonel laughs. 'Plus, of course, we receive generous help with our expenses from the organisers. In the end, it's all to do with money, and the purse is also much bigger here than for a novice hurdle at Fontwell.'

He drifts away to speak to someone else while I make for the exit. But Jerry is having none of that. He intercepts me as I sidle towards the door.

'Come on,' he says, taking me by the arm. 'There's plenty more people wanting to speak to you.'

Short of physically fighting him off, I have no choice.

Once upon a time, and mostly because of who my father had been, I had some minor celebrity status in racing, and Jerry is doing his best to resurrect it, telling everyone what a great jockey I was.

His memory must be failing.

Over the next half-hour, he brings a stream of people over to be introduced to me, some I know vaguely and some I've never seen in my life before. One of those is the boss of White Turf's main sponsor, a Swiss luxury watch company. This is his party.

'So, are you looking forward to the races tomorrow?' he asks.

What do I say? I have absolutely no intention of being at the races, yet here I am this evening, availing myself of his hospitality.

'Of course.'

'Good. Then you must come and have a drink with us in our chalet next to the track. No, better still, come and have lunch.' He turns to the young woman standing by his side. 'Elena, tell Claude we have another guest for tomorrow's lunch. Mr Pussett, here.'

'Yes, sir,' replies Elena, making a note on a clipboard.

I force a smile. 'Thank you.'

Oh God! Why did I come?

And my torment goes on, with everyone else getting tipsy from the free-flowing champagne, while I stick religiously to my sparkling water.

I haven't had a drink containing alcohol in more than six years.

I don't make a big thing of it. I just don't drink any more. Maybe my life would have been so much better if I'd never started.

And it was my move back to Lambourn that began it all.

CHAPTER

9

Tʜᴀᴛ ᴡɪɴ ᴀᴛ the Cheltenham Festival in March had a far-reaching effect on my career, and my life.

Rather than just being merely mentioned in *Racing Post* articles, I was now featured in one as an up-and-coming young rider and, of course, I was compared to my father. That in itself was not a bad thing, as I had started this journey with the hope and expectation that I would become him, as his memorial. Indeed, I welcomed the comparison. At least, I did to start with.

I was suddenly being offered more rides by both northern and southern trainers. By the close of my second season at the end of April, I'd had far more than enough winners to have my seven-pound allowance reduced to five, something that made my life a whole lot easier on the starvation front, for a while anyway.

Not that jump racing stops for long.

A short six days after the season finale at Sandown Park, the whole thing starts again and then runs on throughout the year, pausing only briefly for ten days or so in the height of summer, when the ground is often rock hard. However, the major jump races don't return to the calendar until October or November.

But there is barely any let-up for the conditional jockey, who continues to work as a stable hand even when racing takes its holiday. And it was on such a day in early June when my employer came along to the box where I was mucking out and brusquely told me to drop everything and follow him immediately into the stable office.

I wondered what I'd done wrong.

Jerry Dickinson was waiting for us in the office and it wasn't me that my employer was angry with, but him.

'Mr Dickinson here wants you to go and work for him, but I've already told him you don't want to. You're happy working for me, but he insists he won't leave until he's heard it directly from you.' He stared at me as if demanding I agree with him.

I knew Jerry Dickinson by his reputation, and also by his results.

He was one of the leading Lambourn jump trainers. Then in his early-fifties, he had recently launched a campaign to attract many fresh owners to the sport, all of them prepared to invest their considerable wealth in horses for him to train. The opportunities for me were obvious.

He was the younger son of a Birmingham-based former bookmaker. He had ridden a few times as an amateur jockey before becoming too tall and too heavy. So he had then turned to training racehorses instead, near Daventry, and had quickly proved himself a winner. On the retirement of one of the sport's legendary names, he had taken over a major training yard in Lambourn and was forging success on success, including victory in the current year's Cheltenham Gold Cup.

Which jockey wouldn't want to work for him?

'I've been following your career so far,' he said, turning and looking down at me, 'and I like what I see. I'm offering you the opportunity to come and work in the best stable in the country. You may not get the chance again. So what do you say?'

What *did* I say?

My existing employer had been very good to me, taking me on as an untried and untested teenager, and providing me with good coaching and plenty of rides. And he clearly didn't want me to go.

What price did I put on loyalty?

'Thank you, Mr Dickinson. I am very flattered but I can't make such a big decision just like that,' I said diplomatically. 'I need time to talk to my employer and also to my grandparents.'

I thought for a moment that Jerry was going to say that I had to decide right there and then, but he smiled. 'Of course. I'll give you a week. In the meantime, I'll send you the details of what I'm offering. Do you have an agent?'

'No, he doesn't,' said my current boss curtly. Conditional jockeys were not allowed to have agents without the express written permission of their employer, and mine hadn't given his. Not that I'd asked him for it.

But perhaps I needed one now.

In the end, I went south eight months later with the blessing of all concerned, moving into shared digs just down the road from where I had once lived as a child.

I found the whole experience rather a wrench for a number of reasons, not least because Lambourn seemed to me to be far more of a racing pressure cooker than Malton—but maybe that was simply because Jerry Dickinson's set-up was much bigger than I was used to, and he was much more demanding from all his staff, me included.

He had offered me a very attractive package to move but he clearly wanted his money's worth. And I was happy to give it, starting early and finishing late, with precious little time off in between. However, I was now being treated far more like a jockey-cum-assistant trainer than a groom, and I no longer had to muck out or carry bales of bedding. Instead, I spent more afternoons at the races than not, either riding or assisting in the preparation of the mounts for his other stable jockeys.

With almost a hundred and fifty horses in his yard, and with perhaps up to a dozen of them running on a single day, sometimes at three or four different racecourses at the same time, the logistics for simply getting the right horse, ridden by the properly declared jockey, weighing the stipulated amount and wearing the appropriate owner's colours, to the correct starting gate at the appointed time were unbelievable. Never mind about race entries, declarations, vets' inspections, farriers' visits and the transport that was also required, to say nothing of the training of the horses in the first place.

Horseracing was big business, and no mistake.

Hence I very quickly learned how to do everything, from leading a horse around the parade ring, to properly tacking-up for the race, to giving instructions to the jockey, even to representing the trainer in a stewards' enquiry. The only thing I couldn't do was drive the stable's horseboxes to the races—I hadn't passed my normal driving test, let alone the one needed to drive a horsebox. But I could ride in the races themselves, and I did, with increasing frequency.

By my first Christmas back in Lambourn I had ridden enough winners to have my weight allowance reduced to three pounds and I was lying third in the Conditional Jockeys' Championship.

But I was lonely.

When I first arrived, I had moved in with two other conditional jockeys, who were sharing a rented three-bedroomed house, and neither of my older housemates took kindly to me as the young newcomer, especially as I was riding more often and with more winners than they were. And they made it abundantly clear that they didn't like the fact that my father had been a champion jockey. For some reason they believed it gave me an added advantage, with better horses to ride, something they perceived as being unfair on them, and they were damned well going to make me pay.

Hence they tended to socialise just the two of them, purposely shutting me out—not that I had much time to socialise anyway. I was always so tired at the end of the day that I mostly went straight to bed. But my lack of any life away from my work was beginning to have an adverse effect on my happiness.

I wasn't even able to go home to my grandparents' farm for Christmas as I was riding at Kempton on Boxing Day and North Yorkshire was simply too far away.

Each evening, I would walk back to the house I shared, dreading what so-called prank or unkindness the other two had come up with this time. They never seemed to tire of their nasty little games, and the more angry I became with them, the more they seemed to enjoy it.

The route to the house from the stables took me past the local convenience store and I would normally pop in to buy myself a low-calorie microwavable curry to have for supper. One day, a few days before Christmas, I also picked up a six-pack of beers, to drown my sorrows.

If there was one point when I could say my life began to unravel, it would be that moment.

I went straight home, shut myself in my bedroom, and drank three of the cans straight off, even before I switched on the microwave. By the end of the evening, I'd drunk all six.

Did it make me feel any better?

Fleetingly.

The next night, I bought six more.

*   *   *

'More champagne, sir?'

I look at the waiter holding a bottle of Moët.

'No, thank you. I'm on sparkling water.' He isn't to know that I'm now drinking my bubbles from a champagne flute. Better that way. Less obvious. Not that I'm really self-conscious about it, just that it takes the inevitable explaining out of the situation.

It seems easier at home in England—you just say you're driving.

Jerry comes back over towards me and this time he has Susi in tow, and he is holding his phone.

'We need to ask you a little favour,' he says.

Uh-oh.

'Can you help us out tomorrow?' Susi asks, diving straight in. 'Jerry's man has just called to say he's in the local hospital. He's slipped over on the ice and fractured his ankle.'

'I'm not riding,' I say adamantly. 'I haven't got a licence any more.'

Jerry laughs. 'No, not that. You couldn't do the weight, anyway.'

He laughs again and I wonder if he's having a go at me. But, in truth, I have put on a bit since my riding days. A higher body-weight is good for the Cresta. Another of its attractions.

'No, I need someone to saddle Susi's runner while I do Brenda's.'

'Can't you saddle them both?' I ask. I knew it was not unusual for a trainer to saddle more than one horse in a race, sometimes three or four.

'I could at a pinch, I suppose, but I can hardly lead both of them from the stables and into the parade ring at the same time. I only brought one groom with me and he's now useless. It's all I could spare from the yard at home. I was going to lead the other one myself anyway.'

Typical Jerry. Always doing things on the cheap.

'Surely there's someone else you could ask,' I say in desperation. This is really *not* on my agenda.

He looks over my shoulder into the room as if looking for someone else, then his eyes fix again onto mine. 'Come on, Miles. I taught you how to do it years ago. Piece of cake for the likes of you. You'll enjoy yourself.'

No, I would not.

'Please,' wails Susi, taking my free hand in hers. 'I'll be so much happier knowing that it's you looking after my baby, rather than someone I don't know.'

I sigh. Why *did* I come here? I knew it was a mistake.

'Oh, all right,' I hear myself saying.

Am I stupid, or something?

'Great.' Jerry slaps me on the back. 'Would you also like to give them a pipe-opener first thing? Just a couple of gentle turns round the track to stretch their legs.'

'I told you I wasn't riding.'

'But you don't need a jockey's licence for that.'

'I thought you said I was too heavy.'

'Not for a little gentle exercise. You'll do well. What do you say?'

It has been ages since I've sat on a horse.

I hesitate.

'I'd do it myself,' Jerry says, 'but I *am* too heavy. And too damn old. Bloody nuisance Herbie injuring himself or he'd have done it. He's been riding them out all week.'

'Can't you get the jockeys to do it—those riding for you in the race later?'

'I'll have to if you won't.'

And he'd have to pay them extra, I thought. And that won't please him.

I hesitate some more. Can it do any harm?

It's not that I'm particularly worried about falling off and getting injured. Hurtling head-first down the Cresta Run is far more dangerous than cantering a horse for a gentle pipe-opener round a racetrack, even one built on a frozen lake. Perhaps I am more worried about making

a complete fool of myself. But why? It's what I used to do
best, and one surely doesn't forget. Just like riding a bike.

'I have no gear.'

Am I fishing for excuses?

Jerry laughs once more. 'Don't worry about that. You
can use Herbie's helmet and back protector, and we have
an exercise saddle. Wear whatever else you like. No one
from the BHA will be watching.'

The British Horseracing Authority have strict regula-
tions concerning what exercise riders must and must not
wear, at least in Great Britain.

'What time?'

I can't believe I'm asking that.

'It gets light about seven-thirty but it's bloody cold so
wrap up. Should only take an hour at most.'

Jerry is getting excited by the prospect. Am I?

'Do I get a fee?'

'Fuck off.'

10

'Pussett. Ten stone, four pounds. That's one pound overweight.' The Clerk of the Scales made a note in his ledger and then looked up at me.

I was at Kempton on Boxing Day, riding in the second race for Jerry Dickinson, and he was standing right next to me, waiting to take my saddle to put on the horse.

'Overweight? At ten-stone-three?' he said with a mixture of anger and irony. 'What the hell have you been eating?'

It wasn't what I'd been eating that was the problem—I'd had next to nothing for my Christmas lunch—it was what I'd been drinking. A single pint of beer is equivalent in calories to a large slice of pizza, and I'd had a lot more than just one. So many, in fact, that I was also a little hung over.

'Sorry,' I mumbled as I handed him the saddle, diving back into the jockeys' changing room before he could say anything more.

Worse was to come.

We were beaten by less than half a length, and Jerry made it quite clear to me in the unsaddling enclosure that it was totally my fault we didn't win because of me being overweight. One of the losing punters clearly thought the same, shouting abuse at me as I went back into the weighing room.

I sat on a bench in the changing room with my head in my hands, wishing I were anywhere but here. But I had another ride in the sixth race, again at ten-stone-three, again for Jerry.

I stripped off and went back into the sauna—where I had already spent some time before racing—hoping to sweat out a pound of fluid. I'd also had no breakfast and was really hungry, but I dared not eat anything.

Accepted medical advice is that you should only remain in a piping-hot sauna for a maximum of twenty minutes at a time, and you should drink plenty of water both beforehand and afterwards. I remained in there throughout the next three races, well over an hour, and, needless to say, I didn't drink any water at all.

'Pussett. Ten stone, three pounds,' said the Clerk of the Scales.

I handed my saddle to Jerry, who raised his eyebrows fractionally but said nothing. I, meanwhile, could hardly put one foot in front of the other, such were the cramps in my legs brought on by dehydration. I hobbled back to the changing room and drank several handfuls of water from the cold tap in the loos; eventually, the cramps eased.

I finished second again, beaten by a head this time, and, if Jerry thought it was because I lacked the strength to ride the best finish I possibly could have, he'd have been right. But he didn't say anything, for which I was grateful.

An hour later, I started back to Lambourn from Kempton in the horsebox, sitting on a bale of straw in the rear with the horses so I didn't have to talk to anyone human, and I popped into the village convenience store for another six-pack on my walk home from the yard.

Just one more beer wouldn't do any harm, surely, and I needed it.

Boy, did I need it.

* * *

Jerry wasn't kidding when he said it is bloody cold at half past seven in the morning in St Moritz. But I suppose the ice on the lake wouldn't be thick enough to race horses on if it wasn't.

Wondering what on earth I am doing, I turn up at the temporary racing stables in jeans, snow boots and a thick ski anorak, with lots of thermal layers beneath. Gloves and a woollen bobble hat make up the rest of my ensemble, and I am still shivering.

Jerry is there ahead of me and he's not happy.

'Bloody Herbie,' he says. 'They've kept him in hospital overnight and now they're saying they need to operate to insert a metal plate in his foot. I've had to muck out both of mine this morning.' He sounds totally exasperated by this state of affairs.

It's as much as I can do not to laugh. It's clearly been a very long time since Jerry has had to do any manual work.

I stamp my left foot in a vain attempt to get some blood to my freezing toes. 'Come on, then. Let's get this show on the road before I change my mind.'

Jerry looks down at my footwear. 'You're surely not riding in those.'

'Why not?'

'Because they'll get stuck in the stirrups if you fall off.'

'But I have no intention of falling off. And these are all I've got.' Other than my Cresta boots with the vicious-looking spikes on the front or indoor moccasins, and I'm not wearing either of those.

We walk down the row of stables to where Jerry's two are housed at the far end. 'Here,' he says, handing me a back protector. 'Wear this.'

'Is that really necessary?'

'Just do it. All my insurance is invalid if you don't.'

I take off my anorak and put the protector on over my clothes, then quickly replace the warm outer layer.

'And this,' Jerry says, tossing me a helmet. 'It's Herbie's but it should fit.'

I adjust the chinstrap to my head size as Jerry tacks up the first horse.

'Is this Susi's or Brenda's?'

'Susi's. His name is Foscote Boy but at home we usually just call him Fossy. Seven-year-old gelding. He's won over hurdles before, but today's race might be too short for him.'

'How far is it?'

'Two thousand metres. About a mile and a quarter.'

Jerry gives me a leg-up onto Fossy's back. It is the first time I've been on a horse in more than seven years but, somehow, it feels entirely natural. What had I been so worried about? I instinctively gather the reins and slip the toes of my snow boots into the irons.

'Just a gentle canter twice round the track followed by a short sharp gallop for a furlong or so up past the finish line,' Jerry says. 'Just to give him a stretch and a warm-up. But don't needlessly tire him out. He'll need all his energies for this afternoon.'

'Aye, aye, sir,' I reply, giving him an ironic mock salute.

I know what a pipe-opener is and Jerry is treating me like the young wet-behind-the-ears conditional jockey that I'd been when I first turned up at his stable yard. But, I suppose, it is only fair. I hadn't exactly covered myself in glory on the last few occasions I'd ridden for him.

* * *

If that Boxing Day at Kempton had been a low point in my life, it was only the first of many.

After that Christmas of excesses with the beers, I managed to hold things together over the New Year and into the following months such that, by the beginning of April, I'd moved up to second in the Conditional Jockeys' Championship, albeit still six winners behind the leader. But, with Jerry's support, I was doing everything I could to catch up, criss-crossing the country to ride at as many meetings as possible.

One major highlight at this time was my first ever visit as a jockey to the Grand National meeting—three days of top-class steeplechasing over the famous Aintree Racecourse on the edge of Liverpool—not that I went north with any huge excitement, as I didn't have a ride booked for the National itself.

Jerry drove us from Lambourn early on Thursday morning and we checked in to a budget hotel not far from the racecourse.

'Best to do it first, prior to racing,' Jerry said. 'I've had rooms nicked by others before now. Especially if I get back late after having had a runner in the last. Some people will try every trick in the book, including using my name and paying extra with cash—anything to get a bed. I always book two rooms here during the previous year's meeting to get the best rates so close to the racecourse. If I don't use the second one, I sub-let it at a profit. Means I effectively get my room for free.' Jerry smiled at me as if to emphasise how clever he was.

Always the cheapskate. Did he expect me to pay?

But worrying about that did little to dampen my anticipation and delight as we finally turned into the Aintree owners' and trainers' car park. I stood up out of Jerry's Mercedes and breathed in deeply, savouring the atmosphere and history of the place.

Aintree. The venue for so many of our sport's most iconic moments—Red Rum winning three Grand Nationals and finishing second in two more, Foinavon succeeding where everyone else failed at the 23rd fence, Devon Loch's collapse with just forty yards to run for a right royal victory, to say nothing of Captain Becher falling into the brook now famously named after him, or Bob Champion coming back from near-terminal cancer to win the big prize on Aldaniti.

But today I am concerned with more mundane matters, like riding in the first race, a handicap hurdle, and also in the last, a National Hunt flat race, a bumper.

Aintree for the Grand National weekend is like no other race meeting anywhere in the world, with the possible exception of Flemington on Melbourne Cup day.

It is like Cheltenham on steroids.

Swathes of Liverpool's young men and women, dressed up in their finery, make their way by train, bus and stretch limo to the racecourse, often totally inappropriately dressed for the overhead conditions.

Open-toed high-heeled sandals regularly splash through puddles on the concourse behind the grandstands, and goose-bumped areas of bare skin abound, under backless or shoulderless chiffon more suited to high summer than the vagaries of the English weather in early April.

But they are here to see and be seen, to gamble on the horses, to have fun and, of course, to drink—copiously.

By the end of the day many will have had far too much and it was not unusual to see young women, still wearing stiletto heels, slumped down on the damp ground, legs splayed wide, with their very short skirts failing to cover their embarrassment. The men were no better, their ultra-slim-cut short suit jackets and leg-hugging drainpipe trousers all beer-splattered and much the worse for wear.

And all around them, the business of horseracing would continue.

Jerry and I walked the course, not the Grand National course itself, but the shorter inside track used for the races I was riding in. And then I went to get ready in the jockeys' changing room, where little brass plaques screwed to the walls indicated the pegs used by those lucky enough to have won the big one.

I knew that my father had ridden eight times in the Grand National but the closest he had come to winning was second, so there would be no little plaque with 'Pussett' engraved on it.

Maybe one day, I thought. Maybe one day.

I weighed out for the first race and skipped excitedly down the steps from the weighing room to join Jerry and the owner in the parade ring.

'Do your best,' Jerry said quietly to me as he gave me a leg-up. 'I fear he's poorly handicapped in this company, but the owner insisted on him running just to get the free entry tickets.'

This rather dampened my excitement, and didn't instil any great confidence, but Jerry's comment was well founded as the horse finished twelfth of the sixteen runners, some fifty lengths or so behind the winner. And I fared little better in the last race, finishing somewhat closer but still outside the prizes.

However, Friday was a different day altogether.

I won the three-and-a-half-mile novice hurdle on a sixteen-to-one outsider, overhauling the tiring favourite in the final stride. And then I received the news that would keep me awake most of the night.

Jerry's stable had two runners in the Grand National and the jockey he had previously declared for one of them had had a fall in the Topham Chase, breaking his left collarbone.

'So you will now ride Malvernian in the National tomorrow,' Jerry said to me in the car on the way back to our hotel, sending my adrenalin level through the roof. 'He's low in the weights, mind. Due to carry ten-stone-four.'

'No problem.' I said. I knew that there were no weight allowances for conditional jockeys in the Grand National, and I could do ten-four. Just!

'Good. We'll walk the course in the morning. We'll leave here at seven.'

I spent the evening alone in my room, not daring to eat or drink for fear of being too heavy. I tried to watch the television to take my mind off things but I was too nervous to concentrate on anything else.

Malvernian was a ten-year-old bay gelding that had qualified to run in the Grand National by finishing second in a three-mile chase at Doncaster in January, not that I'd been riding him then. Indeed, I'd never sat on his back before, not even at home, but that didn't particularly worry me. Like all jockeys, I'd ridden lots of horses in races that I hadn't been on previously.

Just to have any ride in the Grand National as a 21-year-old conditional jockey was a real feather in my cap, but only if I didn't mess it up. But I wouldn't be the youngest to ride in the race, far from it. Bruce Hobbs had been just sixteen his first time, and he is still the youngest jockey ever to win it, steering Battleship to victory only three months after his seventeenth birthday.

I set the alarm on my phone for six o'clock but I was awake long before it went off; in fact I didn't feel that I'd slept much at all. But I was relieved to be able to get up and dress, to be finally doing something rather than simply lying there in bed churning over and over everything that could go wrong.

Not that I was worried about the horse falling. I was concerned more about failure due to my own shortcomings.

'Treat it just like any other race,' Jerry said as we walked down the line of fences towards Becher's Brook. 'But keep out of trouble if you can. Stay wide on the first circuit and don't go into the first fence too fast. The landing sides on these first six are all lower than the take-off sides, and that will tend to pitch your horse down onto its nose. Give him a chance to get used to it. Four miles is a long way and you can't win it in the first mile, but you can certainly lose it if you fall or are brought down.'

We moved on to the Canal Turn, where the racecourse turns abruptly left through ninety degrees. 'Try to jump this fence on the angle,' Jerry told me. 'Doing so can save you many lengths but be careful not to get squeezed on the inside by others cutting across you.'

We completed our walk at The Chair, the most for-midable fence in all of British steeplechasing: five feet two inches high, three feet thick and preceded by a deep, six-foot-wide ditch. 'Kick on hard into this,' Jerry instructed. 'Those that hesitate won't get across and they'll either end up on top of the fence or fall backwards into the ditch.'

I swallowed my fear and wondered if the 600 had 'kicked on hard' into the 'Valley of Death' at Balaclava.

11

THE WAITING WAS the worst part. Nervous tension in the Aintree changing room before the Grand National put everyone on edge. For the old hands with many Nationals to their name, it was a time to reflect on past victories or failures over the big fences. But for the debutants like me, it was just a time to worry.

I tried to busy myself and spent twenty minutes in the sauna to sweat off a few ounces. I then changed early into Malvernian's maroon and white silks, making sure for the umpteenth time that all my kit was in order. Next, I weighed out—ten-stone-four, on the dot—and gave my saddle to Jerry to take away and put on the horse.

About half an hour before the race was due to start, all the jockeys were told to go outside for a group photo in the winner's circle.

'It's in case one of us dies,' one of the old lags joked as we trooped back in. 'So they have a recent picture to put on the TV news.'

No one laughed.

Finally, the call for jockeys was made and I went out to the parade ring to meet Jerry and Malvernian's owner, a large, moustached man wearing a camel-coloured cashmere coat and a dark-blue fedora.

'Best of luck,' he said nervously.

'Thank you, sir,' I replied in the same manner.

Everyone was nervous, even Jerry.

Treat it just like any other race.

That's what he'd told me this morning, but the Grand National wasn't just any other race. Events of the next half-hour could put you into the history books for ever—as either a hero, or a villain.

The bell was rung and Jerry tossed me up into the saddle.

'Just remember what we talked about earlier.'

I nodded at him and he disappeared off to sort out his other runner.

Malvernian was led out through the tunnel beneath the grandstands and onto the track. There was a parade for the race so we had to sort ourselves out into the correct order before being led past the enthusiastic crowd for inspection.

Sitting there on Malvernian's back, staring across at the sixty thousand expectant faces, was quite a strange feeling: part excitement, part apprehension and part dread of what was to come. It felt like a dream but then we were released back into reality, cantering down, away from the clamour, to the quiet of the first fence for the horses to have a look.

The lull before the storm.

Back to the starting point in front of the packed stands, circle, circle, girths tightened, circle, circle, all the while keeping one eye on the starter, who was already standing on his rostrum, waiting for the appointed time. Finally, he raised his flag and the forty runners spread out across the course and walked in.

'Come on, then,' shouted the starter, simultaneously lowering his flag and releasing the tape.

We were off, encouraged on our way by a huge roar from the crowd behind us.

As Jerry had instructed, I lined up towards the outside and took it fairly steady on the long run to the first, not that every jockey had heeded the warning given to us all earlier in the weighing room about going too fast. And some of them had paid the price.

By the time Malvernian and I jumped the fence there were already five horses and riders prostrate on the turf although, thankfully, none of them were in our way.

I stayed out wide and avoided trouble all the way down to Becher's, running about mid-field, and I was enjoying myself immensely. At the Canal Turn we jumped the fence at an angle while avoiding being squeezed on the inside, and at The Chair I kicked on hard and Malvernian cleared it with ease.

Jumping the water in front of the stands, I counted just nine horses in front of us, but that number steadily increased as we went towards Becher's for the second time, and the race began to develop in earnest around us.

I could tell that, short of a Foinavon-style disaster again at the 23rd fence, we were not going to win this race, and by the time we jumped the Canal Turn on the angle for the second time, Malvernian was losing ground even more rapidly.

'Time to call it a day, old boy,' I said into his ear, and pulled him up before the last open ditch, four fences from home. He didn't object.

I'd been neither a hero nor a villain.

But, oh my goodness, what fun I'd had!

* * *

I trot Foscote Boy down from the stables and out onto the frozen St Moritz Lake.

It is the first time I have ever ridden a horse on ice and I am initially wary that it might be slippery in the same way as the hard glassy surface of the Cresta Run. But the ice on the lake is covered with a layer of compacted snow and that, combined with special protrusions on his shoes, means that the horse has no difficulty in keeping its footing.

I am not alone on the ice. Several of the day's other runners are also being given a warm-up and I follow a group round the track at a gentle canter.

I am surprised by how good it feels to be back on a horse and I almost begin to wish that it *was* me riding him later in the day, especially when I ask Foscote Boy to quicken and he surges forward.

'There's a good boy, Fossy,' I say into his ear as I pull him up after a short gallop. 'Save the rest for later.'

I walk him back towards the stables and find that Jerry has come down to watch, leading the other horse.

'Still got it, then?' he says. 'You look like you've never been away.'

I smile at him and slide down onto the snow.

Jerry transfers the saddle.

'What's this one called?'

'His full name is Cliveden Proposal. We usually just call him Cliveden.'

Jerry gives me a leg-up onto the second horse's back and I repeat the process, enjoying myself hugely. But, all too soon, it is over and we return to the stables.

'Which one will win?' I ask.

'Why? Thinking of placing a bet?'

'I might,' I reply, although I'd never placed a bet in my life, not on horses anyway. But Jerry was a big gambler. Always had been through the years I'd ridden for him. His stable was well known for it.

'So which one are you on?' I ask.

He laughs. 'That's for me to know and you to worry about. On past form, Cliveden should be the better of these two by far, and he should be good enough to beat the others as well. But I'm not saying he will, although he won here last year and he may well start this afternoon as the favourite. But we'll all find out later.'

Indeed we would.

* * *

Two days after my ride in the horseracing Grand National at Aintree, I finally passed my driving test at the third attempt and instantly invested some of my win bonuses into a blue, second-hand, three-door Volkswagen Golf.

Having my own wheels suddenly gave me much greater freedom, even if I now spent more time driving on the motor-ways than I did actually riding.

By the middle of April, I had halved the deficit to the championship leader, who was, unfortunately for him, laid up with an injury, and there were just ten days left of the season when I was engaged to ride four horses at Newton Abbot, three fairly fancied runners for Jerry and one other no-hoper for a local Devon trainer.

I'd ridden at Newton Abbot before, often, but had always travelled there either on the train from Newbury or with Jerry in his Mercedes. This was the very first time that I'd driven myself, and what a foul day it was to be driving anywhere. The heavy rain and low cloud, together with the steady stream of headlights coming towards me on the other carriageway, made it appear more like dusk than midday.

Headlights!

Approaching junction 26 on the M5, south of Taunton, I had the sudden realisation that this was the precise spot where my father had been killed.

Images and memories, imprisoned for so long in my subconscious, now suddenly broke free and invaded my reality, such that my hands began to shake and all I could see ahead was the brick lorry, its headlights also ablaze, with smoke pouring from its wheels.

How I didn't hit something or cause another frightful disaster in the same place, I don't know. One moment I was in the outside lane travelling at seventy miles per hour and, the next, I was stationary at an obscure angle on the hard shoulder with other vehicles' horns and drivers' curses still ringing in my ears.

Not that I really heard them. All I could hear in my head was the tearing of metal and scraping of the car door on the tarmac as the lorry slammed into my father's Jaguar. And his truncated scream.

I was not sure how long I sat there in the Golf—certainly many minutes, but it felt like hours. My pulse rate shot up and my fingertips began to tingle and then rapidly went numb. Then my breathing became laboured and I had stabbing pains across my chest. I feared I was having a heart attack.

I reached for my mobile phone to call for help but my fingers felt like alien sausages, and they were unable to push the buttons.

I forced myself to breathe slowly and deeply through my mouth. Gradually, the attack subsided and the real world returned. Little by little, the feeling came back to my fingers, along with painful pins and needles, and my heart rate gradually dropped back to a more normal rhythm as the discomfort in my chest subsided.

I'd heard about other people having panic attacks and had always thought that they should simply get a grip of themselves and stop being so overdramatic. It came as a big surprise for me to discover that a disturbance in the brain could cause such intense physical manifestations, to the point of total paralysis of normal function, and there was no action whatsoever I could have taken to prevent it.

I leaned back in my seat and closed my eyes, thankful that it was over.

But then I was startled by someone tapping loudly on the passenger-side window of my Golf.

I lowered the glass.

'Are you all right, sir?' asked a man wearing a dark uniform plus a bright-yellow high-vis jacket. A policeman.

'Yes, officer,' I replied. 'Thank you. Quite all right. I wasn't feeling very well so I pulled over.'

'Do you need medical assistance?'

'No,' I said. 'Thank you, but I've recovered now.'

I'm not sure he believed me about feeling unwell in the first place.

'The motorway hard shoulder is for emergencies only,' he said sternly. 'It's not there for you just to have a snooze.'

Perhaps I should have told him that my panic attack had been a full-blown emergency and I could have easily caused a major accident, but I didn't really want him calling an ambulance. Not now.

'Sorry,' I said.

'Now get yourself going. It's not safe to be stopped here.'

I started the car and drove on very carefully, all the way to Newton Abbot, wary that the same thing might happen again.

And it did, but thankfully not on that journey.

12

I DIDN'T WIN ANY of the four races that afternoon at Newton Abbot. Indeed, I didn't win another race before the end of the season, in spite of having rides every day. Hence, I finished runner-up in the Conditional Jockeys' Championship.

'Better luck next year,' everyone said—everyone except Jerry, who was furious.

'What the fuck's the matter with you?' he demanded loudly in the unsaddling enclosure after a particularly bad race I'd ridden at Warwick. I should have won it easily but had left my run far too late, such that I was a fast-finishing second, beaten by only a short head, when Jerry had wagered a fortune on the nose.

'I don't know,' I had mumbled as I went to weigh in.

But I did know—I was hardly sleeping.

After my trip down the motorway to Devon, unwelcome images had suddenly begun to invade my dreams, and on a nightly basis. So much so that I was afraid to go to bed and would finally fall into a restless slumber in an armchair, still fully clothed.

Then I would wake in a cold sweat, reliving the death of my dad or my mum, sometimes both of them together, with my mother's cold and stiff body in the Jaguar with me as the brick lorry bore down upon us, and, all around, people shouting that it was all my fault.

And so I began to drink again, to numb the searing agony. Beer at first but then wine and finally spirits, anything with alcohol in it. Anything that would shut out the nightmares.

It wasn't doing wonders for my weight but I could just about cope if I reduced my food intake still further. I was now eating only three proper meals a week, that is if a low-calorie microwavable curry could ever be considered to be a proper meal.

Then one of my housemates told me he could get hold of some Lasix tablets without a doctor's prescription. It seemed that there was someone in the village with a supply who'd be prepared to sell some to him, for the right price, which I would then have to double to provide him with his cut, naturally.

Lasix has been a drug widely used in horseracing in the United States for many decades, although there is a current legal attempt to restrict its use on race day. It can prevent bleeding into the lungs, a problem some horses have due to the huge rise in their blood pressure during hard exercise.

But it also acts as a diuretic and one of the main arguments against the use of Lasix in horses on race day is that it is therefore, in itself, performance enhancing, never mind what other illicit substances the diuretic effect might be masking.

An intravenous dose of Lasix, given a few hours before a race, will cause a horse to excrete as much as three gallons of urine before it runs. This in turn makes the horse more than thirty pounds lighter, a vast amount when you consider a single pound extra carried on its back is enough to make the difference between winning and losing. Hence horses that don't need Lasix for valid medical reasons are given it anyway, else they would be at a massive disadvantage against the others.

Lasix is also a human diuretic and is prescribed to many people with heart problems to reduce a build-up of fluid in their legs.

And fluid is heavy, so getting rid of it makes you lighter.

In British and Irish racing, the use of Lasix, or any other diuretic for that matter, is outlawed both for the horses and the riders. Not that that has stopped jockeys from sometimes using them. Before they were banned, many would simply swallow a handful of pee-pills, as they were known, as their only breakfast. Laxatives, too. Even cocaine, which suppresses appetite. Anything to win the ongoing battle with weight.

One Saturday in early May, I received a major wake-up call at Bangor-on-Dee Racecourse.

I had been engaged by a local Shropshire trainer to ride his horse in a steeplechase at the North Wales racecourse, and it was very low in the handicap. With my three-pound allowance, I had to weigh out at nine-stone-twelve.

In desperation, I swallowed two of the four Lasix tablets I'd bought via my housemate and, as a consequence, I'd had to stop three times on the journey north to relieve myself. When I arrived at the course, I went straight into the sauna to try and lose even more fluid.

And it was while I was sitting in there that a rumour spread rapidly around the jockeys' changing room that the dreaded drug-testing team had arrived.

I suddenly began to sweat in more ways than one.

Dope-testing of racehorses takes place on a daily basis at all race meetings, with every winner routinely required to provide a urine sample. The first four home in major races are also tested, plus any other horse the stewards may nominate either before or after the race. There is also a major programme of testing away from the racecourse, such that any horse in training can be tested at any time, and at any venue.

For jockeys, the regime is not quite so rigorous, not least because a single jockey may ride many times in an afternoon and providing a urine sample after each one is simply not practicable. However, increasing determination to keep the sport drug-free has resulted in many more unannounced jockey-testing days both at racecourses and elsewhere.

Those at the races are split into one of two types—breath-test-only days and urine-test-only days. On breath-test days, all jockeys riding on that day are required to have their breath analysed for alcohol content; on urine-test days, riders are selected at random to provide samples to be sent off to the laboratories.

I sat in the sauna, terrified that I would be one of those selected for a urine test, something that would undoubtedly confirm to the authorities that I had taken a diuretic, so I was hugely relieved when it was announced that it would be a breath-test-only day.

But my relief was short-lived.

'Twenty micrograms of alcohol per hundred millilitres of breath,' said the tester, holding up the breathalyser for me to see the read-out. 'That's a fail.'

'A fail?' I went all hot and cold. 'What's the limit?'

'Not more than seventeen.'

'I thought it was thirty-five.'

'That's for driving. Seventeen is the limit for riding in races.'

So it had been legal for me to travel at up to seventy miles per hour along the road from Lambourn in a one-ton metal box, but not for me to ride at less than half that speed over fences without one.

'So what happens now?' I asked.

'You will be tested again within fifteen minutes, after I have done these others.' He indicated to the line of my fellow jocks waiting behind me. 'If you fail again, you will

be stood down from riding today, and you will be reported
to the racing authority. It will be up to them to decide on
your penalty.' His self-righteous manner made it clear he
thought me a very naughty boy.

How could I have failed the test? I hadn't had a drink
since the previous evening. That must be the problem. I'd
consumed a whole bottle of red wine to help me sleep, and
the alcohol must still be in my system.

What could I do to reduce it in only fifteen minutes?

'Hyperventilate,' one of the other jockeys told me
quietly as he went back into the changing room having
passed the test. 'My sister swears it helped her beat a
driving ban.'

So I stood there and breathed in and out as deeply and
as quickly as I could, but it seemed to make things worse.
Whereas before I hadn't felt in the slightest bit drunk, now
I was almost paralytic from excess oxygen in my brain,
totally light-headed, with bright stars floating in front of
my eyes.

'Pussett!' shouted the tester.

I took another couple of deep breaths and walked
unsteadily over to him.

'Blow in here until I tell you to stop.'

I placed my lips around the white tube and, with rising
fear and trepidation, I began to blow.

'Keep going,' he said. 'Keep going.'

The machine beeped and he pulled it away.

My eyes, and his, were firmly fixed on the read-out.

There was a short delay as the machine did its
business—only a couple of seconds, but it felt like for ever
to me, my life in its hands.

'Seventeen,' the tester said, a huge degree of disbelief
clearly audible in his tone.

'That will do,' I said, turning away before he had a
chance to suggest a third test or, worse still, to provide a
urine sample instead.

I went back into the changing room shaking, but I was laughing, too. I'd beaten the system, but how could I have been so stupid?

How? Because at times I didn't seem to care, and it might have been much better in the long run if I had failed that second breath test. Maybe then I would have received the help I needed sooner, before my life finally went into total meltdown.

* * *

White Turf is a strange cocktail of two parts frozen Glorious Goodwood mixed with one part haute couture, a large slice of cordon bleu, with just a dash of Yorkshire point-to-point for taste.

Point-to-point because, just like at Duncombe Park, where I'd had my first-ever race ride, the racecourse here is transitory. Large tents act as hospitality areas, weighing room, press accommodation and betting halls. Temporary scaffolding structures provide grandstand seating, commentary box and TV towers, while smaller tents are utilised as shops, bars and cafés.

In just a few days the whole lot will have disappeared, taken away by a fleet of trucks to provide similar functions elsewhere. Indeed, come the spring, the very surface that the horses race upon will also go, melting away to become the playground of yachts and powerboats.

But for now, the frozen lake is the centre of attention, with a steady flow of people making their way down from the town onto the ice.

In all the years I have been coming to St Moritz, this is the first time I have ever been to White Turf, and I'm already beginning to regret it. Horseracing was a life I had promised myself to leave behind, a life that had brought me so much heartache and pain.

So what am I doing here?

Was it simply out of vanity? Or was it due to some strange unconscious desire to regain something I had lost, something that I'd once held so dear?

I am confused, but here I am nevertheless.

'Meet me in the weighing-room tent in two hours' time,' Jerry had said as I was leaving the stables at eight-thirty this morning.

'I'm not so sure,' I'd replied. I could feel the stress rising in me. 'I don't think I want to do this after all.'

Jerry was not happy, to put it mildly. 'You can't let me down now. Who else could I get? And you'd be letting Susi Ashcroft down too.'

I didn't reply.

'OK. I'll pay you a bloody fee. Is that what you're after?'

No, it's not. Although it would be useful.

'How much?' I ask.

'Twenty quid.'

I almost laughed. 'Twenty quid. That's an insult. Make it a hundred and I might reconsider.'

I could see that Jerry was close to exploding, with his legendary temper boiling just beneath the surface. But he held it in check. He needed me and he knew it.

'I'll give you thirty. Final offer.'

'Seventy.'

'Fifty, and that's really all I can afford.'

'OK. Fifty it is.'

I held out my hand and, reluctantly, he took a wad of English twenty-pound notes from his pocket and peeled three of them off. The wad wasn't much reduced.

'I thought you said you couldn't afford more.'

'I can't. This is all spoken for.'

I didn't believe him. It would be his gambling money.

He handed over the three twenties. 'I need ten change.'

I took the notes. 'I'll owe it you.'

He didn't like that.

'Then be at the weighing-room tent at ten-thirty. And don't be late,' he grumbled.

'Isn't ten-thirty rather early?'

'Our race is not until one forty-five, but racing starts before noon, and I like to declare early. It's not quite the same as in the UK and I want you there to see it.'

More likely, he wanted to make sure I'd actually turn up. He knew that if he gave me too long to think about it, I probably wouldn't, fee or no fee.

So here I am at the weighing-room tent just before ten-thirty, but Jerry is ahead of me and watching out for my arrival.

'Ah, there you are. You still know what to do, don't you?' He seems uncommonly nervous.

'Of course I do. You taught me and I haven't forgotten.' I smile at him but he doesn't smile back.

'Both mine will be running in a breast girth today. It's what they're used to. Do you also know how to fix one of those?'

'Yes, Jerry, I do. Now calm down.'

I'd fixed breast girths many a time when I'd worked for him. Most of his horses ran in them. It's a wide strap around the front of the horse's chest that is fixed to the belly girth on either side, where it meets the saddle. It is also held in place with a thin leather strap that goes over the horse's neck. It prevents the saddle from slipping backwards. They are more often used in steeplechasing than on the flat, but not exclusively.

'Right. Good. There are no saddling boxes here so we have to collect the saddles from the jockeys after they weigh out and take them all the way over to the stables and tack-up there. Then we have to lead the horses back to the parade ring here. We need to give ourselves plenty of time. It's a long way.'

'OK,' I say. 'But I do need to pop into the lunch I've been invited to. Just to show my face. It would be rude not to.'

Jerry wrinkles his nose as if any thought of human hospitality on a race day is secondary to what needs to be done for the horses and, as he's paid me, I should be at his beck and call.

Tough.

'At least it won't take so long today,' he says. 'Not like last year. There'd been more than a foot of fresh snow the night before the race, and it nearly killed me trudging through it.'

So Jerry and I had also been together in St Moritz twelve months ago, and neither of us had known it. But that was not really surprising, because I'd kept well away from White Turf then, and maybe I should have done so again this year.

Back then, I'd not been in such a good place mentally as I am now. The brick-lorry nightmares had returned yet again and I had very nearly not come to St Moritz at all. However, I had decided that spending a few weeks hurling myself down an ice chute at insane speeds on a daily basis would be more beneficial to my mental health than the three sessions of group therapy I would have received from the NHS in the same period back in England. And I'd been right. A week after my arrival, the demons had receded—and without me having to touch a single drop of alcohol.

But, from past experience, I knew it was mostly horseracing that triggered my psychotic episodes, which is why I stayed away from the tracks.

Except that I hadn't—not today, anyway.

CHAPTER

13

AFTER THE DRUG-TESTING scare at Bangor-on-Dee, I
did try to mend my ways. I convinced myself that
I was drinking less, even if it wasn't true, and I refused
several offers of rides from other trainers when I knew the
weight to be carried was too low.

Except that I couldn't refuse those that Jerry trained—
he was my employer.

He told me I'd be riding a six-year-old gelding of his
called Wisden at Huntingdon on the spring bank holiday
Monday at the end of May. He had entered it in the three-
mile Conditional Jockeys' Handicap Hurdle, the first race
of the day, specifically for me to ride.

I'd ridden the same horse in his three previous races,
without any success, and Wisden had slipped down the
handicap to such a degree that this time he was only scheduled to carry ten-stone-two. With my allowance, that made
for another under-ten-stone situation.

I spent the two days prior to the race starving myself
even more than normal, and going for runs in the warm
evenings wearing thermal underwear and the plastic sweatsuit but, even so, the pounds were failing to come off. In
desperation, and remembering how cross Jerry had been

at Kempton when I put up overweight, I took the last two Lasix pills and hoped for the best.

'Pussett, nine stone, thirteen pounds,' said the Clerk of the Scales.

'Well done,' Jerry said, taking my saddle.

I scarcely had enough energy to walk, let alone ride over three miles. Why did I go through all this pain and effort to ride a useless no-hoper that would probably finish tailed off, if he finished at all?

I went back into the changing room, ate a chocolate bar and had a high-energy caffeine drink that promised to give me wings. So, by the time I went out to join Jerry and the horse's owner in the parade ring, there was a renewed bounce in my stride.

There was plenty of nervous tension around and, with sudden alarm, I realised that both Jerry and the owner had heavily backed Wisden to win.

Were they crazy?

'Keep handy,' Jerry said, 'and then push on from two out.'

'Yes, sir,' I said, thinking he must have lost his senses. The only thing 'handy' that this horse had shown me in the past was how quickly he could stop when I decided to pull him up.

The bell was rung and Jerry gave me a leg-up.

'Good luck,' Jerry said. 'And remember to keep him handy to give him the best chance. He's a sure thing.' He nodded at me to check I'd understood. I nodded back.

A sure thing? Was there something I didn't know?

The horse certainly seemed to be going fairly easily as we cantered down to the three-mile start at the far end of the finishing straight, but I thought the race itself might be another matter altogether.

But I was wrong.

Wisden set off well as the starter dropped his flag and, as instructed, I kept him handy just behind the two leaders as we jumped the first two hurdles and passed the grand-stand for the first time, with two complete circuits still to go. Nothing unusual about that, but in our previous out-ings he had simply run out of puff well before the others.

But not this time. As we passed the judge for the sec-ond time, we were again in third place, just a length or two behind, and the horse beneath me seemed so full of run-ning that I still had a strong hold on his reins.

The pace quickened over the two flights in the back straight and still Wisden was keeping up as we swung right-handed into the final bend and skipped over the third last.

Those in front began to tire as we straightened up for the final two hurdles, such that Wisden passed one of them in the air with a spectacular jump.

'Go on, boy,' I shouted in his ear as I kicked him hard.

It wasn't so much me that had the wings but my horse, and he flew over the last flight without breaking stride. I drove him hard towards the finish line and he ran on so well that he overtook the short-priced favourite halfway up the run-in.

We won easily by three lengths. Remarkable.

To say that the large bank-holiday crowd was ecstatic with our victory would be totally wide of the mark, and we returned to the unsaddling enclosure in complete silence, save for a few shouted comments from disgruntled punt-ers claiming the race must have been fixed. But Jerry and the owner didn't seem to mind about that. They both had grins on their faces as wide as the Cheshire Cat and, with a starting price of forty-to-one, I could see why.

I slid down off the horse and undid the girths.

'Don't forget to weigh in,' Jerry said seriously.

That worried me. Would the chocolate bar and energy drink I'd consumed before the race make me too heavy?

Even though the Clerk of the Scales may require any jockey who completes the course to weigh in, it is usually only those that finish in the positions with prize money, in this case the first four. I hadn't expected to be one of those so hadn't been too concerned about eating and drinking something after weighing out.

But we had then gone on to win.

I wouldn't be very popular with Jerry, or the owner, if Wisden was now disqualified because his jockey was the wrong weight. I stepped nervously onto the scale and looked up at the read-out with apprehension, but I needn't have worried.

'Ten stone exactly.' The Clerk nodded and made a note in his ledger. 'Next.'

One pound over, but within the allowable extra-weight limit.

I went back into the changing room and sat down on the bench, but after a couple of minutes, an official put his head round the door. 'Pussett,' he shouted, 'you're wanted in the stewards' room.'

Oh hell!

There were four other men in the room when I went in, three sitting in a row behind a table and Jerry standing in front of it. He was nervously rocking from side to side.

'Ah, Pussett,' said one of the men seated—the one in the middle, the chairman. 'We have asked Mr Dickinson here to explain why his horse, Wisden, appeared to show such a huge improvement over its previous showing. Mr Dickinson says he is unable to do so. You rode Wisden today and on his three previous runs when, on each occasion, you saw the need to pull the horse up before completing the course. Perhaps you can tell us why you think Wisden showed such a dramatic change of form today.'

'Maybe it was the ground, sir,' I said. 'He seemed to enjoy the improved going compared to those previous runs. The ground today was good, good to firm in places, whereas he has only run in the mud before.'

'Exactly,' said Jerry, who had suddenly found his tongue. 'It must have been the firmer ground. And also he was better suited by being ridden more positively in a genuinely run race, as I had instructed Miles Pussett, here, to do.'

I nodded at the panel.

The chairman looked briefly to his colleagues on either side before turning back to Jerry and me.

'Wait outside,' he said to both of us, 'while we discuss our course of action.'

Jerry and I went out of the room. Jerry was sweating, and not just because of the heat of the day. We waited in silence and even *my* palms began to sweat. The last thing I wanted was a suspension from riding just for doing my job well.

Eventually the door reopened and we were ushered back in.

'Your explanations have been noted for future reference,' said the chairman. 'We have decided to take no further action at this time other than to order Wisden to be routinely dope-tested. That is all. You may go.'

I breathed a sigh of relief as we went out.

'So will the dope test be positive or negative?' I asked Jerry quietly.

He looked at me. 'Negative, of course.'

But he was grinning. He knew, as I did, that something strange had just happened—and he had known it before the race.

That was a sure thing.

14

THE FIRST RACE of the day at White Turf is not like any
horse race that I am used to. It is a trotting race with
the horses using a harness to pull a one-seat lightweight
vehicle set on two short skis rather than wheels.

I am standing with Jerry near the finish line to watch,
having nipped into the lunch with the sponsors, wolfed
down a starter, and made my apologies for missing the rest.

The field of eight trotters are ushered out onto the
track and suddenly they are off, the horses' legs going nineteen to the dozen as they charge down towards us in line
abreast.

The drivers wear bright-coloured silks and cap-covered
helmets, just like their riding counterparts, and most also
sport goggles and facemasks more akin to those used by
motorbike riders in speedway or motocross. And I can see
why. The kickback of ice and snow is tremendous, but it
doesn't seem to worry the horses too much. Perhaps that is
because they tend to trot with their heads held unnaturally
high, at least to my eyes.

'Strange-looking race,' Jerry says.

I suppose it may appear strange if you're more used to
watching horses gallop, but I am surprised how fast these

animals can trot without breaking into a canter. And it's a close finish too, with four of them racing side by side down the home straight to the line. The crowd cheer their approval and stamp their feet loudly on the temporary grandstand, although that may well have more to do with keeping warm than anything else.

'Come on,' Jerry says. 'It's time for us to get going.'

We go back to the weighing tent to collect the saddles for Foscote Boy and Cliveden Proposal from their respective jockeys, and then we make the long trek over to the temporary racecourse stables.

'You do Fossy, I'll do Cliveden,' Jerry says. 'I've put everything out ready.'

I go into Foscote Boy's stall. But will I remember what to do?

The horse is tied to a ring on the wall with a rope to his head collar. I remove the collar and put on the bridle, taking care to insert the metal bit correctly in his mouth. Next, off comes the thick rug he has been wearing to keep him warm. Then it's time for the saddle to go on, together with the saddle pad and the number cloth, which I have carried over from weighing out. Finally, I attach the breast girth and tighten everything up. As Jerry had said—piece of cake. Even after all this time, the whole process had felt spontaneous and quite natural. What had I been worried about?

I'm just finished when Jerry comes in.

'Well done,' he says, seeing I've done everything correctly, but he checks all the buckles nevertheless.

'That's a very smart breast girth,' I say, admiring its bright-white sheepskin sleeve.

'Helps me see them easier in the race,' Jerry replies. 'Some trainers use sheepskin nosebands for the same purpose. I always use sheepskin breast girths. It's the Dickinson trademark.'

I remembered.

He puts the thick rug back on Foscote Boy, over the saddle. 'It'll keep him warm on the walk over. And for after the race. They can all too easily get chilled very quickly in these conditions.'

I'm not surprised. My feet are already chilled and I'm wearing snow boots and two pairs of thick socks. The horse, meanwhile, has on metal horseshoes.

'How come their feet don't freeze?' I ask.

'There's an insulating pad inserted between the shoe and the hoof. The farrier here is brilliant. He designed it years ago especially for racing on ice.' He looks at his watch. 'Time to go over.'

The third race of the day is about to start as we lead our two horses over towards the racecourse and, if I thought the first race of the day was different, this is like nothing I have ever seen before.

The jockeys, if that is the right word for them, are neither riding the horses nor driving them from little sleds. They are being dragged on skis behind the horses like water skiers behind a boat, except that these are steering with the reins as well as being pulled along by them.

'It's called *skikjöring*,' Jerry says. 'It's completely crazy.'

And he's right, but it looks like fun too.

The horses are loaded into the starting stalls with the jockeys out the back. And then the gates fly open and they're off, thundering along the ice in spectacular fashion. How the horses and the men don't trip over each other, I don't know, but they all somehow manage to avoid any disasters. Two and a half circuits of the course with an exciting blanket finish at the end, which the photo-finish camera has to sort out.

'You wouldn't get me doing that,' I say. 'It's far too dangerous.'

Jerry laughs. 'So speaks someone who hurtles himself down the Cresta Run at far more than twice the speed.'

I wonder how he knows that. I purposely hadn't told him but there had been plenty of others at the drinks party who knew. One of them must have mentioned it to him.

'Yeah, as maybe,' I say. 'But at least there are no metal-clad flying hooves to contend with.'

Some of the worst injuries jockeys sustain are often those where a following horse strikes them when they are already on the ground after a fall. A horseshoe is invariably more damaging to the human body than the turf, especially if it's landing at speed from a great height with half a ton of horse attached.

Susi Ashcroft and Brenda Fenton are waiting for us in the parade ring, each of them looking splendid in their respective fur coats. Not that they are talking to each other. Brenda is with her grandsons and Susi is alone, standing about five yards away trying to give the impression she hasn't seen the others.

David Maitland-Butler is also there, standing rigid with his chin held high as if on an army parade square, assuming the air of someone who is supremely confident that the result of this race is a forgone conclusion—it is all done and dusted bar the actual running.

When the jockeys appear even their mothers wouldn't be able tell them apart other than by their different-coloured silks. Every square inch of flesh is covered, with gloves, scarves, goggles and facemasks acting as protection against both the cold and the kickback. Many even wear special slip-on overshoes to keep their feet warm when walking on the ice, their riding boots beneath being wafer-thin.

Jerry has already given his instructions to his two jockeys at the weigh-out and it is not long before a bell is rung and they mount up.

Foscote Boy's rider is wearing Susi Ashcroft's gold and black racing colours and I give him a leg-up, peeling off the horse's thick rug in the process.

'Good luck,' I say, as I lead them out of the parade ring and across to the track. I receive a muffled reply through the jockey's face covering that might be anything, and in any language, for all I can grasp of his actual words.

Do I long for me to be sitting on the horse's back instead of him?

Maybe I do.

But anyway, as Jerry had said at last night's drinks party, I couldn't do the weight. Foscote Boy is carrying 56 kilograms, about eight-stone-eleven, and, even at my lightest as a jockey, that would have been impossible. I haven't been that low since I was a fourteen-year-old schoolboy.

Jerry, Susi, Brenda and her grandsons go onto the stand reserved for owners and trainers, while I remain by the exit onto the course where the horses go out. I tell Jerry that I will stay and look after the horses' rugs, but I am also happier here, not having to make small talk with him and the ladies.

The start is way to my right down the far end of a long chute, and soon all the horses are loaded into the stalls and ready. And then there is a huge cheer as the gates open and the most valuable race of the meeting is under way— the prize to the winner being over 53,000 Swiss francs, some 40,000 pounds sterling, which is more than enough even to pay the extortionate room rates for a week at the Badrutt's Palace.

The twelve runners gallop down towards me, the very ice beneath my feet trembling with the vibration. It makes me grateful to know that the thickness of the ice is measured every day, checking that it is strong enough to support both the horses and the crowd before racing can take place.

As the field passes the winning post for the first time, Cliveden Proposal is running third with Foscote Boy a couple of places further back, racing on the wide outside to avoid ice and snow being kicked up into his face, but the whole group is well bunched. They swing right-handed away from us into the back straight, where the pace quickens, and this begins to stretch them out.

On the final turn, Foscote Boy, still on the outside, starts to make headway forward while Cliveden Proposal seems to be labouring and going the other way, the dark-cherry-with-white-disc silks falling further and further behind. So much for Jerry saying he was the better one of the two.

Susi is going to get her wish to beat Brenda after all.

But Foscote Boy does even better than just that. He runs on strongly in the straight, overtaking the Maitland-Butler horse in the last few strides to win the race by a neck

That won't please the colonel.

Meanwhile, Cliveden Proposal, in spite of his jockey's best efforts, fades further to finish eighth.

I can see that Susi is ecstatic, throwing her arms around Jerry's neck in excitement, not that he looks very happy with the victory. Meanwhile, Brenda and her grandsons look on with faces like thunder. Losing is bad enough, but losing to Susi . . . A disaster.

Jerry and Susi come down to the track side to greet their victor, but there is concern written on Jerry's face as he looks about for his other runner.

'Don't worry,' I say to him, giving him one of the rugs. 'You go with Susi and Fossy. I'll look after Cliveden for you.'

If anything, this makes Jerry appear even more worried, but he has no choice as Susi links her arm through his and pulls him off towards the winner's circle, leading her steaming horse with the other hand.

I watch them go, part of me almost wishing I could join them and savour their success—after all, it was me who had saddled Foscote Boy in the first place. But, in truth, I am much happier out of the limelight, drifting off into the background, and letting Jerry and Susi take the glory. Although I have to admit that I'm hugely enjoying being at the races again, albeit ones on snow and ice.

Jerry gives me one last glance over his shoulder as he is dragged away through the throng, and there is something about his body language that shouts fear rather than elation.

Terror, more like.

Slightly confused by this reaction, I walk out onto the track to meet Cliveden Proposal, who looks exhausted.

'The poor boy did his best,' says the jockey, pulling off his facemask. 'He just wasn't good enough today.'

I lead him to the place reserved for the unsaddling of those horses that didn't finish in the first three. The jockey slides down and undoes the girths to remove his saddle while I remove the breast girth.

Something isn't right. Not right at all.

And Jerry would have known that I'd discover it. That's obviously why he looked terrified.

The breast girth is heavy, and not just because the horse's sweat has soaked into the sheepskin. Indeed, it is very heavy, with half a dozen flat lead weights actually stitched inside the sleeve, beneath the wool.

The jockey takes himself and his saddle to the weighing-intent, leaving me holding the horse, plus the leaden breast girth.

A breast girth is part of the 'excluded equipment', the things that are not weighed with the jockey. They also include the bridle and anything that the animal is wearing on its head or legs such as blinkers, horseshoes and leg bandages.

I hang the offending item over the horse's withers and then put the thick warm rug over the top of it. No one else has seen or noticed. I decide that it is better if it remains that way—at least until Jerry has a chance to explain.

I look around to see if I can spot him anywhere, but he is still occupied in the winner's enclosure, no doubt collecting his prize for having trained the winner, something that was clearly as much of a surprise for him as it was for Susi.

I decide to take Cliveden Proposal back to the racecourse stables on the far side of the lake rather than waiting out here in the cold breeze. Jerry can find me there.

But at the stables, I discover that the weighted breast girth is not the only strange thing about Cliveden's tack.

First, I take off his bridle and apply a head collar. The bridle is similar to the one I put on Foscote Boy earlier but with one major difference. Whereas Fossy's bridle has a hollow, lightweight racing bit attached, this one is big, solid and heavy, more in keeping with those normally used for dressage, when running fast is not the aim.

And there is more.

The horse is wearing leather boots surrounding a cotton pad on both his fore legs. But these boots don't actually cover the horse's foot. Instead they wrap around the cannon bone between the knee and fetlock joints to provide support and protection for the bone and also for the tendon that runs down its back. A racehorse wearing such boots in a race is not uncommon, especially if they have a tendency to strike into their front legs with their rear when galloping. However, in this case, I find that there is something else hidden between the boots and the cotton pads. Something that certainly shouldn't be there.

Chain-mail.

Strips of it, about four inches wide and eighteen inches long, carefully wound round each leg.

Heavy and invisible.

In all, what with the lead-filled breast girth, the heavy bridle bit and now this, I estimate that the horse has carried at least a stone over and above what it needed to, probably more.

No wonder it didn't win. It was like asking Usain Bolt to run the Olympic 100m final wearing water-filled wellingtons and with a ten-pin bowling ball hanging round his neck.

And Jerry had to have put it all on the poor animal.

But why didn't he want it to win?

I sit on a bail of bedding outside Cliveden's box, staring at the evidence laid out on the floor in front of me, and wait for Jerry to appear with his explanation.

To be honest, I don't know whether he has actually broken any regulation. Certainly in Great Britain there are very strict rules of racing that ensure that a horse must run on its merits and be given every opportunity to achieve the best possible placing, but those rules specifically refer to the manner in which it is ridden in a race rather than to what it is wearing.

I still know the rules pretty well—all jockeys would as their livelihoods depend on them—and I cannot think of anything in them that states a trainer must use the lightest possible equipment that's available.

I remain sitting there for quite a while, mulling over the questions in my head, before I hear horseshoes clattering on the ground outside. Jerry must be back with Foscote Boy.

But he isn't. Foscote Boy has arrived by himself.

The horse walks right past me and into his open stable, wearing his thick rug and another one over it with 'Winner Grand Prix St Moritz' printed large on each side. He is still wearing his bridle and seems unconcerned, pulling the few remaining strands of hay from his net on the wall.

I know that Jerry won't want to speak to me but this is ridiculous. He surely can't have simply let the horse loose to make its own way back. He must be here somewhere, hiding from the inevitable.

I close the stable door—before the horse bolts—and go outside to look for him.

'Jerry,' I call. 'Jerry, where are you? We need to talk.'

But there is no reply.

I walk down towards the frozen lake and find him there, on the edge of the ice. He is face down with his left arm outstretched to the side, and he is not moving. For a dreadful moment, I have the vision in my head of finding my mother lying in a similar fashion, dead and cold to the touch.

I hang back, afraid, but then Jerry emits a groan and moves his arm.

'Come on, you silly sod,' I say. 'Had too many celebratory schnapps?'

I try and help him up but I only manage to turn him over onto his back.

A surfeit of alcohol is not his problem.

The surface beneath his head is red with his blood, the warm liquid turning the snow mushy. Fleetingly, it reminds me of that strawberry-flavoured iced-sugar drink served from churning machines in petrol stations.

At first I think Jerry must have slipped and fallen, and his nose bleed is from hitting the ice, but closer inspection also reveals a nasty cut above his left eye, with general bruising and puffiness all over his face.

Jerry has been mugged.

15

'No police,' Jerry mumbles through his ever-swelling lips.

'For God's sake, man,' I say. 'You've been attacked. We must call the police.'

'No!' He is adamant.

I have helped him back to the stables and he is now sitting on the bale of bedding outside Cliveden Proposal's stall.

'An ambulance, then?'

'You have to pay for an ambulance in Switzerland. And, anyway, the paramedics might call the police.'

'But that cut will need stitches.'

'Then call me a taxi,' Jerry orders. 'I'll go to a hospital in that. I'll tell them I was bashed by a horse.'

'And were you?'

He looks up at me but doesn't answer. I take that to mean, 'No, it wasn't the horse.'

'So *who* did do this to you?'

He again doesn't answer but simply drops his head.

Laid out on the floor in front of him are the two strips of chain-mail and the weighted breast girth. He stares at them.

'Jerry,' I say, 'what the hell is going on?'

'Just get me that fucking taxi.'

* * *

The dope test on Wisden after the win at Huntingdon was negative, just as Jerry had predicted it would be. And he was smug about it, refusing to give me any reasons why Wisden had so suddenly improved his form.

But he had much else to talk to me about.

The win on Wisden had been my first for more than a month, since before my panic attack on my journey to Newton Abbot and, that win apart, Jerry was not at all happy with my form, which did not improve as the summer progressed.

'What has got into you?' he said one morning when I'd badly misjudged a work gallop on the Downs.

Alcohol, I thought, but decided not to say so. That, and lack of sleep.

I was increasingly troubled by the nightmares and, if anything, they were getting worse. Almost every night, they woke me multiple times, and tiredness was affecting my judgement, both on and off a horse.

And Jerry wasn't the only one who had noticed.

The racing press had turned against me too, or at least that was how it seemed.

'PUSSETT LOSES AGAIN AND AGAIN AND AGAIN,' read one headline in the *Racing Post* after a particularly bad afternoon at Uttoxeter in mid-June, when I'd ridden three of Jerry's fancied horses and failed to convert any of them into a place, let alone a win. The article beneath had pulled no punches either, with the journalist referring to me, as they always did, as the son of a former multi-times champion jockey, before going on to give his opinion that I wasn't nearly as good as my father had been.

It was like a knife thrust between my ribs.

I suppose it is the price a son must sometimes pay for following in his father's profession, especially if the father had been exceptional and the son less so.

My childhood plan to become a living memorial to my dad was beginning to unravel, with some people even tweeting that it was a good thing the father hadn't lived long enough to see how badly the son was now performing.

And with it all came the abuse, especially from those who blamed me entirely for them losing money on a horse they had backed, even if, as in one case, the horse in question had been brought down by another falling right in front of us.

I am sure that social media does have the ability to do some good, but it can also do so much harm, with some people clearly believing that sending abusive comments, and even death threats, is totally acceptable behaviour, without any consideration for the damage they might be doing to the recipient.

And damage me they did.

Any residual confidence I might have had drained away under the onslaught. My loneliness and unhappiness deepened sharply into depression, and worries about my future escalated into a full-scale anxiety disorder.

Part of the problem was that I had no one I could talk to. Perhaps I should have gone to see a doctor but, above all else, I was ashamed of what I had become—a reclusive drunk—and the thought of having to expose my most intimate thoughts and actions to a stranger was anathema to me.

Previously, my success as an up-and-coming jockey had kept the worst of the effects at bay but now, with my current loss of riding form, I felt I was being overwhelmed by a gigantic wave of hopelessness, made even worse by the continued success of the stable's horses when ridden by others.

Several times I tried to speak to Jerry about my issues, but he couldn't really comprehend what was happening to me, and it seemed to make things worse.

'Just pull yourself together, boy, for goodness' sake,' he would say unhelpfully. 'Get back to how you were.'

But that was much easier said than done, and I didn't know where else to turn for help.

I asked Jerry for some time off work to go and speak to my grandparents, but he wasn't keen as many of the other stable staff were away on their summer holidays and it would leave him short-handed. In the end, he begrudgingly allowed me a long weekend in late July to go to Yorkshire, but in the event that wasn't any use anyway as my grandfather was taken seriously ill on my first evening at the farm, and was rushed to hospital in Scarborough with a suspected stroke.

The doctor there tut-tutted and kept going on about my grandfather's advanced years. Eventually, he bluntly told my grandmother to prepare for the worst, as he considered that it wasn't in the patient's best interest to treat someone that old, and that she should agree to his no-resuscitation order. I, meanwhile, wondered if the young doctor would think the same way if and when he reached such an age himself.

My own troubles seemed minor compared to my grandfather's, so I just kept quiet about them and tried to support my grandmother, who was confused and severely distressed at the thought of losing her husband of nearly sixty years.

My uncle was equally useless. He was only interested in securing the farm for himself. He claimed it was ridiculous that, as things stood, half of it would come to me after his parents died.

I told him that he could always buy out my share, but that didn't go down at all well. He claimed he couldn't afford to, and it would be solely my fault if the farm was lost after six generations in the same family.

It did absolutely nothing to reduce my anxiety level.

My grandfather was still just hanging on to life when I climbed into my Golf on Monday morning for the drive south, and I had spoken not a word to anyone about my own problems. The whole trip had been a waste of time and had made me feel so much worse.

I found myself on the M1 near Sheffield wondering whether I would experience any pain if I removed my seatbelt and simply drove my Golf straight into a concrete motorway bridge support at seventy miles per hour.

No one would mourn me much. I was twenty-one years old, with no friends and precious little family. Indeed, my uncle might have been delighted.

I'd not had a girlfriend since those heady pubescent days when I'd sneaked a kiss and a cuddle in the hayloft with the daughter of the riding-school owner in Malton, and there seemed little or no prospect of me acquiring any romantic liaisons in the immediate future. I was too damn busy with the horses for that.

Maybe my mother had shown me the only way out of the ongoing misery of loneliness and despair.

But I couldn't find a bridge support without a crash barrier in the way protecting it, and the prospect of ending up still alive but paralysed frightened me far more than dying.

An hour and a half later, when I left the motorway at Northampton, that day's particular urge to kill myself had receded, although it was to return often in the months ahead.

* * *

I go with Jerry in the taxi to the emergency private medical clinic in St Moritz town centre, but he remains reluctant to talk about anything, and especially not about who has attacked him and why, or the reasons why he made Cliveden Proposal carry so much extra weight in the race. Or, indeed, whether the two are connected.

'That's my business,' is all he will say.

I personally think that, as an accessory after the fact, it is *my* business too, but decide to keep quiet, at least until the stitches are inserted in his head wound.

But it is not just stitches.

A doctor at the clinic is concerned that Jerry has concussion and that he is internally bleeding into his left eye, which has gone bright red where it should have been white. The doctor wants to keep Jerry in overnight for observation in case treatment is needed to reduce any increased pressure in his eye. However, the patient is not at all keen.

'It's just a way of increasing their bill,' he says to me when the doctor goes out of the room.

'But you must have travel insurance,' I point out. 'They will surely pay.'

Jerry looks at me with his one good eye and I realise that not having travel insurance is another of his cost-saving initiatives, except that this one is not going to be cost-saving in the long run.

'I'll be fine,' he says to the returning doctor. 'Just put some stitches in the cut and I'll be off.'

'It's up to you,' replies the doctor in perfect English, 'but you have what we call a hyphema in that eye. It is a serious condition, so don't blame me if you go blind.'

'Blind?' Jerry is clearly shaken.

'Yes, blind. At least in your right eye, maybe both.'

Jerry goes silent for a moment, then looks at me. 'I think I'd better stay here after all, don't you? You'll look after the horses for me?'

Why on earth did I go to that drinks party?

CHAPTER

16

M Y GRANDFATHER DIED five days after having had the stroke—that's if you count dying as the moment when his heart stopped.

The doctors at Scarborough Hospital had performed lots of tests and had determined that he was already brain-dead due to the stroke having caused a blockage in the artery that should deliver oxygenated blood to the brain. However, and in spite of the initial doctor's do-not-resuscitate order, he had been placed on a life-support machine that continued his breathing, and his heartbeat.

My uncle called to give me the bad news and also to tell me that it was planned to turn off the life support on the following morning, and would I be coming to the hospital to join him and my grandmother at the bedside?

I was badly torn.

My love for my grandparents was absolute, but I felt that the stress of watching yet another of my close relatives die would simply be too much for me to bear, especially in my already vulnerable condition.

So I didn't go, but part of me regretted it. The more so when my uncle called the following afternoon to berate me for not being there to support my grandmother.

'Was it very bad?' I asked.

'What do you think?' he retorted. 'They turned off the machine and he never breathed again.' He was choking back tears. 'You should have been there.'

No, I shouldn't, I thought. My anxiety levels were quite high enough already.

'When's the funeral?' I asked.

'Sometime next week. I'll let you know when it's finalised.'

'Right,' I said. 'I'll get time off from work.'

It shouldn't be too much of a problem. My rides for other trainers had almost completely dried up and even Jerry was using me less and less, but he hadn't quite deserted me altogether.

'I've declared you to ride Gasfitter at Market Rasen on Sunday in the two-mile-seven-furlong handicap hurdle,' Jerry told me two days after my grandfather died.

'Market Rasen? That's a long way north for you.'

Market Rasen is a small town on the edge of the Lincolnshire Wolds, not far south of the Yorkshire border. Almost back in my old stamping ground.

'It's the last jump meeting before the two-week August break and he's ready now, so I don't want to wait.'

Gasfitter was one of the three horses I'd ridden at Uttoxeter on that disastrous afternoon in June. Then I'd pulled him up before the last.

'OK,' I said. 'What weight has he got?'

'After his last poor run, he's fairly well handicapped at ten-stone-five.'

With my three-pound allowance that meant ten-two. I could just about do that all right, with a day's wasting and some time in the sauna.

'Fine,' I said.

And so I went north again just six days after coming south, but this time with Jerry in his Mercedes because I was short of both petrol and the money to buy some, not least because most of my spare cash was going on booze.

This was my first ride at Market Rasen and, although Gasfitter's race wasn't until four o'clock, Jerry and I left Lambourn early enough so we could walk the course together before racing started at two.

'It's quite deceptive,' Jerry said as we set off round the track on foot. 'It looks fairly flat from the stands but there are plenty of dips and undulations that can unbalance a horse, and the far-end turn is a steep downhill run that tends to throw horses out wide coming into the straight.'

I nodded at him, taking it all in.

The start was at the far end of the finishing straight and Gasfitter and I would complete more than two full circuits, jumping twelve flights of hurdles in all, the three down the back twice and the two in the home straight three times, with sharp right-hand bends to negotiate between.

'It's a good galloping course,' Jerry said as we finished our walk. 'It's not an easy place to make up ground so keep him handy.'

I thought back to the same 'keep him handy' instruction he had given to me when Wisden had won unexpectedly at Huntingdon in May.

Was something strange afoot again?

*   *   *

Foscote Boy and Cliveden Proposal are standing quietly in their stalls when I make my way back to the stables from the clinic in St Moritz town centre.

Jerry has refused point-blank to discuss the question of the over-weighted tack, claiming he isn't feeling well enough, but that hasn't stopped him giving me the key to his lock-up store in the stable building, along with a detailed set of instructions concerning what the horses must be given to eat and how they should be settled for the night.

They are due to start the long journey home to England in the morning and Jerry had already asked me if I would go with them in the horsebox he is sharing with David Maitland-Butler, the only other UK-based trainer at the meeting.

'No,' I said flatly. 'I will not.'

'But bloody Herbie is still in hospital with his broken ankle. And I've no one else I can ask. You'd get a free passage home.'

That might be tempting if I didn't already possess a fully paid return air ticket.

'How about asking the colonel? He must have a stable lad travelling with his horse. Surely he could look after yours as well?'

He looked up at me with his good eye.

'You've got to be fucking joking. You know what Maitland-Butler's like. It's a bloody miracle he let me share his horsebox in the first place—not without a hefty fee, mind.'

Indeed, I did know what the colonel was like—he was almost as miserly as Jerry himself. And he could be extremely touchy even at the best of times, and we both knew that he wouldn't co-operate one iota in this instance, not having been beaten by Jerry in the big race.

'He would simply see it as his way of getting back at me.'

'Too bad,' I said. 'I'm still not going. I will go and feed them for you tonight but that's it. No more. You'll have to arrange for one of your staff from home to come and collect them. Either that or employ a local groom to go with them and then fly him home afterwards.'

Jerry looked absolutely horrified that I should suggest anything that was so expensive.

I use his keys to open the store and then I measure out two bowls of high-energy mixed-feed racehorse nuts.

Horses generally eat approximately one pound in weight of mixed feed per day for every hand they stand high at the withers. Most are between sixteen and seventeen hands, so they need sixteen to seventeen pounds of nuts each day, plus some hay to chew on for added fibre, a total daily energy intake of some 35,000 calories—equivalent to eating about 500 Weetabix.

They also drink between six and eight gallons of water every twenty-four hours, so as well as putting the feed in their mangers and re-stuffing their hay nets, I refill their water troughs.

The two horses seem quite happy and do not appear distressed by their earlier exertions out on the frozen lake, whatever weight they may have actually carried. I pat their necks, add a second rug to their backs against the cold of the night, and use a large fork and a bucket to collect a few droppings for disposal.

Finally, I put everything away in the store, including the weighted breast girth and the chain-mail boots, but not before I use my phone to take a few photos of them first.

*   *   *

Gasfitter was sent off in the two-mile-seven-furlong handicap hurdle at Market Rasen at a price of twenty-to-one—quite long odds for a previous winner over hurdles, even if that had been some time ago and his recent form had been indifferent to bad.

'Keep him handy,' Jerry had again said to me in earnest as we stood in the parade ring.

I had simply raised my eyebrows at him but without reaction. However, there was an aura of anticipation in the air, which he couldn't help but express in his body language, just as he had done at Huntingdon.

I wondered how much he had staked on Gasfitter's nose, and that greatly worried me.

I had ridden for Jerry in twenty races since my win on Wisden in May and I hadn't finished in the first two in any of them. My confidence was at rock bottom, yet here I was with the weight of Jerry's expectation resting very heavily once more on my shoulders.

I felt sick.

All the nerves that had plagued me so much in my early rides returned with a vengeance and I almost missed the start, being left flat-footed and some six lengths behind the rest of the eleven-runner field.

So much for keeping him handy. I could almost hear Jerry's groan coming from the grandstands.

'No need to panic,' I said to myself. 'Plenty of time to catch up.' So I didn't try to regain the lost lengths too quickly and unnecessarily tire my horse.

By the end of the first circuit I was back in the pack, lying in seventh or eighth. Hardly handy, but better.

Turning right-handed into the back stretch for the second time, I found that Gasfitter was still moving effortlessly and we gradually gained another place, up to sixth, on the inside where I was hugging the rail.

In previous races his engine had begun to run out of petrol after about halfway, but not this time. But why was I not surprised?

I felt that his improvement in form was all going to be wasted—I had surely lost the race at the beginning. It had to be too much to have given our opponents a six-length start, even if we were going better than I had expected.

Jumping the last of the three flights down the back, I had moved up into fifth, but the four horses in front of me also seemed to be on the bridle and travelling well.

As we began the turn back into the home straight, I was badly boxed in by those ahead, two of which had finally begun to weaken.

Just as Jerry had told me earlier during our walk around the course, the sharp downhill final turn threw the horses in front out wide. I was ready and kept Gasfitter on a tight right rein, sticking like glue to the inside rail. Not only did this give me some room for my finishing run, it meant I took the shortest route, gaining several lengths over those outside me.

We jumped the last flight upsides with the long-time leader and I drove hard for the winning post, both of us flashing neck-and-neck over the line such that neither jockey knew which had won. Nor did the judge.

'Photograph, photograph,' he called over the public-address system.

In the past, if the result was very close, the judge would call for a positive print to be made from the negative in order to make his decision. That could take several minutes to produce. However, digital video technology has now taken over from the old film-loaded photo-finish cameras and the result is generally given quickly.

But not on this day. The crowd went strangely quiet as they waited for the result to be announced. And then they waited some more, so much so that there developed a hubbub in the stands as everyone began discussing possible reasons for why it was taking so long.

Please, can I have won. Please, can I have won.

'It must be really tight,' said Gasfitter's stable lad as he came out to lead him in. 'It'll be on the nod.'

As horses gallop, their action causes their heads to alternately stretch out forwards and then lift up and back. When two horses cross the finish line together it is often the horse whose head just happens to be stretched out at that particular instant that wins 'on the nod'.

Dead heats are rare, especially since the widespread introduction of photo finishes in the mid-twentieth century, but they are not so rare as to not happen. At Aqueduct Racetrack in New York in 2006, amazingly, there were three dead heats in a single afternoon.

Perhaps this would be another, I thought—not that Jerry would be very happy with that because his gambling winnings would be halved.

'Here is the result of the photo finish,' said the judge eventually over the speakers, causing the crowd to go quiet again.

I held my breath.

'First number one, second number ten.'

Gasfitter was number ten.

We had lost.

My shoulders slumped with disappointment. Another loser.

Jerry would be less than happy too, especially after the debacle at the start.

And he was.

His face was puce with rage and he said absolutely nothing to me as I slid down to the ground, removed my saddle, and took it to weigh in.

In contrast, the majority of the crowd seemed delighted by the result, the well-backed favourite having just clung on to take the honours by the smallest of margins.

Losing by less than an inch after running for over two and a half miles didn't seem very fair. But racing wasn't fair. I should have known that by now from past experiences. It had a habit of kicking you in the teeth when you were already down, and this was just one of those occasions.

I sat on the bench in the jockeys' changing room with my head in my hands. Devastated.

The first real chance I'd had in weeks to break my barren spell and I'd blown it, and all because I'd been careless at the start. There was, of course, no certainty that I would have won without my error, but that was what everyone would think, and they would undoubtedly say so at length on social media, and in the racing press.

At least my phone was currently switched off, as was required by the rules during racing, so no abusive messages or comments could get through.

Perhaps I'd leave it off for a while longer, or even for ever.

I sat there for a long time, as other riders went out for the remaining two races of the day.

There was an official who stood guard at the door to keep non-jockeys from entering, and at one point he came over to inform me that the trainer, Mr Dickinson, was outside and he wanted to speak to me.

'Please tell Mr Dickinson that I don't want to speak to him.'

The official seemed somewhat surprised that a jockey should want to say such a thing to a trainer but he disappeared and, presumably, passed on the message because he returned a couple of minutes later to say that Mr Dickinson wanted to know how long I would be, as he was waiting outside for me and it was a long drive home.

'Please tell him that I'm not coming and he should leave without me.'

The official disappeared again to pass on this next message, while I remained seated on the bench feeling wretched.

Was I being unreasonable and foolish? Or pragmatic?

Several hours in a car with Jerry was more than I felt I could cope with at the moment, especially after the afternoon's events. I was truly afraid of what he might say.

But how would I get home otherwise?

Did I care?

I went on sitting on the bench.

And so started the worst twenty-four hours of my life—and, in other ways, the best twenty-four hours of my life as well.

SUSI ASHCROFT ARRIVES at the White Turf stables just as I am locking up to leave.

'Where's Jerry?' she demands.

'He's had a slight accident. Hurt his eye. The doctors have kept him in overnight for observation.'

She is not remotely sympathetic. Indeed, she is annoyed. 'Then why didn't he bloody call me? I've been waiting for him in the bar at my hotel for over an hour. We were going to celebrate our win.'

'I'm sorry,' I say, although I have nothing really to be sorry about.

'And I have dinner booked for us at The K. Does he have the slightest idea how difficult it is to get a table in there at such short notice?'

The K is the hugely expensive and exclusive Michelin-starred restaurant at the Kulm Hotel. Even I know how difficult it is to get in, not that I'd ever been. I assume that Jerry didn't offer to pay, even with his share of the race purse.

'I'm sure Jerry didn't hurt himself on purpose.'

'But it's most inconvenient.' She purses her lips in irritation. 'I don't suppose you would like to join me?'

She's right—I wouldn't—but, once again, my mother's insistence of being polite to a woman raises its head. Hence I don't simply say 'no' outright. Instead, I try to make up an excuse.

'I have to look after the horses for Jerry.' I wave over my right shoulder, towards where they are standing quietly in their stables.

'Don't be silly,' Susi says with a hollow laugh. 'The horses can damn well look after themselves, at least for the next few hours, and you know it. I'm not stupid. If you don't want to come and have dinner with me, just say so. But if you won't, I'll have to eat for two anyway as I had to pre-pay for the five-course tasting menu in order to secure the table.'

I mentally compare the five-course tasting menu at The K to my usual evening fare of a take-away lamb wrap from the döner kebab stall near my lodgings.

'OK, Susi, I'd love to join you for dinner.'

* * *

Eventually, a member of the racecourse security staff asked me to leave the jockeys' changing room at Market Rasen so that he could lock up.

At least, by then, I had changed from my riding britches into my street clothes. I still had no idea where I was going, or why, but I collected my kit, stuffed it into my holdall and walked out with it over my shoulder.

The racecourse is just a mile away from the town centre and that seemed to be as good a place as any, so I set off in that direction.

It was a warm early August summer's evening and the sun was still high in the sky when I reached the market square. There were sounds of revelry spilling out from the open front door of the Aston Arms on the northern edge of the square and, suddenly, a drink seemed to me to be a very good idea—a stiff one.

'Gin and tonic,' I said to the barman in the pub. 'Make it a double. No, a triple.'

He pushed a glass up three times on the optic. 'Slimline or regular tonic?'

'Regular,' I said. I didn't care about the calories. After refusing to speak to my employer, I reckoned my race-riding career was over for good, so why should I worry about putting on a few pounds?

I slid a ten-pound note across the bar.

'Been at the races?'

I nodded, taking a big slug of the drink. 'How do you know?'

He pointed down at my holdall on the floor, which had my whip sticking out through a gap in the zip. 'Riding, were you?'

I nodded again and drained my drink. 'Same again,' I said, slamming the glass down onto the bar top.

He pushed the optic up three times more, splashed in a little more tonic, and passed the new drink across to me in exchange for another tenner.

I took another deep slug.

'That bad, was it?'

'Worse.'

I could feel the first welcome effects of alcohol on my brain, accelerated by the fact that I'd had nothing to eat all day.

'Do you do food?' I asked the barman.

'Not on Sunday evenings,' he replied. 'We only have crisps or nuts.'

I had a bag of salt and vinegar.

'Which way to the train station?'

'Across the square, down John Street opposite. Left into Chapel Street and it's on your right. You can't miss it.'

I drained my glass and picked up my holdall.

'Thanks.'

'Won't do you any good, mind.'

'Why not?'

'There are no trains from Rasen on a Sunday.'

* * *

'Tell me about Brenda Fenton's grandsons,' I say to Susi over our starter course at The K.

'You mean the terrible twins, Ronnie and Reggie.'

I laugh. 'You must be joking.'

The infamous Kray twins, murderous gangsters in London during the 1960s, were called Ronnie and Reggie.

'Yes, I am,' Susi says with a wry smile. 'Their real names are Declan and Justin but they're nicknamed Ronnie and Reggie. Tweedledum and Tweedledee, more like. But don't be saying that to their faces, mind. They're not averse to chucking their weight around and using their fists on those who they think don't pay them or their grandmother sufficient respect.'

'Nice.' My voice is heavy with sarcasm.

'That is one word I have never heard in connection with those two.'

'What do they do for a living?'

'Your guess is as good as mine. Some say they simply live off their grandmother, but there are also rumours they're involved in organised crime—you know, protection rackets and such. Plus they gamble a lot on boxing. They're very keen on their boxing.'

Hence the use of their fists.

'Are they ever in trouble with the law?'

Susi laughs loudly. 'When are they not? But, sadly, nothing serious enough to put them in prison. They keep getting off. Probably by intimidating witnesses. They claim they're misunderstood and that they are nice boys at heart.' She laughs again but she is not amused.

'You seem to know a lot about them.'

She sighs. 'Brenda and I used to be friends—good friends.'

'What happened?'

'It's a long story.'

'That's OK,' I say. 'This is a long dinner.'

And what a superb one it is too.

Our starter is a trio of a black truffle salad, a goose foie gras terrine, and wasabi rock lobster with mango and chilli sauce. And Susi has ordered a bottle of very expensive Chablis Grand Cru to help wash it all down, not that I'm having any of that.

She lifts her wine glass. 'To Foscote Boy.'

I raise my glass of sparkling water. 'Foscote Boy.'

'Don't you ever drink?' Susi asks.

'All the time,' I say, taking another sip of water. 'Just not alcohol.'

'The only friends I have who don't drink are all recovering alcoholics.'

She doesn't exactly ask outright if I am one, she just looks at me and leaves the comment hanging in the air, as if waiting for a response.

'Poor them,' I say.

I am not any more forthcoming and Susi eventually drops her eyes from my face to her food.

'You were telling me how you and Brenda fell out.'

'I wouldn't say we fell out, as such. We just drifted apart.' Susi takes another sip of her wine. 'You see, we're both very competitive. That's the problem.' She goes silent for a while, staring into space, before continuing. 'As you know, I've had horses with Jerry for ever, but Brenda only bought her first one about six years ago.' She smiles. 'The whole thing is ironic, really. It was me who invited her to come along to the October horses-in-training sale at Newmarket in the first place. Before that she wasn't the slightest bit interested in horses.' She pauses, sips some more. 'I love the sales. Many people use bloodstock agents to buy horses for them, but there's a real thrill about bidding yourself in the auction. And Brenda loved it too, so much so that she stuck her hand up on that very first day and bought one there and then.'

'A jumper?'

'Well, it was a flat horse at the time—a four-year-old bay gelding—but I introduced Brenda to Jerry and she sent the horse to him for jumping.'

'And hence you became rivals rather than friends.'

'We were friendly rivals at first. We laughed a lot, but she was, nevertheless, always keen to outdo me. I think she bought more horses at the sales just so she could tell people that she owned more than I did. She even outbid me several times on the same horse.'

I feel it must cost an awful lot to outbid Susi Ashcroft at anything. And I don't suppose it went down well.

A waiter arrives to take away our empty plates and then replace them with full ones. 'Sangohachi pikeperch,' he says, 'with sake beurre-blanc, green radish and sorrel. Enjoy.'

I can't remember ever having had sorrel before but it has a sharp, lemony taste and complements the fish, which is delicious, and a huge upgrade from a döner kebab. And we still have quail and Wagyu beef to come, plus the dessert.

'It's all a big shame,' Susi says sadly, going back to Brenda. 'We used to have lots of fun together, but that really changed after the twins arrived.'

'Arrived?'

'They grew up in America with their father—Brenda's son—but he died of cancer so they came to live with their grandmother in her big house in St John's Wood. That was about four years ago. I think the boys were eighteen at the time.'

'In what way did that change things between you and Brenda?' I ask, taking another mouthful of pikeperch.

'The twins brought their brash New York ways across the Atlantic to London with them. They were determined to get their own way at whatever cost to everyone else's feelings. They even threatened *me* once. At the sales. They told me in no uncertain terms that I was not to bid on a certain lot because their grandmother wanted it. One of them even said to me—with considerable malice, I can assure you—that I had a beautiful face and it would be such a shame to lose it over a horse.' She shivers at the memory. 'I complained to Brenda about what he'd said but she insisted he was only joking. But he bloody wasn't.'

No wonder Susi and Brenda had drifted apart.

* * *

'So where is the nearest station that does have trains on Sundays?'

'Lincoln,' said the barman of the Aston Arms.

'Does Market Rasen have taxis?'

The barman sucked through his teeth. 'Not on a Sunday.'

I'd just have to get one from Lincoln to come and fetch me.

I took my phone out of my pocket and turned it on. It rang almost immediately—voicemail. 'You have five new messages,' said the computer-generated voice. They were all from Jerry Dickinson.

'Miles, I'm outside,' said the first one. 'Ready to go when you are.'

'I've just been told,' said the second in a slightly raised tone, 'that you don't want to speak to me. I'm not surprised, either, after that performance. But I'm still waiting outside to drive you home.'

'OK, then,' said the third message angrily. 'Make your own bloody way home.'

The fourth was from a little later, during his drive. It was echoey and had obviously been recorded using a hands-free system. And he'd had time to build up a head of steam. 'Now listen to me, you little shit. Jockeys don't send officials out to tell trainers that they won't speak to them. Not even McCoy does that. And especially not a conditional who's in my employment. So watch your step, young man.'

The final one was from just a few minutes earlier and was more measured, but still blunt in its meaning. 'Miles, I'm just home. First lot goes out at seven o'clock tomorrow morning. If you're not here then, you can collect your cards.'

I clearly needed that taxi if I wanted to keep my job.

But was being a jump jockey still my passion?

Hardly. At the moment, I was hating every minute of it.

My extended run of poor results had more than dented my confidence, it had torn it into shreds and flushed it down the toilet. But what hurt me more were the continuous, unfavourable and spiteful comparisons with my father.

'Such a shame,' one of the regular columnists had written in the *Racing Post* during the week. 'Miles is devaluing the Pussett name. It would be better for everyone if this flawed son of a great champion found something else to do for a living.'

I found the comment incredibly hurtful but maybe he was right. Goodness knows what he would say after that afternoon's debacle.

But I didn't feel that I was doing anything different from eight months previously when my standard had been flying high and the very same pressman had hailed me as a possible future champion.

Nothing different, that was, other than my alcohol intake. Maybe that was the problem, although I didn't feel that it had adversely affected my riding. It wasn't as if I was drinking before I went to the races—I hadn't quite stooped to that level.

Time to decide if I wanted to keep my job or not.

I rang a firm of Lincoln taxis and booked one to come and get me. Next, I looked up the train times. The last train that could get me home tonight had left Lincoln half an hour ago. Perhaps biting the bullet and going with Jerry wouldn't have been such a bad idea after all.

'I wonder how much a taxi is to Lambourn,' I said, counting the remaining cash in my pocket.

'Where's Lambourn?' asked the barman.

'Between Swindon and Newbury.'

'Blimey. That's bloody hours away.'

Too many hours. Even if the taxi driver was prepared to take me all the way there at this time on a Sunday evening, it would cost more than I could afford. But could I afford not to?

I looked up more train times and found that I could get a train from Lincoln at half past nine tonight and, after a change at Newark, I could be at King's Cross in London by midnight. Then there were night trains from Paddington to Reading and an early-morning service from Reading would get me to Hungerford by twenty to six in the morning. I could run the eight miles from Hungerford Station to Lambourn and still be at work by seven.

I looked at the time readout on my phone.

20:27.

I grabbed my bag and went outside to wait for the taxi. Getting to Lincoln station within the next hour might be tight.

18

AFTER THE FIRST four courses at The K, I am completely stuffed. So much so that I scarcely have room to force down the Felchlin chocolate tart, together with Vietnamese coffee ice cream and liquorice caramel.

'Magnificent,' I say, leaning back in my chair and holding my bulging stomach. 'It's a good job I'm not riding light tomorrow.'

Indeed, it's a good job I'm not riding at all.

'Do you ride much these days?' Susi asks over coffee.

'Only the ice,' I reply with a laugh. 'This morning was the first time I've been on a horse in over seven years.'

'What do you mean by riding the ice?'

'I certainly didn't come to St Moritz for the horseracing. I'm here to ride the Cresta Run.'

Susi looks at me quizzically, so I explain to her how grown men, wearing skin-tight Lycra sliding suits, hurl themselves head-first down a frighteningly steep ice chute at speeds close to eighty miles per hour just for the fun of it—no pay or prize money—with the daily risk of concussion, broken bones and even death.

As I speak, her big eyes get even bigger and her eyebrows climb steadily towards her hairline.

'How often do you do it?'

'As often as I can. The Cresta season runs from the week before Christmas until the first week in March, give or take, depending on the weather conditions. The ice is not artificially cooled so, when it gets too warm, the ice melts and the season's over. But I'm usually long gone by then. I'll only be here for a few more days this year.'

That's actually because my money is running out rather than any change in the temperature, but I decide not to tell her that.

'But do you ride the ice every day you're here?'

I nod. 'Several times a day if I can. Unless the weather's too bad—heavy snow or fog are the worst. Tower has to be able to see that the track is clear before allowing someone to start. It's too dangerous otherwise.'

She shakes her head in disbelief.

'I only didn't ride it today because I was at White Turf, but I'll be there tomorrow morning trying to go quicker than I did yesterday, or the day before. A little bit faster every day, that's my aim, and I love it.' I smile at her.

'You must be mad,' she says.

Indeed, I am, but my madness long preceded my first visit to the ice in St Moritz. Zipping along the ice at eighty miles per hour is therapy for, not the cause of, my mental health problems.

They are the result of other factors.

* * *

I made it to Lincoln Station with only a minute to spare, having unsuccessfully implored the taxi driver to go a bit faster.

'More than my job's worth to get a speeding ticket,' he replied dryly as he drove along sedately at twenty-five miles per hour.

At that rate, even if he had been prepared to take me all the way to Lambourn—which he wasn't, I'd asked him—I'd probably have arrived too late anyway.

I paid him with no tip, then jumped out of the taxi and ran into the station, skipping through the open ticket barriers and onto the single-carriage train only seconds before its doors closed.

I was laughing. At least I'd won that race by a short head.

We set off and I began to feel a little better.

I took out my phone and looked again at my journey details. I had twenty minutes to change trains at Newark. I'd buy a ticket there.

But I never did.

It was meant to be a half-hour journey between Lincoln and Newark, with three scheduled stops, but the train actually made four, grinding to a halt in the middle of nowhere with only darkness visible through the windows.

After about ten minutes of inaction, the driver came out of his cab into the coach to inform me, plus the other three people on the train, that there was a signalling problem and he couldn't move until he received the go-ahead. 'The tracks cross just ahead,' he said with a laugh, 'and we don't want to be run into by the Edinburgh to London express on the main line, now do we?'

Personally, I'd have taken the chance, as the Edinburgh to London express wasn't due to arrive yet and it was the one I needed to catch from Newark, but the driver wasn't shifting in spite of my pleading. The train remained resolutely stationary for the next half an hour.

Eventually we trundled slowly into Newark North Gate station but, by this time, the horse had already bolted, departing five minutes previously for King's Cross.

Could anything else go wrong for me today?

'What time's the next train from here to London?' I asked forlornly, already knowing the answer.

'There isn't one. Not until half past six tomorrow morning,' said the driver. 'In fact, there are no more trains to anywhere from here tonight.' He was totally unapologetic, almost as if he was quite enjoying my discomfort. 'But, if you send your ticket in, you'll get your money back.'

How about my job? Did I get that back too?

He walked off, whistling happily, his work over for the day.

The other three passengers had already drifted away and I now followed them out through the exit onto the road, wondering where I should go now.

There were no taxis waiting on the rank to take me anywhere. Why would there be with no more trains?

I sat down on a bench outside the station building. I was cold, hungry and miserable. Everything I had done on that day had been a disaster. But I knew that sitting there feeling sorry for myself was not going to make things any better. It may have been August but the nights were still chilly in rural Nottinghamshire and I was only wearing a thin waterproof jacket over a short-sleeved shirt. The only thing I could be sure of was that it would get colder as the night went on.

So I picked up my holdall and went to investigate what Newark had to offer me at eleven o'clock on a Sunday evening.

The answer was not much, other than pain and despair.

*　*　*

The Fenton twins, Declan and Justin, aka Ronnie and Reggie, are waiting for me outside when I exit the Kulm Hotel after my dinner with Susi Ashcroft.

I don't notice them at first but they fall into step with me, one on either side, as I walk down the hill from the hotel.

'Hello, boys,' I say, without stopping. 'What can I do for you?'

They don't answer. They just walk with me towards the town centre.

Even this late on a Sunday evening there are plenty of people around, tourists coming out of the bars and restaurants, making their way back to their accommodations. Should I call out to them for help?

A door opens right in front of us and a group of half a dozen or so spills out onto the pavement. I decide that action is required and make a sharp left to go in through the still-open door.

Ronnie and Reggie are ready for me. They must have sensed my slight change in step. They each grab me by an arm and lock theirs through mine, frogmarching me forwards.

'We wanna talk to you, Pussett,' says Tweedledum on my right, his rich New York accent sounding slightly incongruous here among the Swiss chalet architecture.

But I don't want to talk to him. I take a deep breath to call out to the group for help but it's cut short by a vice-like squeeze on my left bicep.

'If you shout,' Tweedledee hisses with real menace into my ear, 'you might get seriously hurt.'

I stay quiet.

'Just shut up and walk,' says Tweedledum. It sounds like 'wark'.

So the three of us stride, arm in arm, through the town centre and on down towards the frozen lake. Am I, like Jerry, destined to end up face down on the ice with a bloody face and a hyphema in my eye? Or maybe worse?

The twins turn me down a side street away from the bright lights. Is this it? But why? What have I done to them?

Round another corner and we are well away from any witnesses.

They stop and push my back up against a wall so I'm facing them.

'Now then, Pussett,' says one. 'We wanna ask you some questions.'

'What about?' I ask, trying unsuccessfully to keep a nervous quiver out of my voice.

'We wanna know why our grandma's horse didn't win.'

'That's simple,' I say. 'It didn't win because some of the others were faster.'

'But, before the race, that Dickinson guy said her horse was a sure thing.'

I almost laugh. Jerry had a habit of saying his horses are a 'sure thing' before races, especially to their owners. Except, of course, in this particular case, it wasn't true. Their grandmother's horse couldn't have been a sure thing because it had been carrying an overweight breast girth and chain-mail boots, to say nothing of the needlessly heavy bridle bit.

I decide not to mention those. Not least because these two morons would think that I was responsible.

'Racehorses are not machines, you know. There's no such thing as a *sure thing* in racing. Perhaps your grand-mother's horse was having an off day.'

'We think Dickinson fixed it,' says the other twin, 'with your help.'

Whereas he might be right about the first bit, he is wrong about the second. I had nothing to do with it until after the event. But if I confirm the first, would they believe me about the second? Not a chance. So I just shrug my shoulders and bluster on.

'That's ridiculous,' I say. 'Both Jerry Dickinson's horses were clearly trying to win. Sometimes in racing things just don't turn out as you expect.'

And I rather hope that this encounter doesn't turn out as I expect either.

I begin to think that I'm convincing them, but maybe not.

'We don't believe you,' Tweedledee says suddenly. 'Dickinson as much as admitted it when we saw him earlier.'

I wonder if that was before or after they beat him up.

'And what does your grandmother think?' I ask.

They are suddenly angry. 'It doesn't matter what Grandma thinks,' one of them retorts loudly. '*We* are the ones who look after her interests.'

And more fool her, I think, if she lets them do so by intimidating her friends.

'Perhaps you need a reminder that it is the owners of the horses that pay the money and therefore it is they that call the shots, not some snivelling trainer and his hanger-on ass-kissers like you.'

There are not many racehorse trainers I've come across who would agree with that assessment of the relative hierarchy, and I also rather object to being referred to as Jerry's hanger-on ass-kisser. But I keep quiet about it because I am far more worried by what he means by 'a reminder'.

'Look,' I say, 'the fact that your grandmother's horse didn't win has absolutely nothing to do with me. I was just asked by Mr Dickinson to help out by leading a horse over from the stables. If you have any problems, you'll have to take them up with him. Now, I'm going back to my hotel.'

I try to walk forwards but they throw me back heavily against the wall. 'Not so fast.'

They are smiling as if they are enjoying themselves. One of them is even cupping his fist in his other hand, as if warming it up ready for action. Beating people up is clearly fun for them. Well, it would be, wouldn't it, with odds of two against one, especially as they love their boxing.

How did I get into this mess? More to the point, how do I get out of it?

I can hear voices speaking German, getting nearer. Two men come round the corner deep in conversation. Ronnie and Reggie both step back from me a fraction so as to not look too threatening.

'*Guten Abend,*' I call loudly to the newcomers, drawing deeply on my very limited knowledge of their language.

The men stop walking and look across at the three of us. One of them says something lengthy that I do not understand, but that doesn't stop me. '*Jawohl,*' I say, and push past the twins, walking towards the men with my right hand outstretched and, as everyone would, they shake it. Indeed, I greet them warmly, as if they are long-lost family, and I position myself between them, facing back. If Ronnie and Reggie are going to hit me now, there will be witnesses.

But the twins don't even try. They simply smile at the newcomers, wave farewell in my direction, and walk nonchalantly away. But not before one of them turns back to threaten me. 'Our business is unfinished here,' he says. 'You'd better watch your back.'

The twins finally disappear around the corner and I breathe a huge sigh of relief.

'*Danke,*' I say to my new best mates. '*Danke schön.*'

'*Bitte schön. Wer sind diese Männer?*'

'Sorry,' I reply. 'I don't actually speak German.'

'Who are those men?' he asks again in perfect English. 'Are they your friends?'

Hardly.

19

A T ELEVEN O'CLOCK on a Sunday night, Newark-on-Trent town centre was, as the Bard himself might have said, as dead as a doornail.

Even the pubs were shut.

I wandered aimlessly around the empty streets, not knowing where I was going or what I should do.

Was this what it was like to be homeless, as undoubtedly I would be when I failed to turn up for work in the morning?

I fleetingly wondered if I should call Jerry and explain my predicament, but I dismissed the notion almost as soon as I thought of it. For a start, he would be asleep by now, and secondly it would give him another reason to shout at me, and I didn't think I could take that.

Instead I started looking for a place to bed down for the night, and somewhere more appealing than a shop doorway.

At least I still had a few pounds left in my pocket, and a debit card with which I supposed I could increase my overdraft. But I worried about the bank coming after me for that money now that I wouldn't be earning.

They would force me to sell my Golf. So I worried about how I would get around. But maybe I wouldn't have any need to get around, and I worried about that too.

In fact, I worried about everything, but top of my immediate agenda was finding myself a proper bed for the night. And that was a lot easier said than done, because the only hotel I could find in the town centre was closed for renovation, with scaffolding covering the frontage.

It felt like the whole world was against me.

I was cold, I was hungry and I was tired, at rock bottom, and the night seemed to stretch ahead of me like a long dark tunnel with not even the slightest glimmer visible at the end.

I sat down on the edge of the pavement wondering what the hell I should do.

I thought about going back to the railway station. Maybe a waiting room would be open. But what was the point? There weren't any trains—not even one to step in front of to end all this misery.

And then things got even worse.

A car swept into view, catching me slightly unawares. As it turned, its headlights illuminated me briefly and my mind jumped back again to the M5 near Taunton all those years ago, and the brick lorry.

There was a warning tingling in my fingers, but that accelerated rapidly into a full-on panic attack, similar to the one I'd had when driving to Newton Abbot, but this one was far more intense.

I lay back onto the cold stone as a searing pain spread across my chest and down my arms. I was in such agony that, at one point, it caused me to arch my back so only my feet and head were in contact with the ground.

I couldn't breathe. I was convinced I was dying and just hoped that the end would come quickly.

Gradually the pain eased a fraction and I rolled over onto my side and lay in the road, shivering uncontrollably, with my head down on the tarmac.

Part of my brain was in turmoil and part was working normally. I seemed unable to master my own movements yet I was aware of what was happening, and the lack of control was terrifying. But my mind was also racing with images of impending doom and dread, of tearing metal and broken bodies, of sleeping-pill overdoses and rigor mortis.

A second pair of headlights appeared in my limited arc of vision and I was convinced that this was the brick lorry, coming back to claim my life as well as that of my father. I tried to scream but no sound emanated from my mouth— I didn't have the breath.

But these particular headlights stopped before they hit me and, suddenly, there were two sets of voices above me.

'Is he drunk?' one of them asked.

I tried to shake my head but, such were my trembles, they probably wouldn't have realised. True, I'd had a couple of stiff drinks, but that had been hours ago. I wasn't drunk. Maybe I wished I was.

'I'll call an ambulance,' said a different voice. 'He'll have to go to hospital.'

Good idea, I thought.

Hospitals are warm. They also have beds.

*   *   *

I stick like glue to my new-found friends as I make my way back towards my lodgings in St Moritz. Fortunately they are going my way, not that I don't also keep a keen eye open for the terrible twins.

'What did those men want?'

It is a good question. What did they want? Do they have any evidence that Jerry had fixed the race or were they just spoiling for a fight with whoever they could find, and on any pretext?

'I have no idea,' I say. 'But I'm very grateful to you both for coming to my rescue. Goodness knows what would have happened otherwise.'

They seem quite shocked by my intimation.

'Are you saying they might have hurt you if we hadn't arrived?'

I force a laugh. 'I don't expect so.' But I don't believe myself for a second, and nor do they.

'Was it to do with drugs?' one of them asks boldly, and, instantly, the atmosphere changes. 'We don't want foreign drug dealers in Switzerland, and certainly not in our town.' His tone is suddenly quite hostile and maybe he's wishing they'd left me to fend for myself.

'No,' I assure them, pulling the pockets of my jacket inside out. 'No drugs. Those men are just upset that their horse didn't win the race this afternoon.'

They laugh. Our friendship is restored.

I make it to my *Gasthaus* unscathed and I ensure that my bedroom door is well and truly locked, because I can't watch my back and sleep at the same time.

* * *

Ironically, the ambulance took me back to Lincoln, to the emergency department at Lincoln County Hospital, little more than a mile from the station where I'd narrowly caught the fateful train only two hours before.

By the time the ambulance arrived to scoop me off the tarmac in Newark, I'd recovered somewhat and had also discovered that the voices above me belonged to two policemen who'd been on a late-night patrol through the town centre in their squad car.

I was assessed at the scene by the paramedics, who concluded that I'd *simply* had a panic attack—a mental aberration, as they called it. However, after consultation between themselves and the two policemen, they decided it would probably still be best if I went with them to hospital, just to be on the safe side. I didn't argue. I was all for it, laying on my concern, especially over the dreadful pain that I'd experienced in my chest.

And it wasn't all pretence. I still considered it remarkable that a 'mental aberration' occurring high up in my brain could have such devastatingly painful physical effects lower down in my body.

I remained seriously worried about my heart.

One of the paramedics drove the ambulance while the other took my blood pressure and then rigged me up to an electrocardiograph machine as I lay on the stretcher in the back.

'I can assure you, Mr Pussett,' he said, scanning the readouts, 'you've not had a heart attack. Everything is quite normal.'

That was a relief. Something had finally gone my way.

But why was I so pleased by the news? Indeed, why should I care about my health at all? Less than an hour previously, I'd seriously considered the possibility of killing myself by walking in front of a train. A fatal heart attack would surely have saved me the trouble.

I was clearly confused.

Did I want to die or not?

Not just at that moment, I decided.

But tomorrow would be another day.

*   *   *

Mornings on the Cresta start early, not least because, by noon, the warmth of the sun's rays will soften the surface of the ice, and that will make you go slower. The early birds catch more than the worm here, they catch personal bests, and that's what I'm seeking, day in and day out.

Mondays are for practice, with competitions occurring mostly at weekends or on Wednesdays. But practice is still a competition as far as I'm concerned.

I'm competing against myself.

Go faster—*go faster*. Every day of the week and twice on Sundays.

There is a lightening of the eastern sky as I walk up through the town towards the clubhouse. According to the almanacs, the sun rises at about half past seven in St Moritz in the middle of February, but it's always a long while after that before the fiery globe makes a warming appearance above the surrounding peaks.

As I walk, I keep my eyes peeled for the pugnacious twins, but no one in their right mind would be out in this freezing air unless they had to be—except me, of course, but then, I'm not in my right mind anyway.

A crystal-clear sky overhead has let the mercury drop rapidly overnight and a flashing neon sign informs me that it is twenty degrees below zero. At least the track will be nice and hard.

The St Moritz Tobogganing Club is a tiny slice of England set in the middle of Switzerland, with its Union Jack flying high above the control tower. It was the British that first started this high-risk foolishness and, while other nationalities are welcome and numerous as members, the president is almost always a Brit, as decreed by the club founder, a Swiss, back in 1887.

Practice starts at eight o'clock, just as soon as it is sufficiently light for the total course length to be seen from the tower. It's now seven-thirty so I go into the clubhouse for a quick coffee and a croissant.

A number of other crazy people are there ahead of me—new wannabe riders already kitted out in borrowed boots with rakes attached, plus knee and elbow pads and tough gloves, some even dressed in tweed jackets and plus-fours, reminiscent of the early pioneers of the 1880s and 90s.

They are all waiting for their first-day 'death talk' from the club secretary about how dangerous it is, and the X-ray montage of members' injuries is getting plenty of attention. One or two of the group have gone rather pale, perhaps thinking that this may not be such a good idea after all, in spite of having already paid a large, non-returnable deposit.

I remembered back to my first day on the Cresta.

Just like these here today, I was apprehensive and a little bit scared, but not so much of injuring myself, more of being seen to be a fool.

Perhaps I still am.

On that first day I had ridden a club toboggan from Junction, as beginners and novices always do. Junction is the name given to the section of the run as it passes the clubhouse. It is about a third of the way down from Top, from where only those who have qualified with fast enough times from Junction are permitted to start.

It took me two whole seasons to become a Top rider, and every year I have to do a qualifying time from Junction when I first arrive, in order to maintain my status.

The Cresta Run is one of the few sporting activities where people can go faster with increasing age, and there are some long-standing club members, now in their sixties, who are still producing their personal-best times. The current record time from Top was set by someone in their mid-forties.

Nowadays, I am seen as one of the more seasoned riders, but even the most stalwart of us would have to admit to being a touch afraid every time we are called by Tower to 'the box'.

Practice today will initially start from Top, meaning those anxious beginners will have a little longer for their nerves to fray before they are permitted onto the ice.

It is a quiet morning at the club.

Last evening, while I was enjoying the culinary delights of The K with Susi Ashcroft, members of the Shuttlecock Club were elsewhere in the Kulm Hotel for the annual Shuttlecock Dinner, and many are still sleeping off the effects.

Membership of that particular club is restricted to those who have crashed at Shuttlecock, and that means most who have ever ridden the Cresta.

Although I qualify many times over, I have only been to the Shuttlecock Dinner on one previous occasion, in my first season. I tell myself that it is too expensive and that is why I don't go but, if I were being honest, it is actually because of the vast amount of alcohol that is expected to be consumed by all attendees.

Lead me not into temptation—so I now stay away.

I change into my protective sliding gear, collect my toboggan and helmet, and take the camion up to Top. I am one of only three riders in the transport so it's looking promising for multiple runs today.

On a good practice day there can be as many as two hundred total rides on the ice, including those from both Top and Junction, and it is not unheard of for some riders to get in six or seven runs just for themselves, that's if they are exceptionally brave—or stupid.

'Miles Pussett to the box,' is announced through the Tannoy.

I drag my toboggan onto the ice.

'Take it easy,' I tell myself. 'This is a practice not a competition and, remember, last time down you fell at Shuttlecock. Just use this run to get your confidence back.'

But will I take any notice of my own advice? Unlikely.

Out of sight, down at the control tower, the bell is rung to indicate that the track is clear. The start officer lifts the wooden barrier and I'm away, the familiar surge of adrenalin again coursing through my veins.

Boy, am I living my life to the full!

20

THE ACCIDENT AND emergency department of Lincoln County Hospital was surprisingly busy for so late on a Sunday night.

Rather than taking me straight in for treatment on the stretcher, as I had hoped, the paramedics decided I was well enough to walk in through the main door and join the throng of others sitting patiently—or not so patiently—in the waiting room. That way, they explained, it released them to go and help someone else in greater need.

At least it was warmer in the waiting room than out on the streets of Newark, and I found a corner where I could lean up against the wall and go to sleep, all the while clutching my holdall to my chest.

'Mr Pussett?' called a female voice, rousing me from my slumbers. 'Mr Miles Pussett?' An attractive young woman in blue scrubs stood in the middle of the waiting room, her blonde hair tied back in a ponytail.

'Here,' I shouted, standing up.

'Good.' She smiled. 'Follow me.'

She led me through a door and into a cubicle, where she pulled the curtains around us.

'I'm Rachel,' she said, turning and smiling broadly at me again. 'I'm one of the emergency night nurses here. I'm so sorry you've had to wait. It's always rather busy in here after the pubs close, even on a Sunday.' She laughed. 'Now it's your turn, so how can I help you?' She smiled at me again and indicated towards a chair for me to sit on.

It was too much.

My outer veneer cracked and I couldn't stop myself from crying, huge sobs wracking through my body. Perhaps it was just relief at feeling safe, or maybe it was because there was finally someone else who seemed to care.

'There, there,' Rachel said, placing a comforting arm across my shoulders. 'You have a good cry. It will make you feel better.'

After five minutes or so the weeping eased and I really did feel better. And, throughout, Rachel had just stood there quietly, not placing any pressure on me or urging me to 'pull yourself together', as my grandfather had always done whenever I'd cried as a young boy.

'I've looked at the paramedic's report,' Rachel said finally, pulling up a second chair for her to sit down next to me. 'It shows your blood pressure is fine and your heart trace is normal. But it also says that you had some sort of panic attack.'

I told her all about the intense pain in my chest and my inability to move. I also told her about my fear, not only of the attack but of the headlights, and why. I told her of my thoughts about killing myself and I explained to her what had happened at Market Rasen races, and why I would now lose my job, and my home.

In all, I must have spoken to her for almost an hour, but she didn't hurry me to finish, or say that she had something more important to attend to.

When I'd run out of things to say, Rachel stood up.

'How about a cup of tea?' she said. 'And some toast?'

'That sounds wonderful.'

She disappeared and, presently, returned with a tray holding a cup of tea and a plate of buttered toast. I tucked in eagerly.

'You need to see our specialist mental health team,' Rachel said.

'Mental health?' I said, surprised. 'But I'm not crazy.'

She smiled at me again. 'Of course not. But there is definitely something not quite right and it might be useful for you to see someone, to talk things through, just like we have done tonight.'

Maybe she had a point. Having someone to talk to did seem to have unburdened much of the stress I was carrying. I had felt it gradually lift off my aching shoulders, as if my heavy load was now being shared.

'I'm training to be a psychiatric nurse myself,' Rachel said. 'And I think it would be a good idea.'

'OK,' I said. After her kindness, and the toast, how could I refuse? 'Wheel them in.'

'They're not on duty right now. But they'll be here at seven in the morning.'

Seven in the morning.

My stress levels began to rise again as I thought of Jerry's reaction I failed to turn up at that exact time for first lot.

'I can't wait until then. I need to get to Lambourn tonight.'

'You're not going anywhere tonight,' Rachel said decisively. 'You need to stay right here.'

'But I can't.' My stress levels went higher still.

'Yes, you can. I will telephone your employer before I go off-duty to tell him you have been detained here in hospital. I'm sure he'll understand.'

She obviously didn't know Jerry Dickinson.

'What time do you go off-duty?' I asked.

'Seven-thirty.'

'So what do I do now?'

'You stay here. We're not very busy now so you can either stay right here in the department on a trolley, or I can see if I can find you a bed on a ward.'

'Here is perfectly fine by me.'

Anywhere close to her would be perfectly fine by me, but I didn't say so.

She made up a bed for me on a trolley and I lay down.

'Please come and see me before you go off-duty,' I said.

'Sure will.' She smiled at me once more.

I was almost asleep before she was out of sight . . . not completely, but almost.

*　　*　　*

I make it through Shuttlecock with no problems on my first run of the day, partly because I have heeded my own advice at the top and have taken it fairly easy, raking hard into the turn.

'Pussett down in five-three point four-one,' says Tower.

Not bad. Slower than my two completed runs in the Grand National, but it's still not bad. I'll try and go faster next time.

I lift my toboggan from the track and load it onto the camion for the ride back to Top. With luck I'll get in a couple of runs before the control tower decides to switch the start point to Junction for the beginners' first attempts.

The camion waits for a couple more riders and then we are off, negotiating the 514ft change in altitude between Top and the finish, a vertical separation of more than three times the drop over Niagara Falls.

I sit on a bench in the waiting hut until it is my turn.

'Miles Pussett to the box,' comes the call.

It's pulse-racing time once more—and how I love it.

Shuttlecock spares me again, but only just.

I am beginning to master the line I should take at these speeds—surprisingly starting the turn slightly higher on the wall so that I can use gravity to steer left and down as it tightens.

I am laughing out loud as I speed down Bledisloe Straight, streaking under the road bridge and on towards the finish.

At long last, I am beginning to understand this ice.

This time the camion takes me back to the clubhouse—my fun temporarily on hold as the start switches for the next hour from Top to Junction.

Time for a coffee.

Sitting in the clubhouse bar is David Maitland-Butler.

'Hello, Colonel, what brings you here?'

He seems as surprised to see me as I him. 'I'm a member.'

'Really? Since when?'

'Since before you were born.' He says it in a manner that is designed to make me feel foolish. 'I used to be a regular here. I was in the Army team that won the Inter-Services Cup back in the eighties.'

'Has it changed much?'

'We never had any of these fancy sliding suits or full-face helmets they use now. Just a pair of coveralls and an old motor-cycle dispatch rider's helmet with leather sides. That was good enough for us.'

He makes it sound like the change to more modern and safer equipment is definitely for the worse.

'I thought you'd be supervising the loading of your horse.'

'Not leaving now until tomorrow. Dickinson told me he has some trouble with his staff. Damned nuisance. Something to do with a broken ankle.'

'How's Jerry doing?'

'It's not he who has the broken ankle.'

'I know. But he also had a fall on the ice yesterday. He hurt his face and spent last night in the local clinic.'

'Did he? How strange. He didn't mention it to me.'

I wonder why I don't tell the colonel the truth, that Jerry was beaten up by the Fenton twins. Maybe it is out of loyalty to my former employer and the knowledge that the colonel would think it funny. Perhaps I shouldn't have mentioned anything in the first place.

'Did you actually see him?' I ask.

'We spoke on the phone. Last night. He asked if I could provide a groom to look after his two on the way home. I said no. I've only one boy here and he's quite busy enough with mine.'

So Jerry had called the colonel after all—and with the predicted outcome.

'He's arranging for someone to fly out today to take his home tomorrow.' He smiles. 'But it's actually quite fortuitous. My horsebox has developed an engine fault that won't be fixed until tomorrow anyway.'

'Does Jerry Dickinson know that?'

He doesn't answer, but the supercilious smirk on his face tells me everything. If I know the colonel, which I do, he'll have made Jerry pay for the extra night's accommodation for his horse, plus for him and the stable lad.

It's not that the colonel couldn't afford it—he could easily. But it's one more example of racing's competitive nature. The colonel simply looks upon it as an opportunity to get one over another trainer—similar to beating him on the track.

I suppose I shouldn't be surprised. Jerry would have done exactly the same to him if the roles had been reversed.

'So, are you here to ride the ice?' I ask, changing the subject.

'I think I'm too old for that now, don't you?'

'Nonsense. You're what, in your mid-sixties? Lord Bra-bazon won the Coronation Cup here when he was seventy-one. And the oldest person ever to complete the course was a sprightly ninety-year-old.'

'You seem to know a lot,' the colonel says, dryly.

'I'm just fascinated by the history of the run, that's all.' Why wouldn't I be? The Cresta has been my saviour.

'Well, I'm still not going down,' the colonel says emphatically. 'I value my health too much these days. As someone once said: *When the exhilaration is worth the fright, then you must ride the Cresta. But when the exhilaration is not worth the fright, then you must give it up.* Well, the fright for me is far too much these days, so I've given it up.'

He clears his throat as if he has become somewhat emotional.

'But I thought I'd pop along for a Bullshot, just for old time's sake. I still pay my club dues every year, so I might as well make some use of the place.' He raises a glass of brown liquid towards his lips. 'Fancy one?'

'No, thanks.' A Bullshot is a mixture of beef stock and vodka, a Cresta classic, but not my tipple. Not any more. 'I'll just have a coffee.'

'As you like.' He takes a large swig of his drink and stares at my own fancy sliding suit visible beneath my open anorak. 'Have you been down today?'

'I certainly have. Twice from Top already this morning, and I'll be going down again later.'

'Oh, the joy of being young and fearless,' quips the colonel. 'But you'll learn.'

I hope not.

21

T RUE TO HER word, Nurse Rachel came to see me before she went off-duty at seven-thirty, and she brought more tea and toast with her.

I was still in the A & E department at Lincoln County Hospital, having spent the remainder of the night on a trolley in one of their cubicles, fast asleep with neither a brick lorry nor a pair of headlights to be found anywhere in my dreams.

'I phoned Mr Dickinson,' she said.

'And?'

'He seemed quite angry at first, told me to tell you not to bother coming back.'

'At first?'

'Yes, well, I can get angry too, and I gave him a right earful about how employers could get into serious trouble for bullying their employees.'

'I bet that didn't go down well.'

'No, it didn't, but then I explained that you had wanted to leave in order to get back to work on time this morning, but we insisted you should remain here to see our specialist team.'

'Did he ask why?'

'He certainly did.'

'And what did you say?'

She looked a bit sheepish. 'I shouldn't have said anything, not without your permission.'

'But you did.'

She nodded.

'It's all right,' I said, smiling at her. 'I give you my permission now.'

She looked relieved.

'What did you actually say to him?'

'I really shouldn't have said anything at all, but he kept going on and on at me about how you had simply not done as you were told and it was all your own fault. He was being quite nasty so, in the end, I told him you had to see the specialist mental-health team because we were worried about you. I'm so sorry. It just slipped out. It was so unprofessional of me.'

'It's all right,' I said again, smiling at her.

Now give me your phone number. I didn't actually say it but I so wanted to.

'What did he say then?' I asked instead.

'He just suddenly shut up. He then wanted to know when you would be ready to come home. He said he'd send a car for you.'

Blimey!

'And what time will I be ready to go home?'

'You can go any time you want. Irrespective of what I told Mr Dickinson, we are not forcing you to stay here, just advising it. The mental-health team are here now and they will come and see you shortly. You should be able to go home by eleven o'clock at the very latest. I can't think they'll want to keep you in. That's what I told Mr Dickinson.'

'Thank you.'

'Right,' she said. 'I'm off home myself now. Good luck.'

She smiled at me once again and made my heart rate rise in delight.

'How do I contact you?' I said, just a tad too eagerly as she started to leave the cubicle. 'To let you know how I get on.'

And do you have a boyfriend? Or are you married? With kids?

There was no ring on her wedding finger but that meant nothing. Rings might not be allowed because they were a potential infection risk.

'I'm here four nights a week. Seven-thirty PM to seven-thirty AM, Sunday through to Thursday morning,' she said, smiling. 'You can always call the department.'

'Thanks,' I said. 'I will.'

*   *   *

The mental health team consisted of a doctor and a clinical psychologist—at least, they were the two that came to see me.

I had been shifted off my comfortable A&E trolley and into a small windowless room containing four typical hospital arm-chairs, with bright-green, faux-leather upholstery, plus a small oval coffee table.

I sat down facing them both.

'Now tell us,' said the doctor, 'what is it that you think brings on these attacks you've been having?'

'I've only had two of them,' I said. 'But they have both been rather intense. I really thought I was dying last night.'

'In what way?'

I gave them the details of the attacks and how headlights seemed to have been the trigger in both cases, and why that was. I told them of the brick lorry and how I had been in my father's car when he'd been killed, and also how I had found my mother dead and stiff on her bed from an overdose of sleeping pills.

Somehow it was easier telling it for a second time after having already told the whole story to Rachel.

They sat patiently and listened, not interrupting or asking any questions, until I finally stopped.

'And how do you feel about your life in general, during those times when you are not having an attack?' asked the doctor.

'Depressed,' I said. 'Especially recently.'

'Why do you think that is?'

I spoke about the bad run of form I'd been having at the track and how, when I did get the chance to win, my confidence was so low that I often made a hash of it. I told him about the race at Market Rasen the previous day and how it was my fault that I hadn't won it, and how angry my employer had been.

'Yes,' he said. 'I've heard all about his anger from Nurse Valentine.'

'Nurse Valentine?'

'Rachel Valentine,' he replied. 'I think you spoke to her last night.'

Valentine! Oh, Rachel, please be my valentine.

'And having to control my weight so much doesn't help either.'

'In what way?'

'Yesterday I had to ride at ten stone two pounds and that includes five pounds for my clothes, my boots and my saddle. So I had to be nine-stone-ten stripped. I stand five foot nine inches in my socks, that's tall for a jockey, which means that my body mass index is about twenty.

'You may think that sounds pretty healthy, but I have to be strong to be able to control a horse over fences at thirty miles per hour, so I have big muscles. Hence, I have no fat on me and, in order to keep it that way, I scarcely eat anything at all.

'My whole life is governed, controlled and determined by my bathroom scales. I stand on them every morning in trepidation, terrified that I will have put on a pound since yesterday.

'And, if I have to do really light, say at nine-five body weight, I have to waste, rapidly losing even more weight by eating absolutely nothing and getting rid of body fluid by long hours of sweating in a sauna, and then not drinking anything to replace it. That can also make you pretty miserable.'

It can also directly affect the balance of your mind. Fred Archer, champion jockey for thirteen consecutive years and perhaps the most successful jockey of all time with a career win percentage of an incredible 33 per cent, shot himself dead at the height of his considerable fame, still aged only twenty-nine, while delirious from having wasted for three whole days to ride at an unnaturally low weight, even for him.

'Have you spoken to your own doctor about how you feel?'

'I don't have my own doctor.'

'You must be registered with the health service.'

'I was with a surgery in Yorkshire but never changed it when I moved back to Lambourn. I suppose that technically makes the Malton doctor still mine. But I see doctors all the time, mind. Every time I have a fall, I have to pass a doctor in order to ride again. That's about once a fortnight on average over the past year. I'd speak to one of them about something if I needed to.'

But maybe not about my mental health, I thought. I wouldn't want any busybody racecourse doctor telling the authorities I wasn't fit to ride because I was going crazy.

'Well,' said this doctor, half-turning towards the psychologist as if seeking her approval, 'we think that you should register with a GP near where you live now and ask for an appointment. You need some help. Panic attacks can be very debilitating, as well as potentially dangerous, and yours may be as a consequence of some other underlying psychological problem, possibly PTSD.'

'PTSD?' I asked.

'Post-traumatic stress disorder.'

'Isn't that what soldiers get?'

'Others can suffer from it too. It's brought on by traumatic events. It's best known for affecting the military but it's also quite common elsewhere. In your own case, it may be a response to what happened when your parents died, and your current depressive state has made things come to a head. Only a full psychiatric assessment will determine if PTSD is the cause of these attacks, or if there's some other reason. And, for that, you'll need to be referred by your GP.'

I didn't particularly like the sound of a full psychiatric assessment.

'And what if I do have this PTSD thing? What then? Can it be cured?'

'Psychotherapy and medication can alleviate most of the symptoms and make things easier to bear. You should be able to return to a normal productive life.'

I took that to mean, 'No, it can't be cured.'

'And what if I tell you that I'm perfectly fine and I don't need some quack messing about inside my head?'

He smiled at me in a kindly manner. 'It is often the patient who is the last to realise that something is wrong, when all around them can see it clearly. I hope that you agree that it's better to find out for sure. If you do indeed have PTSD, research shows that without treatment, attacks like you had last night are likely to get more frequent and more severe.'

Not much to look forward to there, then.

CHAPTER

22

'MILES PUSSETT to the box.'
My third run of the morning and it's still only
ten-forty. Maybe there will be time for another—perhaps
two more. The most I have ever managed in a day was five,
but they'd all been from Junction. Now I am starting at
Top.

My heart rate rises a notch or two in anticipation and
also with a touch of fear. But for me, unlike the colonel, the
exhilaration is still definitely worth the fright. And long may
it be so.

The bell on the tower is rung and the barrier across the
track is lifted.

Time to go.

The track ahead of me glistens due to a very slight
thaw, producing a thin layer of water over the still-hard ice
surface beneath. Perfect conditions for fast times.

'Right,' I say to myself. 'You now know the line to take
into Shuttlecock, so let's go for it.'

I lean down and push my toboggan fast along the ice,
leaping on at the last moment, and I'm away. I almost fly
over Church Leap, and then I'm on through the upper

bends and along Junction Straight, all the time picking up speed.

Again the question rises in my head—do I rake or not? Not.

I use my new-found line into Shuttlecock and make the turn with ease, pulling myself forward on the toboggan for extra speed as I hurtle down Bledisloe Straight.

Such is the vibration that it is impossible to see more than five to eight yards ahead and I am relying mostly on my memory of how the run twists and turns—just three slight curves and the Cresta Leap to go.

Hello, hello. Personal-best time, here I come . . . maybe even membership of the Five-O Club, joining that handful of elite members who have been down in under fifty-one seconds, hence posting a five-o something time.

However, it is not my back I should have been watching out for.

It's my front.

There is an object lying on the track. Something dark, in the shadow of the road bridge. I see it only at the very last instant and, at the speed I am travelling, there is simply no way to avoid it.

I hit it full-on at eighty miles per hour. I don't have time to rake or even to roll off my toboggan.

One moment I'm hurtling along in expectation of my personal-best time and the next I am flying through the air like a rag doll before crashing back onto the ice at least fifteen to twenty yards further on.

I land heavily, first on my right shoulder and then on my back, the force of the latter impact driving the air from my lungs. I instantly know I've done some serious damage, as the pain that shoots through me is excruciating.

But I still don't stop moving.

I slide on down to the bottom of the run on my back, feet first, but without my toboggan, which appears to have gone elsewhere. At least that's a relief, as I don't fancy the thirty-five kilograms of it crashing into me as well.

Finally, I come to a halt at the lowest point and I lie stationary on the ice in total agony, unable to move, waiting for help to arrive.

The first person to appear is one of the men from the company that construct the track each year from scratch, and maintain it throughout the season.

'You OK?' he asks in heavily accented English.

But I am unable to reply because the pain is making breathing difficult.

The man is soon joined by two others and they radio to Tower that medical help is urgently needed.

Someone else then arrives holding my toboggan and we can all see that it is badly deformed at the front, bent out of shape by the force of the collision.

They look horrified, as am I.

Suddenly, all sorts of people are around me, including the hierarchy of the club, and all of them want to know what happened.

'I hit something,' I finally manage to say, although my words are muffled by my helmet.

Someone bends down to remove it.

'Don't touch me!' I shout. 'Wait for the medics.'

They hear that all right, and back off. If my time as a jockey has taught me anything it is that you don't move an injured rider without using the proper medical procedure, for fear of doing them even more harm.

I can hear them talking about what I hit—a bag of cement has been found lying in the middle of the track.

If there was horror before, there is now uncontrolled anger.

'How could that possibly happen?' I hear someone say forcefully.

How indeed?

'But Jock came down before him, just a minute earlier. He didn't encounter anything.'

Lucky Jock.

The club secretary comes into my limited field of view.

'Miles,' he says, crouching down. 'I'm so very sorry about this. Medical help is on the way.'

'I'm cold.'

The secretary takes off his own coat and places it over me. He must be really worried, as he's now standing in only his shirt sleeves with the air temperature still close to freezing. Fortunately for him, blankets are found and he can put his coat back on again. But my back is still in contact with the ice and it's getting very cold indeed.

Finally, after what seems like an age, two medical personnel in bright-red uniforms arrive.

'Where does it hurt?' one of them says to me in English with a German accent.

'My right shoulder and my neck.'

Mention of my neck gets them very agitated.

'Can you feel your legs?' He squeezes one of my ankles.

'I can feel that.'

They relax a little.

Gingerly they remove my helmet, replacing it with a stiff surgical collar tight round my neck. Then they support my head as they roll me onto my left side to place a stretcher underneath.

The sides of the track add to their problems but they manage it eventually, but not before I have uttered a few choice Anglo-Saxon expletives both at the pain of being moved and the discomfort of having to lie on the back protector under my sliding suit.

'We will give you something for the pain,' says one of the medics.

I wonder why he didn't do that before moving me.

All the while the group from the Cresta have been standing around watching. I catch a few snippets of their conversations.

'How could such a thing happen?'

'This could close down the club. It could be the end of the Cresta Run as we know it.'

'Where did the bag of cement come from?'

And, of course, the really big question: 'Was it done on purpose?'

*   *   *

The car Jerry sent to pick me up at eleven o'clock from Lincoln County Hospital was his own Mercedes, but he wasn't driving it. Somewhat surprisingly, it was his wife behind the wheel.

I had only met her a few times, either at the races or occasionally when I'd waited in their back porch for Jerry to drive me to a racecourse. To my knowledge, she had never visited the stable yard during my time there.

'Hello, Mrs Dickinson,' I said, putting my holdall on the back seat and climbing in the front.

'Call me Sabrina,' she replied with a smile.

She drove in silence for quite a long while, right through Lincoln city centre, past the grandeur of Lincoln Cathedral with its three tall bell towers, and then out on the road towards—where else?—Newark.

'Can you recommend a doctor?' I asked her eventually.

'What sort of doctor?' Sabrina replied, keeping her eyes on the road.

'I need a GP.'

'Aren't you registered with the surgery in Lambourn? That's where everyone in the village goes.'

'No,' I said. 'I suppose I must have been registered there when I was a kid, but I never bothered when I moved back from Yorkshire.'

'It's dead easy to switch surgeries,' Sabrina said. 'Just pop in to the reception and fill out a form. They'll do the rest.'

'I can't even recall where it is?'

'On Bockhampton Road. Not far from the primary school.'

'Right. I'll pop in sometime.'

She drove on further in silence, round the Newark bypass, and on towards Leicester, where we joined the southbound M1.

'Why do you need a GP?' Sabrina asked as we passed the exit for Rugby. 'Is it something I can help you with?'

I sat there without speaking.

'I'm sorry,' Sabrina said, after a minute or so. 'I didn't mean to pry.'

'It's all right,' I said. 'And it is nice to know that some-one cares. It's just that I'm not quite sure where to start.'

'Take your time. There's no hurry. Nor any need to start at all if you don't want to.'

Did I want to?

It was one thing talking to medical professionals who I didn't know. Quite a different matter talking to the wife of my employer—an employer who had been spitting blood the last time I'd seen him.

We continued on in silence, leaving the M1 at Northampton and taking the road towards Oxford. Only when we had turned off the Oxford bypass onto the road to Wantage did I say anything further.

'They want me to have an assessment.'

'Who does?' Sabrina asked.

'The doctors at Lincoln Hospital.'

'Why?'

'They think I might have something wrong with my brain. The assessment would find out for sure.'

'But why do they think that?'

'I'm having nightmares. And also panic attacks. That's what I had last night. A panic attack. I ended up lying on a street in Newark town centre, at midnight. I thought I was dying. Two policemen found me and called an ambulance. It took me to hospital.'

Sabrina looked over at me briefly and there was real concern in her face.

'But what were you doing on the streets of Newark town centre at midnight? Weren't you in hospital because of a fall at the races?'

'No. I didn't have a fall. I was just trying to get home.'

'But I thought Jerry took you.'

'He did.'

She looked at me again, this time with puzzlement written in her features.

'Are you telling me that Jerry took you to Market Rasen but he didn't bring you home again?' She was obviously angry, and it wasn't with me.

'Yes,' I said. 'But it's not quite that simple.'

I told her about the race I had ridden on Gasfitter and how we had been beaten on the line after I'd been left flat-footed at the start, and how furious Jerry had been with me. I also explained what had happened afterwards.

I told her of my abortive attempt to travel back by train on a Sunday evening, and how everything seemed to have conspired against me.

'Even so, Jerry should never have left without you.'

She drove us round the northern side of Wantage, then up over the Downs, before finally dropping down into the 'Valley of the Racehorse', as the area around Lambourn is styled.

'Do you want to come home with me to our place?' Sabrina asked as we entered the village.

'Will Mr Dickinson be there?' I couldn't keep the anxiety out of my voice.

'I expect so,' Sabrina said. 'I know he wasn't going to the races today.'

'Perhaps I shouldn't then.'

'As you like, but you'll have to face him sometime and it might be better if I'm there to act as a peacemaker.' She looked over and smiled.

I swallowed hard. 'OK. If you say so.'

* * *

I am airlifted by helicopter the short distance to the roof of the Upper Engadin Hospital in the village of Samedan, just beyond Celerina, where most Cresta members have ended up at one time or another. This is my second visit.

The medics are taking no chances as I am strapped tight to a spinal board.

There is considerable commotion going on around me as I am being readied for the transfer. The police have now been called and the Cresta Run has been closed, at least for the rest of the day.

One of them tries to speak to me but he is shooed away by my friends in the red uniforms. They say something to the policeman in German, the only word of which I can catch is 'morphium', which I take to mean morphine.

The drug is helping, not that the pain has gone away completely. It remains concentrated in my right shoulder and I reckon I must have dislocated it. My father once put his out in a fall at Newbury when I was a small child, and he always told me it was far more painful than a break.

He may have been right.

The other thing that is almost as painful is that the emergency staff at the hospital simply use scissors to cut off my very expensive skin-tight aerodynamic sliding suit, something that took me two whole years of saving to afford.

A full body CT scan reveals that my right shoulder is, indeed, dislocated and there is also a crack in my shoulder blade. However, the really good news is that my neck and spine are undamaged and the surgical collar can be removed. Thank the Lord for the back protector after all, uncomfortable to lie on or not.

Overall, I have been very lucky. A collision at eighty miles per hour can easily be fatal. I know that well from past experience.

After what seems like a very long time, one of the doctors comes over to see me, leaning down to where I am lying flat on my back.

'I'm Dr Kaufmann, one of the orthopaedic doctors here, and I am going to put your shoulder back in place now.' He is holding a loaded syringe. 'I'm going to give you a drug called ketamine for the pain. You will not remember anything afterwards.'

That's a relief.

* * *

'You wait in here,' Sabrina said as we went into the Dickinson kitchen through their back door. 'I'll go and fetch Jerry. He'll be in the snug watching the racing on the TV.'

My heart was pounding. Maybe it was because I didn't know whether I still had a job or not, and was about to find out, or perhaps it was because I needed a drink.

Sabrina was taking some time to return and the pounding was getting worse. At one point I almost lost my nerve and walked out. But where would I go? The house I shared with the other conditionals was just that—conditional on me having a job in Jerry's stable.

After about five minutes, which felt like five hours, Sabrina came back into the kitchen. Jerry was with her.

'We have decided,' she said, 'that you should move in here with us, at least for the time being. You can have our son Nigel's old room. He works in New York and hardly ever comes home.'

I looked at Jerry and wondered if he had actually been party to this decision, or whether his wife had simply told him what was happening.

'Do I still have a job here?' I asked.

'Of course you do,' Sabrina said. 'Jerry is very sorry for leaving you behind yesterday. Aren't you, Jerry?'

He didn't look very sorry but, eventually, he nodded.

'I'm very sorry,' he mumbled, biting his lip.

He stepped forward and offered his hand, which I shook.

'I'm sorry, too,' I said.

'Then we'll say nothing more about it. Back to normal.'

The ice was broken, even if relations clearly remained somewhat frosty.

I could really do with that drink.

23

True to Dr Kaufmann's word, I have no recollection of having my shoulder put back into place. It seems that one minute I am in agony and, the very next moment, all is well—or almost.

My right arm is held tight to my body in a restrictive sling, presumably to stop it moving, and my shoulder aches as if it's been kicked by a horse, but it is a huge improvement on what it was like before.

I am lying on a bed in a single room in the hospital with a magnificent view of the Alps through the window—it is almost enough to make anyone feel better.

Hanging over a chair at the foot of the bed is what remains of my sliding suit, the Lycra cut into strips and utterly destroyed beyond repair. I wonder if my insurance will pay for a replacement. Probably not.

After a while, the doctor comes in to see me.

'Ah, you're awake,' he says. 'How are you feeling?'

'Much better, thank you.'

'Good. I would like you to rest here for a while, to allow the effects of the ketamine to wear off completely, but there are a whole host of people outside waiting to talk to you.'

'Who?'

'A policeman for a start. He's the first in line. Then there are the president and secretary of the St Moritz Tobogganing Club, together with most of their committee, plus some reporters who want a quote. It seems you are quite a celebrity. I've managed to hold them all at bay so far, but the policeman is very pressing.'

'What time is it?' I ask.

'About three o'clock.'

It is four and a half hours since I started that last run on the ice.

'Where has all the time gone?'

'That's what ketamine does to you—it steals your life away. But it works. You don't remember anything about having your shoulder reduced, do you?'

I shake my head. Perhaps I could try some more of this ketamine stuff to erase a few other bad memories.

'You had better wheel in the police and then some of the Cresta lot,' I say, 'not that I'll be able to tell them anything useful. But I'm not keen on seeing the reporters.'

'Don't worry. I'll make sure that everyone else is kept out.'

'Thanks.'

The doctor goes out and is soon replaced by a policeman in a smart blue uniform with a gun on his hip. He sits beside my bed, notebook at the ready.

Over the next half-hour he asks me lots of questions about what I did throughout the morning, but he is really only interested in one thing—did I see anyone on the bridge drop a bag of cement onto the track as I was coming down?

'I'm sorry,' I say. 'I saw absolutely no one. The only thing I saw was the bag lying on the track, and then only a fraction of a second before I hit it. Nothing else.'

'Thank you, anyway, Herr Pussett,' says the police-man, clearly frustrated by the lack of help I can give him. 'I hope you recover soon.'

He stands up and put his notebook away in his tunic.

Almost as a parting gesture, he turns back to me as he is leaving, to ask one last question. 'Do you know of any-one who would want to hurt you?'

Ronnie and Reggie? The Fenton twins?

But did they really want to hurt me to the extent of placing a bag of cement in my way when I was travelling at eighty miles per hour?

Maybe they didn't appreciate the danger.

Or maybe they did, and simply didn't care.

'I was threatened last night.' I say it very slowly but it has a galvanising effect on the officer, who instantly returns to his seat, again removing his notebook.

'Who by?' he asks, making a note.

I tell him of my encounter with Declan and Justin Fenton in the backstreets, and how I am convinced that, without the timely arrival of two local gentlemen, I'd have been beaten up.

'What is this "beaten up"?' he asks in confusion.

'Hurt. Punched, or kicked. Probably both.'

His eyes open wider, as if things like that just don't happen in the tranquil streets of St Moritz, not on his watch.

'The twins were unhappy that their grandmother's horse did not win the big race at White Turf yesterday. They believed that I had something to do with it.'

'And did you?'

'No. I did not. It simply didn't win because it wasn't fast enough.'

And that, in turn, was because it was carrying an extra stone in weight. But I don't mention that. I feel it would

complicate the issue too much. And I still need to hear
what Jerry has to say about it before I tell anyone.

'I think I had better go and speak to these Fenton men,'
says the policeman, standing up again. 'Thank you, Herr
Pussett. I will keep you informed of any progress in my
investigation.'

'Do I get any protection?' I ask.

'What do you mean?'

'If the Fenton twins did this to me on purpose they
might come back and have another go.'

'I think that is most unlikely. There would be too
many witnesses.'

Unlikely or not, do I want to take the chance?

The policeman tells me that he will advise the hospital
to take extra care, but I'm not sure it's enough.

He departs and I lie my head back on the pillow.

I have a feeling that Ronnie and Reggie are not going
to be very happy when the Swiss police come a-calling,
asking awkward questions.

I will still need to watch my back, and my front.

* * *

On Monday afternoon, just after getting back from Lincoln
and settling in at the Dickinsons', my uncle called to tell
me that my grandfather's funeral was fixed for the coming
Thursday at two o'clock in their local village church.

'OK,' I said. 'I'll be there.'

I felt I owed it to my grandfather, and also to my
grandmother, to send the old boy off properly. They had,
after all, taken me in and given me a home after my mum
died. But it would be another hugely sad affair, with lots
of tears, and I wasn't at all sure if that was the best thing
for me right now.

'Of course you must go,' Sabrina said when I told her
later. 'I'll fix it with Jerry. Will you drive up?'

I thought back to when I'd last driven back from Yorkshire, how I had searched all the way for a motorway bridge to crash into.

'No,' I said. 'I'll go by train. My uncle will pick me up from Malton.'

Thank goodness, I thought, that the funeral was during the week rather than on a Sunday, so the trains should be better.

Hence, on Thursday morning, dressed in a white shirt, black tie and my only suit, I travelled to Malton, arriving at half past midday.

One of the stops on the way was at Newark, and I had to take some deep breaths and tell myself to remain calm as the train remained in the station for three long minutes. But, with the help of a couple of hefty shots from the on-board buffet, I was fine, and my uncle collected me from Malton for the last ten miles to the tiny church of St Hilda's in Ellerburn, the same venue where my mother's funeral had been held four and a half years previously.

'How's Grannie bearing up?' I asked in the car.

'OK, I suppose,' my uncle replied. 'She obviously misses him. She keeps talking to him as if he's still there in the house. It's very strange.'

I couldn't understand why he thought that was strange. I still sometimes spoke out loud to my father and he'd been gone for years.

In spite of its small size, the church was nowhere near full as my grandfather's coffin was carried in by the undertaker's men and placed in front of the altar. My uncle supported his mother's arm as they followed it and I, in turn, walked behind them.

My uncle read a short passage from St John's Gospel, something about God's house having many rooms and one being prepared for my grandfather. Then the vicar gave a short address, but it was clear to everyone that he'd never even met the person in the coffin about whom he was speaking. And that was about it, other than 'The Lord Is My Shepherd' sung badly by the meagre congregation to pre-recorded organ music.

My grandfather wouldn't have cared. If it had been up to him, there probably wouldn't have been a religious service at all. He had regularly and persistently declared that he didn't believe in God or an afterlife, and he was proud of the fact that he'd only ever been to church for weddings and funerals, plus the odd christening, such as mine. So I suppose it was apt.

The whole thing was over in less than twenty minutes and I spent much of that time wondering why I had come all this way north just for this.

'Thank you. Lovely service,' we all said to the vicar at the church door as we exited, lying through our teeth.

And then we were off in a big car, following the hearse and coffin to the East Riding Crematorium for a quick committal and a rapid shunt into the fiery furnace, before going back to the farmhouse for some cheap sherry and a piece of chocolate cake.

Only then did my uncle approach me about the farm, as I knew he would eventually.

'Why should you have half the farm when it's been me that's lived and worked on it all my life? It's my home. And I intend to make damn sure it stays that way.'

He stormed off outside so, having said goodbye to my grandmother, I called a taxi to take me back to Malton train station. The thought of being alone in a car with my uncle at the moment was almost as bad as being in one with Jerry.

Maybe worse. And I needed another drink, one that was stronger than sherry.

* * *

Whatever Jerry might have said about things being back to normal, life certainly did not return to normal for me in Lambourn.

Perhaps there was no such thing as normality in my life. True, it was good to be finally rid of my sadistic housemates, but I discovered that living in the Dickinson household severely limited my privacy and, in particular, my ability to have a drink when I wanted one.

I took to smuggling in bottles of vodka beneath my coat and hiding them under my clothes in the chest of drawers. But it was fraught with danger, not least because of the eagle-eyed cleaner who came in every day to make my bed after I'd gone to work.

But why was I worried? I was over eighteen. It was legal for me to drink alcohol if I wanted to. So why was I so afraid of being found out? The very thought of it made me angry—angry with the prying cleaner, angry with the Dickinsons, even angry with the world for being so unfair to me. But, mostly, I was angry with myself both for the predicament I found myself in and for not standing up like a 'man' and getting over it.

The degree of anger surging inside me was both a surprise and a worry. I had never been an angry child yet here I was suddenly grinding my teeth and clenching my fists with rage.

And there were other problems too.

Sabrina took it upon herself not only to provide a roof over my head but also to put food for me on her table.

Gone were my three low-calorie microwavable curries a week, replaced with twice-daily wholesome meals made with fresh ingredients.

Of course, they were delicious and, although I begged her to give me small portions, my weight started to creep up alarmingly even after only one week.

I warned Jerry that, at this rate, when jump racing restarted again after its summer break, I would be unlikely to be able to ride anything that was to carry less than ten-stone-six.

He was furious, yet again, but he should have blamed his wife not me. She was feeding me too much. But he would also blame the booze, I thought, if only he knew about it.

Far too many liquid calories were still passing down my throat, late at night, under the bedcovers. But I needed them. I was still having the brick-lorry nightmares and the vodka helped me sleep.

'Have you been to the surgery?' Sabrina asked me at breakfast on Monday morning, a full week after she'd collected me from Lincoln.

'Not yet,' I said, biting back the urge to tell her that it was none of her business. 'I've been too busy, what with my grandpa's funeral.'

She gave me a disapproving look as if that was not a good enough excuse. 'Then you must go today. I'll run you down there, if you like.'

'It's OK,' I said. 'I can walk.'

'I'm going anyway. I have to pick up a prescription.'

Hence, half an hour later, I found myself suppressing another bout of anger as I was chaperoned by Sabrina into the Lambourn surgery.

'Please can I have a form to register as a new patient?' I asked the lady behind the reception desk.

She pulled a sheet of paper out of a filing cabinet and handed it over, together with a pen.

'Do you have your NHS number?'

I shook my head. 'I don't even know if I have one.'

'You get allocated one as a baby and you keep it for the rest of your life. Never mind. I'm sure we can get it from your previous surgery. Make sure you put their details on the form. And do you have any ID with you? A driving licence will do, provided it's got your current address on it.'

It didn't, but who was going to worry about a few hundred yards' difference?

I filled out the form, using the shared house as my current address, and handed it back to the lady along with my driving licence for her to check my details. All seemed to be in order.

'Can I also make an appointment to see a doctor?'

'Not today,' she said. 'We're already full.'

'Soon then, please.'

I forced a smile at her as she tapped the computer keyboard on her desk.

'We've had a cancellation, so I have one free slot tomorrow afternoon at two-thirty, with Dr Rasheed. Will that do?'

'Perfect. Thank you.'

Sabrina drove me back to her house. 'All set?'

'I'm seeing a doctor tomorrow afternoon.'

CHAPTER

24

THE NEXT PEOPLE allowed in to see me at the Upper Engadin hospital are the president of the Cresta Run and the tobogganing club secretary. Both look haggard and worried. Perhaps they think I will sue.

'My dear Miles,' says the president. 'We are so very sorry. We cannot see how this could have happened. We are still asking ourselves how a bag of cement could have ended up on the run.'

'How about the men stationed along the track?' I reply. 'Didn't any of them spot it?'

He sighs. 'As you know, the men are there to maintain the ice and help fallen riders. They therefore position themselves at the corners. It's where most damage is done to the ice and also where riders come off. They don't expect trouble on the straights.'

'How about the CCTV images? They must show something.'

'At that point of the run the cameras are actually attached to the bridge, one looking up and, on the other side, one facing down. They don't show the bridge at all. And the cameras that do are so far away it is impossible to discern anything. We've been looking hard at the images to see if we can see if the bag fell off a truck or something as it went over the bridge.'

I look at them. 'I had a policeman in here just now who seems to believe that it was done on purpose.'

This is clearly not a surprise to either of them. He must have told them the same thing, even if they don't want to believe it.

They clearly haven't met Ronnie and Reggie.

As I've lain here, I've come to the conclusion it is just the sort of thing the twins *would* do. Anything for a laugh, in their warped minds.

'They also think it may have been done to target me personally.'

Now my two visitors *are* surprised.

'But how could anyone be sure it was you who was coming down? We all look the same in our sliding suits and helmets, especially at speed.'

'*Miles Pussett to the box.*' I imitate the Tannoy call. 'It plays over the speakers all the way down the run. Everybody knows who's riding next.'

They both nod in agreement. 'Of course.'

'What bothers me, though,' I said, 'is where anyone would get a bag of cement from in the first place.'

'Ah, well,' says the club secretary, 'we believe they have the answer to that. Some construction work is going on right next to the bridge, the rebuilding of a retaining wall, and there's a stack of similar bags by the side of the road. Twenty-five kilos each. The police seem to think that someone may have simply picked one up, lifted it over the bridge parapet and dropped it onto the run.' He shakes his head, not in a way that indicates he necessarily disagrees with the police, but simply because he can't understand why anyone would do such a thing.

Nor can I.

'But surely they'd have been seen?'

'Not necessarily,' says the president. 'The construction team were not working this morning and that road is always very quiet in the winter. And no one was watching the run from there because today was only for practice. Not like on Saturday for the Grand National when there were lots of spectators on that bridge.'

'And you're sure the CCTV shows nothing?' I still couldn't believe it.

'Positive. There is one point on the footage when something moves rapidly down past the up-facing camera. It's only fleeting and you probably wouldn't notice it without looking carefully. It must have been the bag being dropped. And, the very next instant, you appear in the shot coming onto Bledisloe Straight. There would have been no time to do anything about it even if we had seen it.'

Is he trying to convince me, or himself?

'So is the run going to open again tomorrow?'

'That's up to the police but, if it does, we will have a man standing guard on every bridge to make sure the same thing can't happen again.'

Stable doors and bolting horses once more comes to mind.

*   *   *

Dr Rasheed kept me waiting for nearly twenty minutes at the Lambourn surgery, during which time the angry bile rose again in my throat and I nearly did a runner. As it was, I'd had to stop at the convenience store to buy myself a small bottle of liquid courage in order to make it there in the first place.

What would I say to the doctor?

Did I really need his advice?

I just needed some pills to give me a bit more undisturbed sleep every night. Then everything would surely be better, much better.

During one of my lengthy wakeful periods in the course of Monday night, I'd called the emergency department of Lincoln County Hospital. I found the telephone number online and dialled it several times, except for the last digit, before losing my nerve and hanging up.

What would I say even if she were there?

Finally, I pushed the last digit too, and it started to ring. Even so, I was about to disconnect again when someone answered.

'A & E, can I help?' said a male voice with an Australian accent.

'Can I speak to Nurse Valentine?' I said it quickly before I lost my nerve.

'Sorry, mate,' said the Australian, 'she's not here at present.'

'Could you please give her a message?'

'Sure thing. Fire away.'

'Please tell her that Miles Pussett called. I'm the jockey she helped last week after I had a panic attack in Newark. She might just remember me. I want to thank her for all her help and also to tell her that I'm going to see a doctor about my problems later today.'

'No worries.'

'Can you also give her my number?' I read it out as he wrote it down.

'I'll pass the message on, but she might not get it for a few days. She's off sick this week.'

'Nothing serious, I hope.'

'Chickenpox. Very infectious. One of the kids has got it.'

Kids?

Of course. Why had I thought anything different? Not with my luck.

'Please give her the message when you can.'

'Will do.'

He'd hung up and I'd sat there for quite a while holding my phone, feeling particularly low.

'Miles Pussett,' someone called.

It instantly brought me back to the Lambourn surgery
waiting room. 'Come on in,' Dr Rasheed said, leading me
through the door of his consulting room. 'What seems to
be the matter?'

'Panic attacks,' I blurted out, sitting down and almost
having another one on the spot. 'The mental health team
in Lincoln told me I need to get my GP to refer me for
what they called a full psychiatric assessment. They think
I might have something called PTSD.'

He smiled at me. 'And when was this?'

'When was what?'

'When you were seen in Lincoln?'

'A week ago yesterday, at Lincoln County Hospital. I
was taken there by ambulance from Newark.'

Did he not believe me?

'And what were you doing in Newark?'

Did it matter? I could feel myself getting angry again.

'I was having a panic attack,' I said. 'I was found lying
in the street at midnight by two policemen.'

It all sounded so unlikely. Even I wouldn't have
believed me if I hadn't experienced it.

'You can ask Mrs Dickinson if you don't believe me.
She's a patient here. She's the wife of my employer, Mr Jerry
Dickinson. She drove all the way to Lincoln to collect me.'
I was speaking so fast that I was hardly taking a breath.

The doctor glanced down at his watch. I knew he
was already running late and each appointment was only
meant to last ten minutes. It felt as if he wanted me out so
he could see his next patient.

But I was doing him a huge disservice.

'Miles,' he said with a smile. 'Of course I believe you.
But I'd like you to see one of the other doctors in the

practice. He deals far more in problems of this nature. I'll go and speak to him now. Go to the waiting room and I'll call you from there.'

I went back to the waiting room and, after ten more minutes, just when I was about to give up, Dr Rasheed appeared again, this time with another man who I took to be in his forties.

'Miles,' said Dr Rasheed, 'this is Dr Nixon. He's one of the other doctors here. He would like to have a chat with you.'

'Hello, Miles,' said the new man. 'Shall we go to my room?'

I stood up and followed him along the corridor to the room at the end. He closed the door behind us.

'Dr Rasheed tells me that you need some help.'

'I'm told I do.'

'And what do *you* think?'

'Will it do any good?'

'It depends,' said Dr Nixon. 'You mentioned PTSD to my colleague. I've had some experience of dealing with that from my time spent working with the army. If that is indeed the problem, then we can certainly help. The treatment does work, but it will also take time. There are no overnight solutions. It's like going on an emotional roller-coaster ride, with lots of highs and lows. But we can try to make the lows as shallow as possible, and then, hopefully, force them to go away altogether.'

I sighed loudly and almost started crying. 'Then please help me.'

*   *   *

The next arrival into my room at the Upper Engadin hospital is not a journalist looking for a quote, it is Susi Ashcroft.

'How on earth did you know I was here?' I ask.

She seems slightly uncomfortable. 'After what you told me at dinner last night, I thought about going and watching you in action. I didn't realise the Cresta Run was so close to the hotel until the concierge told me it was just along the road. So I went but, when I got there, the place was crawling with police. I asked for you and someone told me you'd crashed on the ice and been taken to hospital by helicopter. I was very worried.'

'Thank you.'

She smiles. 'Are you going to be in here long?'

'I hope not. I dislocated my shoulder but it's back in place now. They should let me go either later today or tomorrow, but I suspect my Cresta riding days are over for this year. I've cracked my shoulder blade as well.'

'But you'll be back again for more next year?'

'I hope so.'

She smiles again and shakes her head. 'You're quite mad.'

I smile back at her. Little does she know.

'I thought you'd be going home today,' I say.

'I would have, but there's a minimum-stay requirement to get a room at the Kulm. Michael had initially intended coming with me. We were going to make a short holiday of it.' She laughs. 'He now regrets he didn't come to see Foscote Boy win yesterday.'

'So how long are you staying?'

'The suite is booked until Friday but I'll probably go home on Wednesday. I'll just pay for the extra two nights.' She pauses. 'You can use it if you want, it will be paid for anyway.'

Two nights in a suite at the Kulm Hotel is very tempting, but I feel that I'd have to offer a contribution towards the cost, and I'm already well over my budget.

'That's very kind of you, but I'll probably go home myself as soon as they let me out of here.'

'As you like.'

'Have you seen Jerry?' I ask.

'Indeed I have. He came to see me this morning about nine, as I was having breakfast. He wanted to apologise for missing our dinner last night. And he's sporting quite a black eye.'

'I bet he is. The clinic must have discharged him.'

'I think he discharged himself.' She laughs. 'He kept going on about how expensive it was.'

Typical Jerry.

'I told him not to worry about the dinner as I'd had a lovely time with you instead.'

'Was he all right about that?'

'Not wild. He seemed very keen to know exactly what we talked about. He kept pressing me to remember.'

I'm sure he did. He would have been worried that I might have mentioned an overweight breast girth and chain-mail boots.

'He also asked if I knew where you were—said he needed to talk to you. All I know is you're not staying at the Kulm. I told him that.'

I lay my head back on the pillow. The last effects of the ketamine are still with me and I'm tired. Susi sees it.

'I'd better go,' she says. 'They asked me not to be too long.'

'I'm quite surprised they let you in at all. There have been some reporters outside and the doctor assured me that everyone would be kept out.'

Susi smiles at me. 'I told them I'm your mother.'

* * *

Dr Nixon arranged for me to attend the Psychological Medicine Service at the Royal Berkshire Hospital in Reading for my full psychiatric assessment.

I had no idea what to expect and was quite ready to be poked and prodded in every direction, but mostly it was just talking, even though they did take some of my blood and urine at the beginning.

'To eliminate any physical conditions that may be affecting your mental state,' said the nurse taking the samples, 'such as a thyroid problem or vitamin D deficiency.'

After that it was just me sitting in a room for nearly ninety minutes alone with a female psychologist, answering questions about my life and how I felt about certain things. She started by asking me if anyone else in my family had ever had any mental-health issues.

'Not that I'm aware of,' I said. 'But my mother did take her own life.'

She clearly thought that that was a mental health issue and made a note.

'If you feel able, can you tell me about it?'

So I told her how my mother had found her life very difficult after my father had been killed in a car accident when I was twelve. I explained how I'd come home from school one day to find her lying cold and stiff on her bed. I also described my father's accident, and how I had been in his Jaguar with him at the time he died.

'And what is your primary emotion as you recount those events to me now?'

'Guilt.' It just popped out without me really thinking, as if my subconscious was urging the word to escape my lips.

'Why?' she asked.

'I don't know how to explain it.'

'Try.'

'I suppose I feel most guilty that my father died in the crash and I didn't. If I hadn't been with him in the car, he wouldn't have had to make the manoeuvre to save me, which almost certainly killed him. I've felt particularly guilty about that ever since.'

'And your mother? Do you feel guilty about her death too?'

'Yes. I wonder how I didn't see it coming.' I was almost in tears. I took a deep breath and steadied myself. 'My mother and I didn't always see eye to eye when I was a teenager. She didn't approve of much of what I did or wanted to be, so I didn't even realise that she was so desperate. Sometimes, I used to hear her crying in the night but still I didn't go and comfort her.' I took another deep breath. 'Not a day goes by without me thinking of her, and I so wish and pray that I had behaved differently at that time—but I didn't. So, yes, I do feel guilty about her death.'

'And would you say that these feelings of guilt affect your life on a regular basis?'

'Definitely. Every day.'

I told her about the nightmare I was having—how I could see in my head the brick lorry with its blazing headlights bearing down on me, with people standing around shouting that it was all my fault.

'And how long have you been having this nightmare?'

I told her about the panic attack I'd had on the way to Newton Abbot in April and how things had gone downhill from there, with the nightmare recurring most nights since.

'But I was unhappy before that. I haven't really been happy since I moved down here from Yorkshire eighteen months ago. In fact, I haven't been properly happy for a very long time. Maybe not since I was sixteen. But things have got very much worse recently.'

'And why do you think that is?'

'My current bad form has preyed badly on my mind, together with always having to keep my weight down.'

'Keep your weight down?' she said in surprise, looking up from her note-taking. 'But you look absolutely fine to me. Even a bit too thin.'

'I'm a jockey,' I said, slightly irritated with her. 'I ride racehorses for a living. I need to be too thin.'

'Is that also what you meant by your current bad form? You mean your racing form?'

I nodded. I explained how I'd set out to be a living memorial to my father but things hadn't panned out as I'd hoped, making me feel inadequate and hopeless. I also explained how the recent critical articles in the *Racing Post* had badly affected me and how I had become increasingly angry at the slightest criticism or perceived failure.

'There has been the odd high point,' I said, remembering my win on Wisden at Huntingdon, 'but they're rare. Mostly, for the past four months, it's been loser after loser after loser for no apparent reason. I've been at my wits' end.'

'And how have you coped with that?'

'I haven't. Not really.'

'Have you taken anything?'

'You mean drugs?'

She nodded. 'Or alcohol.'

I blushed.

I know I blushed, and so did the psychologist, so there was no point in denying it.

'I have been drinking a little to help me sleep.'

'What do you call a little?'

'A couple of cans of beer. Maybe a swig or two of vodka when I go to bed.'

'How big are the swigs?'

'Well, fairly big, I suppose. But not enough to make me drunk.'

'And in the mornings? Do you ever have a drink for breakfast?'

'No,' I said, emphatically. 'Never.' I was quite shocked that she'd asked. What did she think I was, an alcoholic?

The questioning went on, probing into all aspects of my life, including my childhood and also whether I'd ever had any feelings for anyone else other than members of my family.

'I had a girlfriend once,' I said. 'When I first moved to Malton. It lasted about two years but just sort of fizzled out. It wasn't very serious. Nothing more than a kiss and a cuddle among the hay bales. Her mother didn't approve.'

'Nobody else?'

Nurse Valentine, I thought. But that was mere fantasy, not reality, especially with her having kids.

'No. Not that I wouldn't welcome a romantic liaison.'

'With a girl, or with a boy?'

Clearly nothing was off limits in this interview.

'A girl,' I said. 'Definitely a girl.' Maybe I was a little too emphatic.

'Do you have a problem with people having gay relationships?'

'Not at all,' I replied. 'It's just not my personal cup of tea.'

She moved on, getting me to describe in detail what I felt during and in the run-up to my panic attacks.

'Do you know what triggers them?'

'Headlights,' I said. 'All I can see is the brick lorry.'

Finally, she asked me to do a few cognitive tests—mental arithmetic, word games, and so on—and then we were done.

'Well?' I said as she closed her notebook and stood up.

'All very interesting,' she said. 'I will be writing to your doctor in a day or two with my diagnosis. You will also get a copy of the letter, through the post.'

It will go to the wrong address, I thought.

25

Dr Kaufmann at the Upper Engadin hospital decides that I should remain in their care overnight.

'Your body has suffered quite a severe trauma,' he says. 'And that cracked shoulder blade would benefit from you not moving it too much. We can't do much else about that. It's impossible to put a shoulder blade in plaster so you'll have to keep your arm in that sling for at least a couple of weeks. It may be sore but it will fix on its own. But I think a night of observation here would be wise.'

I agree but, in spite of what the policeman had said, I'm also worried about my safety.

'How secure is this hospital?'

'Secure?'

'The police have told me that they think this was done on purpose, even that I was specifically targeted. If so, then someone tried to kill me today and I don't particularly want them coming back in the dead of night to finish the job.'

The doctor seems quite shocked. 'I will make sure that one of our security team is permanently posted outside your door. Trust me, no one will get in here without your approval.'

'Thank you.' I pause. 'But I also have another problem.'

'What's that?'

'Apart from this,' I touch the thin hospital gown I have on, 'I have nothing to wear.'

He laughs.

I explain that I left my anorak in the hut at the top of the Cresta, my ski pants and snow boots in a locker in the clubhouse changing room, and the rest of my stuff is at my *Gasthaus*.

'I'll see what I can manage,' he says. 'Anything else?'

'My phone is also in the locker at the club, in one of my snow boots. Is there any chance you could contact the club manager and ask for someone to bring it down to me?'

'No problem. I'll give him a call.'

I feel somewhat lost without having any connection with the outside world. I reckon that reuniting me with my phone is the very least the club can do, and I will need it to arrange my flight home.

'I presume this puts paid to my riding of the Cresta for this year?'

'Unless you want that shoulder out again.'

I do not.

'Even though the scan showed no breaks in the joint itself, you will have stretched the muscles and ligaments that hold everything in place. So it's loose. You need to give everything time to tighten up again. That's also why you need to wear that sling.'

'But it will tighten up all right?'

'It will, although I have to tell you that it is never as tight afterwards as it was before. Now it's been out once, I'm afraid it is quite likely to happen again, especially in someone as young and active as you are.'

That is a worry, not only for my future riding of the Cresta but also my livelihood. Setting up deck chairs may not be particularly arduous but it needs two working hands.

'Of course, you can always have it operated on, but we don't usually do that unless the dislocation has become recurrent. The procedure shortens the tendons to tighten the shoulder and keep the joint stable. The outcome is generally pretty good.'

'But not guaranteed?'

'No. Some still come out even after surgery, especially if there's a family history.'

'Surely dislocating shoulders is not hereditary.'

'Inherited instability certainly plays a part. Something like half of those who arrive here from the ski slopes with dislocated shoulders have a parent who's also had one out at sometime or another.'

'My father dislocated his once.'

'There you are then,' says the doctor, spreading his arms wide in satisfaction of a theory well proved. 'And a substantial proportion have had their other shoulder out too. So be careful.'

'Don't worry. I will.'

I clearly now have even more parts of me to watch.

*   *   *

The letter from the psychologist at the Royal Berkshire Hospital arrived four days after my visit there for the psychiatric assessment.

Even though I had already collected all my stuff from the house I'd previously shared with the other two conditional jockeys, I still possessed a front-door key so I'd been popping along each day after morning exercise, to check the post, and there was the letter, lying on the mat.

I decided not to open it immediately as, at that point, my two former housemates returned from their stables. And they were not happy to find me there any more than I was happy to see them.

'What the fuck are you doing here?' one of them asked accusingly, stabbing me in the chest with his finger.

'Just collecting my mail,' I said, stuffing the envelope into my trouser pocket, and my anger back in its box.

'Well, don't. You no longer live here. So give us your key and get out.'

He held out his hand determinedly and, with resignation, I handed it over. What else could I do? Fight them both?

They slammed the door shut and I could hear them laughing together on the other side. I wondered why they were quite so nasty towards me. What I would have given to have had a friendship with them, to have had proper mates with whom I could share experiences and discuss problems.

And all because my father had been a champion jockey and theirs hadn't.

Jealousy could be so destructive.

And it should have been me who was jealous of them, not the other way round.

They both had fathers who were still living, while mine had been dead for ten years. They also had mothers, and siblings. I had no one left in my family except an elderly grandmother who lived over two hundred miles away, plus an uncle who wanted me to forgo my rightful inheritance.

Was it any wonder I was unhappy?

I walked back to the Dickinson house and went straight up to my room to open the letter from the psychologist on my own.

Dear Dr Nixon,

Thank you for referring your patient, Miles Pussett, to me at the Royal Berkshire. I spent some considerable time with him earlier this week and I found our conversation most interesting and enlightening.

*It is my considered opinion that Mr Pussett is suffering
from a combination of post-traumatic stress disorder (PTSD),
together with a psychotic depressive disorder largely brought
on by feelings of inadequacy, and by his perceived guilt over
the death of his parents.*

*He has suffered two major panic attacks, triggered
by memories of the accident that killed his father, which
are indicative of his PTSD, and I see no prospect of them
not continuing without some form of treatment and/or
medication.*

*However, I believe that the depressive disorder is the more
acute problem, and tackling that may also ease the PTSD
symptoms.*

*I recommend that he be referred immediately to one of
our clinical psychiatrists here at the Royal Berkshire, initially
as an outpatient, although I wouldn't rule out the need for
in-patient care at sometime in the future, especially if the
situation with respect to his alcohol consumption were to
deteriorate.*

Yours sincerely,
Charlotte Le Grand, Senior Diagnostic Psychologist

I read it through from start to finish at least three times,
trying to decipher the true meaning behind the jargon.

Eventually, I threw the letter down onto the bed.

Did I really believe it?

The doctor in Lincoln had said that it was often the
patient who was the last to realise they were sick.

If it *were* true then, I suppose, it might be something of
a relief. There would finally be an explanation for why I
had been feeling so dreadful, and maybe a path forward for
me to get better. But I was also hugely embarrassed by the
letter, particularly about its reference to my alcohol intake.

My hands were shaking and I was worried that I was
about to have another panic attack, right there and then.

I took the bottle of vodka out from its hiding place under my socks, and had a generous swig.

Just to calm my nerves.

*   *   *

'There's someone outside from the Cresta club,' says the security guard, putting his head round my hospital-room door. 'He says he has your phone. Shall I let him in?'

'Oh, yes, please.'

His head disappears again and, presently, the door opens wide, but the new arrival is not who I expect. Far from it.

'Hello, Miles,' he says. 'How are you feeling?'

I am shocked, not least because I didn't realise my visitor even knew my first name. He had always before just called me 'Pussett'.

'Fine, thank you, Colonel.'

The Honourable Colonel David Maitland-Butler, OBE. The very last person I would have expected to bring me my phone.

'You seem surprised to see me.'

'I am. Very.'

He laughs. 'To tell you the truth, I'm quite surprised myself. I've had quite a day.'

So had I.

'I was in the Cresta club bar just finishing my second Bullshot when who turns up—one of my old army team-mates from long ago. Couldn't believe it. Seems he's still riding the ice after all these years. Bloody mad, if you ask me. Anyway, we have a couple of drinks together and then the police turn up, and they won't let us leave, so we have a couple more drinks.' He laughs again. 'We ended up being in there all day.'

And, as a result, the colonel is clearly more than slightly the worse for wear.

'I am just leaving when someone yells out that you need your phone at the hospital and will someone take it, so I volunteered.'

I bet the colonel was always volunteering when he was in the army.

'So here it is.' He hands over my phone and salutes somewhat unsteadily.

'Please sit down, Colonel,' I say, pointing at one of the chairs by the bed. I decide not to add 'before you fall down', and just hope he hasn't driven here.

He sits down heavily.

'You caused quite a stir at the club today, make no mistake.'

'Not intentionally.'

'No. No, I can see that.' He is trying very hard to be serious, to see through the alcohol-induced fog in his brain. It is almost funny, but I remember being like that, often, and it is really not something to laugh about.

'So what are they saying about me at the club?' I ask.

'They all reckon you're bloody lucky to be alive.'

I agree with them.

'Were there many people there?' I ask.

'A few, but no one I knew other than my old team-mate. More police than anyone else. Bloody nuisance they were, too, asking questions all day long.'

Personally, I didn't think that was a bloody nuisance. Indeed, I had some important questions of my own to ask.

'Well,' says the colonel, standing up with a bit of a wobble. 'I'd best be off.'

'Why don't you stay a while longer? I'll order some coffee if you like.'

'All right.' He sits down again. 'I have a table booked at eight o'clock for dinner, but it can wait.'

I look at the time on my phone. 'It's only six now. You have plenty of time.'

I use my left hand to push the in-room-service button on the phone by my bed, and ask for two coffees.

'Have they nothing a bit stronger?' asks the colonel.

I laughed. 'No, Colonel. This is a hospital, not a hotel.' And he's had quite enough already.

The coffee arrives and we sit there drinking it in silence, him on the chair and me in the bed.

'Tell me, Colonel,' I say at length. 'Why would a trainer purposely make his horse lose a race?'

'There might be several reasons.'

'Such as?'

'Well, for one thing he might have bet against it.'

'I thought that was against the Rules of Racing.'

He cocks his head and looks at me, as if to say, *Don't be so naïve.*

'Laying a horse is certainly against the rules, such as on an online betting exchange. But simply placing a bet on another horse in the race that you think might win if yours doesn't is not against the letter of the law.'

'But is it against the spirit?'

'If you say so.'

I do.

'For what other reason would you want one to lose?'

'To improve its handicap. We all do that to some extent by entering horses into races when we know the opposition will be too strong. There's nothing in the rules against that. But, years ago, some trainers would enter a horse in a race simply to assist with its conditioning, or to school it over fences. They would tell the jockey to give the horse an easy race, and not expect or want it to win. That's all now been banned. We are not allowed to say anything remotely like that to a jockey any more, and some of them would report me to the stewards if I did, for fear of getting into trouble themselves.'

'But it still goes on?'

Another sideways glance.

'"A trainer is responsible for ensuring that a jockey who rides a horse trained by them in a race is given instructions that shall allow the jockey to ensure that the horse is given a full opportunity to achieve the best possible position.",' he says.

'Is that a direct quote?'

He nods. 'Rule F.39 of the Rules of Racing. It's one all trainers live by.'

'But could you ensure that the horse loses without the jockey even knowing?'

'Of course.'

'How?'

'You could dope it. Give it a breakfast of crushed-up tranquillisers in its bran. But they will almost certainly show up if the horse gets tested.'

'Other than that, then.'

'You could not train it properly, or give it a very hard work-out much too close to the race, like the day before or even the morning of. Or don't feed it enough for a few days beforehand. Things like that will generally slow them down.' He makes it sound like he has tried all of those.

I wonder if he has ever slowed one down by making it carry a huge amount of unofficial overweight.

'Why do you ask?'

'No real reason, Colonel. I'm just interested.'

Very interested.

26

JUMP RACING RESTARTED thirteen days after my awful day at Market Rasen, coincidentally with an evening meeting at the same racecourse, not that Jerry had any runners on that occasion.

Whereas the jump season was technically back under way, the number of meetings was small, sometimes only two or three in a week spread across the entire country. Not like in October or November, when there could be as many as twenty jump meetings during the same period.

Flat racing, however, was in full swing throughout August and Jerry was not averse to entering his predominantly jumping horses in flat races. He especially targeted the long-distance flat handicaps, such as the Chester Cup in May, the Northumberland Plate or Ascot Stakes in June, and the Cesarewitch at Newmarket in October, but he had runners elsewhere too.

So the yard was busy all year round, preparing the hundred and fifty horses for racing, to say nothing of the fact that they also all needed to be fed, watered, mucked out, groomed and exercised every single day.

On the Monday evening, two weeks after I'd moved in to the Dickinsons' house, the three of us sat down, as usual, at their kitchen table for supper at seven forty-five on the dot. Jerry had obviously had words with Sabrina about how much she was giving me to eat, as my portion sizes had reduced dramatically over the past seven days.

I suppose I was grateful, even if I was now back to constantly feeling hungry.

'I've declared you to ride Wisden,' Jerry said. 'This time at Stratford on Thursday.'

'What weight does he carry?' I asked quickly. He'd been handicapped to carry only ten-stone-two when we'd won at Huntingdon and, with my allowance, and Sabrina Dickinson's food, I wasn't at all sure I could do that weight again.

'The bloody handicapper has put him up seven pounds.'

I breathed a sigh of relief, and took another mouthful of my meagre meal. That was OK then.

'You're also going to ride Gasfitter again, on Saturday. I've entered him in the three-and-a-quarter-mile handicap hurdle, at Newton Abbot, so don't make a mess of the start this time.'

Sabrina gave Jerry a very stern glare, which he ignored.

'Norman will be looking after you because I've got one running in the two-mile handicap at Chester, and I'll be going there instead.'

Norman was Jerry's travelling head groom, who would deputise for him when he had runners at more than one racecourse on the same day, as he usually had.

'OK,' I said, trying to keep calm.

At least I was getting rides again.

We finished the meal and, with the early start required in a racing stable, especially in August, we all went up to our rooms about nine-thirty.

I sat on the edge of my bed and re-read, once again, the letter from the diagnostic psychologist and wondered what I should do about it, if anything.

Then I had four or five large swigs of vodka as a night-cap, stuffed the letter into the bedside-table drawer out of sight of the eagle-eyed cleaner, and went to bed.

Gasfitter—at Newton Abbot. The perfect storm for my mental health.

* * *

True to his word, Dr Kaufmann at the Upper Engadin hospital arrives in the morning with some clothes for me to wear for my discharge.

'They're mine,' he says, laying out some underwear, a shirt, ski salopettes and an anorak on my bed. 'So I'd quite like them back.'

'No problem. I'll make sure I return them this afternoon.'

'No hurry, whenever you're ready. I won't need them until the weekend as I'm on duty here every day this week.'

He helps me into the clothes, doing up the shirt buttons over the sling.

'I'm sure I can manage,' I say, even though I can't. 'You must have more important things to do than dressing your patients.'

'It's OK. It is fairly quiet today, so far, and you're a special case. I've never had a victim of an attempted murder to look after before. You're all over the newspapers and on the TV.'

'The TV?'

'Absolutely, and not just the local Swiss channels either. You made the headlines last night on CNN. It's a big story.'

Oh, hell! So much for me trying to keep a low profile.

'Are the reporters still here?' I ask.

'Not today.'

The news that I was neither dead nor fighting for my life had obviously caused the media interest to wane.

Hence, the hacks would have faded away in search of more sensationalist copy elsewhere.

'Do you happen to have any shoes?' I ask the doctor. I can hardly wear the spiked-front Cresta boots I'd arrived in.

'Didn't they bring your snow boots down with your phone? I told them to.'

'No. They didn't.' Clearly, the doctor's full message hadn't made it into the colonel's alcohol-muddled brain.

'Right, give me a minute. What size are you?'

'Eight and a half. That's forty-two in European.'

He disappears out the door and, after five minutes or so, returns with some white wellington-type rubber boots, only much shorter, finishing just above the ankle.

'They're surgeon's boots,' he says with a laugh. 'To keep out the blood. I took them from the operating-theatre store.'

I laugh too. 'I'll make sure you get them back.'

'Don't worry. They arrive from the manufacturer in a sterile pack. These won't be needed again now they're opened.'

I slip on the boots and I'm all ready to go.

'Good luck,' he says, 'and don't come back.'

He holds out his right hand.

I reach out with my left to shake it.

'Sorry,' he says.

'No need, and thank you. I will be back but, I hope, only to return your clothes. But don't I have to pay for you or the hospital?'

'Not at all. The tobogganing club have sorted all that.'

Clearly riding the Cresta Run is not entirely at one's own risk.

* * *

Stratford-on-Avon Racecourse, as it is officially named, is a bit of an anomaly, as the town where it is situated is known as Stratford-*upon*-Avon. But the missing 'up' doesn't seem to worry the locals, or the visitors.

More famous as the birthplace of William Shakespeare in 1564, there has been horseracing at Stratford since at least 1755, when the first results were recorded, and David Garrick, renowned actor and playwright of the eighteenth century, and after whom the Garrick Theatre and Garrick Club in London are still named, organised a horse race here as part of his Shakespearean Jubilee celebrations of 1769.

The fact that torrential rain, plus the subsequent flooding of the river, almost washed out the whole event, and that, as a consequence, Garrick never returned to Stratford from that day forward, has been rather glossed over by the racing historians.

However, on this particular Thursday in late August, the sun shone brightly, there was no rain in the forecast, and the River Avon was well contained within its banks along the far side of the racecourse.

I drove myself the sixty miles from Lambourn to Stratford in my Volkswagen Golf because, although Jerry said he'd be coming too, I decided that, this time, independence of travel was the best option.

I arrived early and, as always, walked the course.

Stratford is a flat, left-handed circuit, about ten furlongs round, with sharp bends and a short finishing straight. The hurdle course runs all the way inside the steeplechase one, which makes the turns all the tighter.

I kept telling myself over and over that, after the summer break, and with a change in my living circumstances, my luck was bound to improve and I would have a new start to my career. Hence, I was feeling more confident as I pulled on Wisden's blue and yellow silks.

I checked myself on the testing scales provided in the jockeys' changing room—ten-stone-six, including my saddle. Perfect. I even managed to smile.

I then waited for Jerry to appear before weighing out and giving him my saddle to take away and put on the horse.

'Jockeys out,' came the call over the speaker system in the changing room, so I made my way to the parade ring. Jerry was already there, waiting with the owner.

'Go steady early on,' Jerry said to me. 'It's a long way, so don't tire him too soon.'

Nothing this time about keeping him 'handy'.

He gave me a leg-up and the stable lad led us out onto the track.

The start was at the beginning of the back straight and we had more than two and a half circuits of the track to complete, plus thirteen flights of hurdles to negotiate.

Clearly, all the jockeys had been given the same instruction to go steady early on, and we were hardly at a gallop as we crossed the first flight.

'Come on, chaps,' one of our number shouted. 'Somebody take it on.'

Not me, I thought. *I'm not contradicting any of my instructions today.*

The pace only quickened slightly as we turned into the finishing straight for the first time, and there were even a few boos from the grandstands as we passed the winning post with two full laps still to run.

In spite of not being told to, I *was* keeping Wisden handy, just a couple of lengths behind the leader, but really only by virtue of the fact that we were all so bunched up by the slow tempo. However, things livened up going down the back straight for the second time and the field began to spread out a little.

Wisden kept up fairly well at this stage, but on the final circuit he began to tire and was well back as we slowly jumped the last and cantered in seventh of the ten runners, beaten a long way by the very same horse we had overtaken on the run-in to win at Huntingdon.

'Those extra seven pounds made all the difference,' Jerry said as he helped me unsaddle the horse in the place reserved for the also-rans.

However, we'd been beaten not by just seven lengths, more like twenty-seven. But at least it hadn't been my fault, and Jerry seemed quite happy, even if I wasn't. All that pre-race confidence, which I had worked so hard to generate, had evaporated almost as quickly as the sweat off Wisden's back in the August sunshine.

*   *   *

You might have thought I was a ghost, if the reaction I receive is anything to go by when I walk into the Cresta club bar at nine o'clock on Tuesday morning.

'Good God, Miles, what are you doing here?' says the club manager. He stands up from behind his desk in the corner and comes over. 'I thought you'd be in hospital for much longer.'

'They've just let me out. Walking wounded.'

I wave the empty sleeve of the doctor's anorak in his direction.

'So I see.'

'Is the run open?' I ask.

'You're surely not wanting to ride?'

'No.' I laugh that he would even suggest it. 'My ice riding is sadly over for this year.'

'The run's not open, anyway. The police are still investigating down at the bridge and, with all the bloody media speculation going on, we thought it best to cancel all practice for today.'

'What media speculation?'

'Crackpot theories, more like.'

'Such as?'

'Anti-British sentiment, what with the Union Jack fly-ing on the roof and such. Some idiot politician even went on the local TV station last night and said it was obvi-ously done by someone who was angry with the British for having left the European Union. What a load of bollocks. Switzerland isn't even a member of the EU.'

'What are the police saying?' I ask.

'Not much. At least, not much to us.'

I wonder if they have spoken to the Fenton twins yet.

'What are you doing here, anyway?' asks the club manager.

'I've come to collect my stuff from my locker. I'll be going home tomorrow or the next day. Depends on when I can get a flight. You don't happen to know if anyone brought my anorak down from Top?'

'Everything left at Top was hung up downstairs in the changing room, as usual.'

'Great. Thanks.'

'I'm just catching up on some paperwork and then I'm off myself. Thought I might go skiing for a change. The club bar won't be opening today either. We thought it was inappropriate under the circumstances.'

But nobody had died.

Not quite, and I intended to make sure it stayed that way.

27

SATURDAY AT NEWTON Abbot was a marginal improvement on Thursday at Stratford, but only just.

The thought of driving all the way to Devon on the last Saturday in August just for one solitary ride didn't fill me with any joy. Traffic on a bank holiday weekend would make the journey a nightmare, and I was having quite enough of those already.

So I drove the twenty miles to Pewsey, parked the Golf in the station car park, and took the train to Newton Abbot, via Exeter. But even the train was packed to the gunwales, crammed full of families off to the seaside for one final outing of the school summer holidays. So I sat on my holdall in the vestibule at the end of one carriage, and thought about the race ahead.

I found it a huge relief that Jerry was 250 miles away in Chester, but I knew that Norman would relate to him all that went on.

I'd seen Norman earlier, when he'd been loading Gasfitter into the stable's small horsebox and setting off south before seven o'clock, hoping to beat the holiday traffic through the major congestion points near Bristol.

'Don't be late,' he'd said to me. 'Our race is the fifth on the card, at four-fifteen.'

'Don't worry. I'll be there.'

He had offered to take me with him in the horsebox, but my mental state was far too fragile to even consider going along the stretch of the M5 motorway south of Taunton. With or without the headlights being on.

The train pulled into Newton Abbot just after one-thirty, and I walked the last mile from the railway station to the racecourse.

The first race of the afternoon was in progress as I used my jockey's pass to gain access to the enclosures. Only five months ago, I would have arrived at least an hour before the first, hanging around the weighing room hoping that a trainer might offer me a spare ride if his declared jockey was stuck in traffic and had failed to appear in time.

But not any more. With my recent poor form and lack of confidence, even I wouldn't have asked me to ride. Indeed, I would be quite happy to forget about Gasfitter all together and climb back on the train home right then, just to save further embarrassment later.

I sat on a bench in the jockeys' changing room through the second and third races before pulling on my britches and silks that had been laid out by the valets.

Gasfitter had been handicapped with a slightly higher rating after his close-run thing at Market Rasen and I even had to have a weight cloth with a couple of pounds of lead inserted to make me up to the right amount.

I weighed out and gave my saddle and the weight cloth to Norman.

'See you in the parade ring,' he said.

When the call came, I moved very slowly, reluctant to leave the safety of the changing room, to again put myself in a situation where I knew I would fail.

In the event, Gasfitter ran reasonably well and, coming to the last flight, I even thought we might have an outside chance of winning, or at least of getting into the first three, but he clipped the top of a hurdle with his front feet and sprawled on landing, sending both of us face down onto the turf.

As racing falls go, it was pretty easy. The horse stood up, uninjured, and galloped away while I just lay there, slightly winded by the impact, but mostly because I didn't want to have to face the music from Norman.

He would know that I could have made Gasfitter lift his feet a little more to clear the obstacle. Perhaps I was not concentrating enough, thinking instead of taking my place in the winner's spot of the unsaddling enclosure. But maybe Norman would also realise that, if I had asked the horse to jump a little higher, we would have likely missed our chance of victory anyway.

It had been a no-win situation either way. And what was new in that?

'Are you OK?' said one of the racecourse doctors, who came running over, going down on his knees next to me with concern on his face.

'Think so, Doc,' I said. 'Just a touch winded, plus a bruise or two.'

'Are you sure? Any pain in your back or neck?'

'None,' I assured him.

I sat up, slowly.

'Careful now,' said the doctor. He helped me to my feet. 'Still feel OK?'

'Yes,' I said. 'I'm fine.'

But I wasn't really. Not mentally. I had a combination of PTSD and a psychotic depressive disorder.

Charlotte Le Grand had said so in her letter.

*　*　*

I switch the thin surgical boots for my much warmer snow ones, collect my things into a plastic carrier bag I find in the club changing room, and make my way back through the centre of St Moritz towards the *Gasthaus*, all the while keeping my eyes peeled for anyone suspicious, and especially for the Fenton twins.

Down on the lake, work is well advanced dismantling the White Turf racetrack, with many of the tents already packed away and the temporary grandstand in a partial state of deconstruction.

For some reason, I make a detour via the stables, but the horses have all gone and only empty stalls remain where Foscote Boy and Cliveden Proposal once stood.

They must have left early.

The storeroom that Jerry had used is also open and emptied, no weighted breast girth or chain-mail boots to be seen, just a few feed nuts spread across the floor and a half-eaten bale of hay lying, *Mary Celeste*-like, in the far corner.

Suddenly, I am overcome with the feeling that it is indeed time to go home, and not just because of my shoulder injury. Maybe it is also time to move on in my life, to finally settle down, and I even wonder whether this will be the last winter I spend here riding the ice.

I will be thirty next birthday and I need to decide what to do for the rest of the time I have available. Hiring out deck chairs on a rainy beach on the Isle of Wight may be a job, but it is hardly a career.

As I arrive at my lodgings, the lady who owns the place, and also cooks the breakfasts, comes dashing out from the kitchen to see me.

'Mr Pussett, I was so worried when you didn't come back last night. Then I heard of your accident and I was even more worried.'

It wasn't an accident, but I don't mention that.

'Thank you, Frau Muller. I am fine now but I will be leaving to go home in a day or so.'

'Of course.'

I go up the stairs.

'Wait,' she calls up after me, as if just remembering. 'I have a message for you. A policeman called here just now but you were out. He asked me to tell you he will come back at eleven o'clock to see you. Is that OK?'

'Yes,' I say. 'Fine. Thank you. Please show him up when he arrives.'

I go to my room and attempt to remove Dr Kaufmann's clothes and replace them with my own.

Only when you lose the use of one hand do you appreciate the difficulties people must have if they only have one in the first place. Buttons are fiddly to undo, and almost impossible to do up again, especially when you are using your weaker, non-dominant hand, as I am.

Even using the phone is a bit of a challenge, but I eventually manage to log into the budget airline's website and convert my flexible return fare into a specific seat on tomorrow afternoon's flight from Zurich to London.

The policeman arrives promptly at eleven o'clock and, as instructed, Frau Muller shows him up to my room. It is the same officer who interviewed me at the hospital yesterday.

He finds me in a state of near total undress.

'I'm so very sorry,' I say. 'But I find I can't dress myself.'

He smiles and helps me into trousers, shirt and a pullover.

'Thank you.'

I sit down on the side of the bed while the officer remains standing.

'So, what have you found out?' I ask him. 'Have you arrested the Fenton boys yet?'

'I have not,' he says. 'When I first went to find them at the Badrutt's Palace, they had already checked out. I put out an alert and they were intercepted attempting to board a plane for London at Zurich.'

'So you have got them?'

He shakes his head. 'They were released. We are able to prove that they had left St Moritz by train at two minutes past ten yesterday morning. Approximately forty minutes before the incident on the Cresta Run.'

'But that's impossible. How could you?'

'Closed-circuit television footage from St Moritz Station clearly shows them boarding the train for Chur at five to ten with their grandmother. They are not seen to get off again before the train departs at two minutes past.'

'But I know that train. It stops in Samedan after just a few minutes. They could have got off there and easily been on the bridge in time. Have you checked the CCTV from there?'

'We have not, and we don't need to. CCTV from Chur clearly shows them disembarking the same train they boarded at St Moritz. Mr Pussett, I am totally satisfied that neither Declan nor Justin Fenton dropped the bag of cement onto the Cresta Run for you to crash into.'

Could they have arranged for someone else to have done it?

But, if so, who?

* * *

My journey back from Newton Abbot races was not without incident, to put it mildly.

I rushed to catch the five-thirty train direct to Pewsey but missed it by a whisker due to having to be cleared by a racecourse doctor in the jockeys' medical room after my fall on Gasfitter.

I yelled angrily at the rear of the departing train as I ran onto the platform.

'Bloody doctor.'

I threw down my kit bag and kicked it. I now had an hour and a half to wait for the next train and, of course, I ended up in the station café.

They served cans of lager. No vodka, but lager would do.

Just one, I thought, to ease the aches and pains from a rough-and-tumble afternoon of eating grass at thirty miles per hour. So I popped a can and enjoyed the cool, refreshing taste as the amber nectar slipped all too easily down my throat.

I thought back over the afternoon's proceedings.

After the race, Norman had actually been quite sympathetic about my fall.

'Hard luck,' he'd said. 'But well done for giving it a go. At one point, I really thought you might win.'

Understandably, Norman was far more concerned about the welfare of the horse than of its rider—after all, they don't shoot the jockey if he is the one who breaks a leg—but, nevertheless, I was fairly confident that his report to Jerry wouldn't be too damning of my performance. Not on this particular occasion.

And, not for the first time, and in spite of my fall at the last hurdle, I had done rather better without Jerry being there to watch me. Perhaps it was because of an unconscious nervous tension that appeared whenever he was present. I couldn't think of any other reason. As far as I was concerned, I was always doing the same thing, which was the best I could.

I'll have just one more can.

It would be hours before I had to drive my Golf and the first one had made me feel so much better.

The train was fifteen minutes late arriving and, by then, I'd drunk four strong lagers. As a result, I almost missed the connection at Exeter through dilly-dallying on the wrong platform.

One of the problems I was having with alcohol was that it created its own destructive positive-feedback loop: the more I drank, the greater it reduced both my inhibitions and my reasoning, so the more I drank . . . ad infinitum until I fell over.

And fall over I did, in the car park at Pewsey station.

It had actually been close to a miracle that I'd got off the train at Pewsey in the first place, and not ended up at Paddington, or in some dark siding somewhere after that. The guard, who'd previously checked my ticket, just happened to be walking past and woke me to tell me we were arriving at my stop. It was time to get off.

And, by that time, I'd also consumed one—or was it two—of the small bottles of wine for sale from the refreshment trolley.

I picked myself up off the ground and weaved a meandering path towards my Golf.

'Come on,' I said to myself out loud. 'Stop being such an idiot.'

I sat in the car as the last of the daylight faded into darkness, wishing myself sober, but with no success.

'Come on,' I shouted to myself again, banging my fists angrily on the steering wheel. 'You can do this.'

But I couldn't.

I almost made it, but some tight bends on the last bit down into Lambourn village on the Baydon Road proved to be my undoing. A sharp left was followed by an even tighter right and, whereas I made the first one, I came upon the second rather too fast and slid off the road and into a deep ditch with a dreadful bang. And all the lights went out.

I sat there in the dark for quite a while, waiting for my mind to clear.

When it didn't, I tried to open the car door next to me, but it wouldn't budge. Next I leaned across but the passenger one wouldn't open either. Nor would the electric windows.

In the end, I decided that I would simply stay there all night and sort out the problem in the morning, when

I could see what I was doing. However, this cunning plan was interrupted when my phone rang.

'Miles,' said a familiar female voice. 'It's Sabrina. Where are you?'

'I'm right here,' I replied, trying my best to sound lucid and as sober as a judge, but without much success.

'Where's here?' she asked. 'You should be home by now.'

'I had a fall,' I said.

'Yes, I know, but Norman said you were OK. And he's been back here for hours.'

'Good for Norman.'

'Miles, have you been drinking?' she asked sharply.

'Just a bit,' I said. I couldn't keep a slight titter out of my voice. 'I'm afraid I've had a slight accident.'

'You're surely not driving?' She sounded slightly horrified.

'Not any more.' I was now laughing fully.

It wasn't amusing but if I hadn't laughed, I'd have cried. Nevertheless, it was a mistake. Sabrina became very angry.

'It's not bloody funny,' she shouted down the phone. 'Where are you right now?'

'In a ditch.'

'Which ditch?' she demanded.

'The ditch on the Baydon Road.'

'What, here, in Lambourn?'

'Just short.'

'Stay right where you are. I'll come and get you.'

She hung up.

I used the flashlight feature on my phone to try and find a way out of the car but without success. So, in the end, just as Sabrina had instructed, I decided to stay right where I was.

I had no choice anyway.

28

For my last night in St Moritz, I decide to splash out and go for supper at the Kulm Hotel, in the Sunny Bar, the spiritual home of the Cresta Run, where sleek toboggans adorn the ceiling as if defying gravity, and the St Moritz Tobogganing Club's race trophies are kept on permanent display.

Supper in the Sunny Bar is an extravagance I can't really afford, but this place has a special memory for me. It was here, less than three weeks ago, that I was presented with a gold and burgundy tie as a new holder of the coveted Club colours. I had earned them by finishing in the top eight of the Morgan Cup, a feat that also qualified me to ride the ice in the Grand National.

If this is to be my last ever evening in this town, I can't think of anywhere I'd rather spend it.

And I am not spending it alone.

I had called the hotel earlier to speak to my 'mother', Susi Ashcroft, to ask her to join me as a payback for the gourmet dinner at The K on Sunday.

I meet her in the lobby and we wind our way through the pillared splendour of the grand saloon, and downstairs to the Sunny.

'I hope you like Peruvian food,' I say.

'I've never tried it,' she replies. 'But I hope we're not eating guinea pig.'

I agree, laughing. They'd be far too fiddly to eat with only one usable hand anyway.

Susi is completely taken by the Sunny Bar and its eccentric decor.

'I never realised that the Cresta Run had such a history,' she says, as she spends ages looking at the hundreds of framed photographs of famous Cresta riders, both past and present, which adorn every available square inch of wall space.

'There's probably one up there somewhere of Errol Flynn,' I say. 'He holds the record for the slowest ever completed run—over three minutes, which allegedly included a stop at Shuttlecock to have a cuddle with a blonde and to drink a glass of champagne handed to him on a silver platter by his waiting butler. Now that's what I call real class.'

She searches for him but without success, so we sit down at our table and I study the menu.

'What are those?' Susi asks, pointing up at a row of seven gymnastic rings hanging on leather straps from the ceiling way above us.

'Ah, the dreaded rings. After Club dinners here, when the members are well oiled, they compete against each other to see who can swing like a monkey back and forth along the line the most times.'

'Have you ever tried it?'

'Once, years ago. During my very first year here.'

'How did you do?'

'Not well. Not well at all. I managed just six rings before coming off. The record is a hundred and fifty—that's nearly twenty times back and forth. So I decided, right there and then, to retire gracefully from that particular activity.'

She laughs. 'That's very unlike you. I thought you would have set up your own set of rings at home, trained hard all summer, then come back to beat them all.'

I look at her. Does she really think that?

Am I truly that competitive?

I shake my head. 'I think you're describing somebody else.'

'I'm not,' she insists. 'As a young jockey riding my horses, you were so determined to win it was frightening.'

'I'm different now.'

A waiter arrives to take our order so, thankfully, our conversation is paused while Susi chooses raw sea bass ceviche as a starter and marinated chicken with a green herb chilli sauce as a main.

'And for you, sir?' asks the waiter.

'What on the menu is easy to eat with only one hand?'

'We can cut up anything into small pieces,' he assures me.

Nevertheless, I choose the crispy pork bites to start and the seafood a lo macho soup as a main course.

'And to drink?'

'Just sparkling water for me,' I say. 'But I'm sure my guest would like some wine.'

'Thank you, I would,' she says. 'The Raveneau Chablis Grand Cru I had the other night in The K was delicious. I'd love some more of that if you have it.'

'Certainly, madam,' says the waiter, who hurries away to fetch it.

I try not to reveal in my facial expression that I know that the Raveneau is hugely expensive, way beyond my pay scale.

'But I'll pay for it,' Susi says, putting her hand on my good arm. 'In fact, I'll pay for the whole meal.'

'No, you won't. This is me returning your kind hospitality of Sunday.'

'You don't need to.'

'Yes, I do.'

'How about we go Dutch on the food then? Would that make it easier for you?'

How does she know that I'm strapped for cash? Was that why she had offered me her suite in the hotel?

'What has Jerry been telling you?'

'He said that you demanded a fee from me for saddling my horse because you're broke.' She pauses. 'Is it true?'

'Is what true?'

'That you're broke?'

'No. It's not. A little short, maybe, but certainly not broke.'

'But you did demand a fee?'

'Not exactly. I didn't ask for anything at all, but Jerry offered me twenty pounds. I thought that was rather insulting, so I said I wanted a hundred. We settled on fifty.'

She chuckles. 'Typical Jerry. He told me at breakfast yesterday that it *was* a hundred and that he would be charging it to my training-fee account.'

I don't know whether to laugh, or be angry on her behalf.

'I'm so sorry.'

'Don't be. I would expect to pay you for doing it. Mind you, I'll only pay Jerry the fifty, not a hundred.'

'He only had twenties on him,' I said. 'So he had to give me sixty, but he wants ten of it back. I haven't given it to him yet.'

We laugh in shared amusement, as the waiter arrives to serve her wine.

'Can I ask you a personal question?' I ask, when he's gone.

'You can ask,' Susi replied. 'But I might not answer.'

'Do you ever bet on your own horses?'

She laughs. 'That's not what I thought you were going to ask.'

'Which was what?'

She laughs again. 'Never you mind.'

In the ensuing pause, Susi takes a sip of her Chablis and I partake of my sparkling water.

'So *do* you bet on your horses?' I ask her again.

'I have the occasional flutter. Maybe a few pounds each way.'

'Not big bets? Hundreds or even thousands?'

'Good God, no. I think the biggest bet I've ever placed was fifty quid to win and it made me feel quite sick. I only did it because Jerry told me the horse was a sure thing.'

Now it's my turn to laugh. 'But Jerry is always telling his owners that their horses are sure things, even when they're not.'

'I know, but that time he was really insistent I should back it. He told me he had. Even showed me his betting slip.'

'And did it win?'

She nodded. 'By three lengths, easing up.'

'How much did you collect?'

'About six hundred pounds, I think.'

'How about Jerry?'

'I don't know. But I'm sure it was a lot more than that.'

The waiter brings our starters and we eat for a while in silence.

'How honest do you think Jerry is?' I ask.

'I wouldn't call charging me over the odds by fifty quid as being dishonest, if that's what you mean. Cheeky, maybe, but not properly dishonest. It's just business. An additional mark-up to maximise his profit. All trainers would do it.'

Perhaps she's right, but I am quite irritated that Jerry had told her that I'd had a hundred pounds from him when it wasn't true.

And it wasn't what I meant, anyway.

*   *   *

Sabrina brought Jerry with her to Baydon Road, but it still took them nearly an hour to find me in the ditch, not helped by the fact that my phone battery had suddenly died from me using the flashlight feature for too long.

I saw the approaching beams from their torches first and shouted out but, with the windows shut, they couldn't hear me. Eventually, a torch was shone through the windscreen straight into my eyes, and I put a thumb up in response. But they couldn't get the doors open from the outside either.

I could see in their torchlight that the Golf had well and truly settled down such that both the driver and the passenger doors were jammed tightly shut by the sides of the ditch. Only the windows and the roof showed above ground level.

'Try the boot,' I shouted.

But that wouldn't open either—it had automatically locked shut when the car was on the move and couldn't be unlocked without the power being on. Oh, for old-fashioned, wind-down windows and mechanical catches.

'Lean away and cover your face and hands,' Jerry shouted. 'I'm going to break the driver's door window.'

Now why hadn't I thought of that?

But it wasn't as easy as it sounded.

First he tried to kick it, but that simply made him fall over. Next he bashed it with his torch, but that didn't have much effect either, other than to stop the bulb from working. Finally, after he must have gone back to his own car, he appeared wielding a hardened-steel wheel wrench and that did the trick with a single blow, shattering the window into many thousands of tiny pieces. Shards showered all over me as he then used the wrench to knock out all the remaining glass, leaving the opening with no sharp edges.

'Can you crawl out now, or have you hurt something?'

Only my self-respect.

I knelt on the driver's seat and went out, head-first, through the gap. Jerry helped me to my feet.

'Come on,' he said. 'Let's go home. We'll sort this fucking mess out in the morning.' He waved a dismissive hand at the car in the ditch.

I sat in the back of their Mercedes as Jerry drove the three of us home. We travelled the couple of miles in total silence—no accusations, no blame, no criticism, nothing.

That all came when we arrived back at the Dickinson house.

'What on earth do you think you were doing?' Jerry said, almost shouting at me as we sat around their kitchen table.

I didn't reply. I just sat there with my head down. I felt quite bad enough already, what with the combined effects of excessive alcohol and huge self-loathing, without him having a go at me too. But I suppose I should be grateful that I wasn't down the local nick getting the third degree from the police about why I had driven a car with far too much alcohol in my system. And I would have deserved it too, and to lose my licence.

'Have you nothing to say for yourself?' Jerry said scornfully.

'Can I have a drink?'

'I think you've had quite enough to drink already,' Jerry said.

'You can have some tea or coffee,' Sabrina said, standing up. 'Or would you prefer just water?'

Vodka would be better, I thought, but decided not to ask for that.

'Coffee would be nice,' I said.

'Make it black and strong,' Jerry said, loudly and sarcastically.

'Please don't shout at me,' I said. 'I'm not well.'

'Got a headache, have you?' Jerry went on shouting. 'I'm not fucking surprised.'

I put my hands up over my ears, and burst into tears.

'Oh, my God!' Jerry shouted again at full volume. 'That's all we bloody need.'

'Shut up!' I shouted back at him, half-choking on my tears. 'Shut up! I tell you, I'm ill. I have something called PTSD and I can't take any more of this.'

I stood up and ran out of the kitchen, up the stairs and into my room. I slammed the door shut.

I scrabbled around in my sock drawer and found a bottle, but it was empty. I whipped the top off and tried to drain any final dregs of vodka into my mouth, but there were none. I searched everywhere in case there was another bottle I'd forgotten about, but I knew there wasn't.

I lay on the bed, face up, crying, the tears stream-ing down the sides of my face, past my ears, and into the pillow.

There was a gentle knock on the door.

'Miles, it's Sabrina. Can I come in?'

I didn't answer but she came in anyway. She was carry-ing a cup of coffee that she put down on my bedside table, right next to the empty vodka bottle.

'What is all this about you being ill?' she asked.

I sat up, took the letter from Charlotte Le Grand out of the bedside drawer and gave it to her. She read it through several times.

'My dear boy,' she said at length. 'Why didn't you show this to me when it first arrived?'

I cried harder. 'Because I feel so ashamed.'

29

After the night of my encounter with the ditch, Sabrina Dickinson took on the responsibility of organising everything in my life, as well as keeping a tight lid on her husband's temper.

But it came at a cost—my privacy, and my freedom.

First, she removed the empty vodka bottle from my bedside table and then conducted a thorough search of my room, going through my clothes in the wardrobe and those in the chest of drawers, looking both under and in the bed, everywhere, even taking the lid off the lavatory cistern in the en-suite shower room to check that the only liquid it contained was water.

'I'm so sorry,' I kept saying over and over as she searched.

'Don't worry,' she said with a smile, finally satisfied that there was no alcohol in the room. 'We'll get you sorted out. You go to sleep now and we'll start the ball rolling in the morning.'

She went out and closed the door.

I took my phone from my pocket and put it on charge. Then I undressed and went to bed.

I felt dreadful and it was some considerable time before I nodded off.

And then I was awake again, seemingly after just a few seconds, but the readout on my phone showed it was ten past three.

My heart was racing and I felt very sweaty.

It was not a new feeling. I had woken at a similar hour on most nights for the past couple of months, and in much the same circumstances. A quick swig or two of vodka would usually calm things down.

But I had no vodka.

When the mind is at war with itself, as mine was, sound reasoning and rational logic are the first casualties. Hence, I decided that, in order to sleep properly, and to be better able to cope with the difficulties that the morning would undoubtedly bring, I had to get myself a drink right now.

My plan was fiendishly simple. I would sneak downstairs to the dining room where several bottles of spirits stood on the Dickinsons' drinks trolley in the corner. I would consume a few mouthfuls of vodka there before replacing the bottle on the trolley and sneaking back to bed for a restful sleep. Jerry and Sabrina would be none the wiser and I would be so much better for it. It surely had to be a great plan.

I got up. I was wearing just a pair of boxers. That would do.

I tiptoed over to my bedroom door, and this is where the plan came terminally unstuck. The door wouldn't open. It was locked. I reached for the key that was always on the inside, but it was gone.

I used my phone to illuminate the lock and there was no doubt, the key was there, but on the outside of the door.

Sabrina had locked me in.

It seemed to me that there were two courses of action I could take. One was to simply go back to bed and try to sleep, and the second was to create merry hell about having had my liberty removed in this way, banging on the door

such that I woke the whole house, and not to stop until I
was released from this prison.

Neither course seemed very attractive, and neither
would result in me getting a drink. Of that I was certain.

I mulled over the two options and the tiny slither of
reasoning that remained in my brain eventually concluded
that the merry-hell alternative would only alienate the only
friend I seemed to have left in the world.

So I went back to bed and lay in the dark for a long
time with sweaty hands and face, before tiredness eventually took over and I dozed off.

I slept soundly for the rest of the night, waking only
when Sabrina unlocked the door and brought me in a cup
of tea at seven o'clock.

'How are you feeling?' she asked, not mentioning having locked me in. Perhaps she didn't realise I knew.

'Much better than last night, thank you.' I threw back
the covers. 'I'd better get up and go to work.'

The horses may not do much in the way of exercise on
a Sunday, but they all had to be mucked out and fed, and
I was on duty on the Sunday shift.

'Jerry says you are to stay here today.'

'Is that all he said?'

She gave me a sideways look as if to say, *Don't go there.*

'Come down when you're ready. I'll get you some
breakfast.'

I showered, dressed and then went downstairs.

Sabrina was in the kitchen, looking out the window
above the sink as she spoke on the phone.

'OK,' she said. 'I'll ask him and get back to you.'

She hung up and turned round.

'Oh, there you are, Miles. Would you like a coffee?'

'Lovely. Thank you.'

She put the kettle on the AGA and spooned instant
granules into two cups.

'I've just spoken to a farmer friend who's agreed to go and pull your car out of the ditch with his tractor before any nosey policemen come a-calling. He says he'll keep it at his place and ask his man who services all his farm vehicles to have a quick look at it to see if it's worth saving. Is it insured?'

'Only third-party. It's all I could afford.'

'Right, I'll tell him.'

'Thank you,' I said again. I was suddenly close to tears once more. 'Why are you being so nice to me?'

'What do you mean?'

'Why are you being so nice when everything I touch is a disaster? Why have I not simply been sacked and thrown out on my ear?'

'Is that what you want?' Sabrina asked.

'No, of course not. I just don't understand.' The tears were flowing freely now. 'You see. I'm so useless I can't even stop crying.'

'You're not useless and, as you said last night, you're not well. I am only doing what any reasonable person would do to help a fellow human being in need. As soon as the doctors' surgery opens tomorrow morning, we will go and sort out your referral to the psychiatrist.'

'But that frightens me,' I said, keeping my eyes firmly on the table.

'There really is no need to be frightened.' She paused for a long while before continuing. 'I had to go and see a psychiatrist once, and it is nothing to be afraid of.' She paused again for almost as long. 'I had obsessive-compulsive disorder when I was a teenager. It completely took over my life for several years.'

I looked up at her in surprise. 'But you did get better?'

'Pretty much. Mostly I was taught how to cope, so that *it* didn't control me, rather I controlled *it*. But I still have to be careful. Even now, I sometimes catch myself doing something that I know is due to the OCD.'

'And seeing a psychiatrist was useful?'

'Undoubtedly. He was brilliant. I saw him or a therapist every fortnight for about six months and they helped me to believe that what I was doing didn't have to take over my life. That I could be in charge of it. But there are still certain things I won't do because I know they are triggers. Like flying, for example. Or going too close to the horses. Any animals, for that matter. I know it's irrational, but I'm afraid of catching germs from them.'

'That must be difficult when your husband is a racehorse trainer.'

But it might explain why I'd never seen her in the stable yard.

'We just about manage,' she said. 'As we do with most things.'

I wasn't entirely sure what she meant by that last comment, but I didn't ask. She'd told me enough, and I knew from experience that it was a considerable strain to talk about one's own mental health.

'Thank you for telling me of your problem. It somehow makes my situation easier to bear. To know that I'm not alone.'

She smiled at me and I could tell from her furrowed brow how difficult it had been for her to talk about it. 'So, what shall we do today?'

'How about Jerry?' I asked. 'What does he want to do?'

'He'll do as he's told.' She smiled at me again. 'Which means he'll be watching the racing from Goodwood in the snug.'

And watch the racing from Goodwood we all did, along with that from Beverley and Yarmouth, on the two large flat-screen televisions situated one above the other on the wall. One television was permanently tuned to the

Sky Sports Racing channel, for Goodwood and Beverley, and the other to Racing TV for Yarmouth. Jerry simply switched the sound from one to the other as the races started at approximately ten-minute intervals, right through from two o'clock until six, during which time he said not a word to me, although I could feel the tension in him.

I reckoned that only Sabrina's presence kept him quiet.

It was the first time I'd ever been in their snug and it wasn't so much *snug* as one huge trophy cabinet, with silver and gold cups everywhere, and racing awards and photos adorning all the available space on both the walls and the tabletops. In one corner stood Jerry's father's old bookmaker's stand holding a dog-eared leather bag with 'M.C. Dickinson, Birmingham' painted on its white side in bold red letters.

It reminded me of Jerry's gambling heritage, as if I needed a reminder.

As the day wore on I became more and more agitated and my hands wouldn't stay still unless I thrust them deep into my jeans pockets. I desperately needed a drink, but I couldn't see how I was going to get one.

Eventually, I could stand it no longer. I had to do something.

'I'm going out for a walk,' I said to Sabrina in the kitchen when the racing had finished and Jerry had gone out to supervise Sunday evening stables. 'I need a breath of fresh air.'

And to get to the village convenience store before it closed.

'Good idea,' she said. 'I'll come with you.'

That was certainly not in my plan.

'There's no need,' I said, just a tad too quickly.

'Miles,' she said, looking straight at me, 'if you think I'm going to let you out on your own to buy more alcohol, you're much mistaken.'

'But I need it,' I whined. 'Look at my hands.'

I took them out of my pockets and they were shaking.

She went out of the kitchen and shortly returned with a cut-glass tumbler containing about an inch depth of clear liquid.

'Drink this,' she ordered, handing it to me.

'What is it?'

'What do you think? It's vodka.'

I knocked it back in one large gulp.

'Take it easy. That's all you're getting.'

It was enough. I could feel the welcoming warmth in my throat and a sudden calmness spreading through my body. After a minute or two, even my hands stopped shaking.

'My goodness. You really did need it,' Sabrina said, noticing the immediate soothing effect the alcohol had on me.

'I did. Thank you.'

'Addiction is very powerful,' she said slowly. 'I was addicted once, to washing my hands. I would scrub them with a nail brush until they were red raw, even though it hurt like hell. I just couldn't stop. Not without help. And that's what we'll get you, starting tomorrow.'

Was I really addicted?

Surely alcohol addiction only applied to people who drank far more than I did—bottles and bottles of the stuff every day. But my hands had definitely been shaking and I'd really needed that drink to stop them.

Perhaps I *was* addicted, and that frightened me, so much so that I quite wanted another drink to calm myself down.

Jerry came back from the stable yard and still he said nothing to me, but I found the atmosphere so oppressive that I decided to go to my room for a bit.

'Supper at a quarter to eight,' Sabrina called after me as I went up.

At twenty-five past seven my phone rang. The readout showed a mobile number I didn't recognise.

'Hello,' I said, answering.

'Is that Miles Pussett?' asked a female voice.

'It is.'

'This is Rachel Valentine,' said the voice. 'From Lincoln County Hospital. I'm returning your call.'

For a moment I was completely tongue-tied.

'Are you still there?' she asked.

'Yes, I am,' I replied quickly. 'How lovely of you to call back.'

'I'm sorry, I've only just got your message. I was off last week. But, tell me, how did the doctor's visit go?'

'Well. He sent me for an assessment and I've now been referred to see a psychiatrist.'

'Good. I'm sure that's the right route.'

'But how are *you*?' I asked. 'Chickenpox all gone?'

She laughed. 'I never caught it. All a waste of time being off work.'

'And your kids? Are they now recovered?'

She laughed again. 'Fully, but they're not *my* kids. They're my sister's. I'm living with her and her husband at the moment. That's partly why I volunteer to do nights. So as not to be in their hair all the time.'

Not her kids. Things were suddenly looking up.

'Look,' she said, 'I've got to start my shift. I just wanted to check that you're OK.'

'I'm very much OK now that you've called. Is this your phone number?'

'Yes.'

'Can I call you again to let you know how I get on with the psychiatrist?'

'Yes,' she said again. 'Please do. I'd like that.'

CHAPTER

30

I CATCH THE 10:02 train from St Moritz to Chur on Wednesday morning, the same train as the Fenton three had taken two days previously.

The bed-and-breakfast owner gives me a lift in her car to the station.

'Will I see you again next year, Mr Pussett?' she says as she helps load my suitcase onto the train. 'When that shoulder of yours is back to normal?'

'Perhaps.' And perhaps not. 'I'll be in touch soon.'

I stare out of the windows at the majestic Alpine peaks as the train meanders its graceful way down the Engadin Valley, through winding tunnels and across numerous bridges and viaducts. At times, the carriages seem almost to float in space, having somehow escaped the pull of the earth.

This must be one of the most beautiful railway lines in the world, especially in the winter when the sun's rays, reflecting off the frosty surface in countless sparkles, make the snow appear as beds of diamonds.

I spend much of the journey thinking, and the magnificence of the scenery seems, for a change, to match that of my mood.

Far from my usual sadness at leaving my ice-covered refuge, this year I am relishing my return to England and the challenges ahead.

Things have clearly come a long way in my recovery, and the time spent in St Moritz this year has been hugely instrumental in that, not least in the last forty-eight hours, when I have been doing a lot of thinking, especially about why someone might want to kill me.

This year I have been more proficient on the ice than I have ever been before, demonstrated by my performances in the Morgan Cup and the Grand National. But, somehow, I have also become more proficient at living. Quite suddenly, I am now looking ahead, towards the future, instead of always staring back at the past. And I am ready to face how things *will* be rather than bemoaning how they *should* be.

For so long I have completely and purposely shut out my previous life, that of horseracing, for fear that the night demons would return, that the feelings of failure and inadequacy would overwhelm me once more, and that I would again be driven to the very brink of suicide, or worse.

But this last week has shown me that there is a way forward that doesn't mean I have to be quite so blinkered. That I don't need to hide myself away on the Isle of Wight, where there are not only no racecourses but not a single licensed racehorse trainer either.

Even if it took an attempt on my life to show it to me.

Not that I have any intention of going back to riding horses in races. That is one avenue that will remain firmly closed, not least because of the weight issue and how that really would throw a fresh spanner into my mental health. And I probably won't get involved in the training of them either, but there are definitely some questions of racing I need to ask, and some answers I expect to receive.

* * *

For my first hour-long session with the psychiatrist at the Royal Berkshire, he mostly invited me to talk while he listened. He made a few interventions but was largely silent. However, he took notes of everything I said.

Sabrina Dickinson had somehow arranged it at high-speed, taking me with her to the surgery in Lambourn first thing on Monday morning and then refusing to leave until the appointment was made. She had an ally in Dr Nixon who, I reckoned, had also pulled in a few of his own favours to get the assessment done so quickly in the first place.

So here I was, just nine days after my fiasco on the Baydon Road, sitting in an armchair in a psychiatrist's consulting room with 'Dr Keith Mitchell' printed on the nameplate screwed to the door.

'I thought you lot used couches,' I said when I went in only to find two chairs facing each other.

'I can get you a couch if you prefer,' said the doctor. 'But I find that a chair is better. Less intimidating. Now, why don't you sit down and explain to me why you're here?'

'I was rather hoping that you might be able to tell me that.'

'OK,' he said. 'Let's start by you describing to me exactly how you feel right now, and why. Feel free to add in anything you might think is useful, like things that have happened to you either recently, or further in the past, that have contributed to how you feel at this precise moment.'

I sat there in silence for a while before saying anything, not knowing quite where to start.

'I suppose I feel lots of things,' I said eventually, 'but mostly I feel embarrassed and ashamed.'

Dr Mitchell made a note in his notebook. He didn't say anything, he just waited patiently for me to go on.

'But I also feel that I'm being treated like a badly behaved schoolboy who's been caught smoking behind the cycle sheds.'

The doctor made more notes.

'And do you resent that?' he asked.

'It makes me angry.'

'Why?'

'Because I'm no longer a child. I'm nearly twenty-two years old.'

'That's still quite young.'

'Tony McCoy was champion jockey before he turned twenty-two.'

'And how does that make you feel?'

I paused, thinking.

'Aggrieved.'

'In what way?'

I paused again. I was finding it very difficult to express myself, to put into words how I was feeling.

'I suppose I believe that people and things are ganging up against me unfairly. Stopping me succeeding. I don't seem to react very well when things don't go my way, and they certainly haven't been going my way lately.'

'Is that your fault?'

'Is what my fault? That things aren't going my way or that I react badly to them?'

'Either.'

I sat there again for several minutes before answering, searching inwards to try and see myself as others might, to determine if I was to blame for my devastating run of bad form. I thought back to my mistake on Gasfitter at the start at Market Rasen, but also to the race at Stratford when Wisden would have failed to keep up whatever I had done.

'Perhaps I feel they are partly my fault but not entirely.'

More note-taking.

'Tell me about your childhood. What is your earliest memory? And were you happy as a child?'

This was easier ground.

'I can remember my mum baking bread when I was very small. It was the smell.' I smiled at the memory. 'I think my childhood was happy.'

'You think?'

'I was certainly happier than I am now, at least until I was twelve.'

'What happened then?'

I told him all about the accident and how I felt responsible for my father's death, and that opened the floodgates, not so much of tears but of words. They just poured out of me. All about my feelings of inadequacy and my failure to become what I had set my heart on being. And the nightmares. Everything.

'Did you love your father when you were a child?'

That brought me up sharp.

'I admired him. As everyone did.'

But did I love him? He hadn't been there for me for most of the time, nor for my mother. His determination to be the best jump jockey of all time was all-consuming. He didn't have time for anything or anybody else. Even when he broke his leg and couldn't ride, he kept the Pussett name in the headlines by joining the TV racing team as a temporary pundit, travelling all over the country—away all day, every Saturday and most Sundays, the very times when I was home from school.

'Do you love him now?'

'I don't know.'

'If someone mentions your father to you, say at the races, what is your instant emotion?'

'Hate.'

I said it without thinking—and it frightened me.

'Why?'

'For dying.'

'But you told me it wasn't his fault.'

'Maybe it was.' I paused. 'But also for leaving me and my mum in dire straits financially.'

'Is that all?'

No, it wasn't. I also hated him for being so successful when I wasn't, but how could I say that?

But I didn't need to. Dr Mitchell was well ahead of me.

'Is it not partly because you are always being unfavourably compared to him?'

I nodded without speaking—too embarrassed to put it into words.

'How about your mother? Did you love her?'

'Hugely when I was a young child. She was brilliant and doted on me. In fact, we doted on each other. We were always laughing.'

'And later?'

I thought back to those dreadful times when I could hear her crying in the night and had purposely not gone to comfort her. Indeed, my mother and I had hardly spoken to each other for the last two years of her life, something I now regretted enormously.

'I feel guilty that I wasn't there for her more at the end, and that she killed herself without asking for my help, or at least talking to me.' I took a deep breath. 'And also because I didn't love her enough to stop her from doing what she did. But, by then, we hadn't been getting on for quite a while. She hadn't approved of my choice of profession.'

And perhaps she'd been right. Had she known all along that emulating my father was always going to be impossible and was therefore best not attempted in the first place?

'I'm afraid our time's up for today,' the doctor said.

'Time's up?' I said incredulously. 'But that surely wasn't an hour.'

'More than. We've run over by five minutes already. But we'll schedule another session for the same time next week.'

'I can't wait until next week,' I implored.

'You'll have to. But, in the meantime, I'll give you something to help you sleep.'

Vodka? Please make it vodka.

It wasn't. And it wasn't Temazepam either, the drug that had killed my mother. It was just some herbal sleep aids that I could have bought over the counter in any chemist.

'These won't help,' I said. 'I need something much stronger than this.'

'Why don't you give these a try first?' the doctor said. 'I don't want to prescribe anything more potent just yet.'

Not until he knows that I'd be safe with them, I thought, and he was right. Swallowing a handful of powerful sleeping pills to make everything go away permanently sounded like a pretty good idea to me at that moment.

Sabrina was waiting for me outside.

'Was that helpful?' she asked as I climbed into the car.

'Not much,' I said. 'It was over too quickly. But he wants me back next week. Same time.'

'Good,' she said. 'At least it's a start.'

I thought about asking her if we could stop at a pub on the way home, just for a quick snifter, but I knew it would be a waste of time. My alcohol intake, while not quite reduced to zero, was being severely limited and highly policed.

Apart from when she locked me in my bedroom at night to sleep, Sabrina hadn't let me out of her sight since she and Jerry had rescued me from the ditch, guarding me more closely than the Yeomen Warders at the Tower of London had guarded Anne Boleyn.

Perhaps I would welcome the chop.

* * *

I change trains at Chur, swapping the slow scenic one from St Moritz for a faster, ultra-sleek, two-storey affair for the onward journey to Zurich Airport. Not that the scenery is any less impressive as we skirt along the shores of the Walensee and Zurichsee.

I gaze out of the window across the lakes to the snow-covered mountains on the far side, but I am not really concentrating on the view. My mind is racing with what lies ahead and the strategy I must employ to uncover the answers I seek. And the first question I want answered is who put a bag of cement on the Cresta for me to run into, and why.

The St Moritz police officer had visited me once more just as I was preparing to leave the *Gasthaus* that morning for the train station.

'What news?' I'd asked, without any great expectation.

'Our enquiries are ongoing,' he had said unhelpfully.

'So you don't have any suspects.'

'No,' he'd agreed. 'We have very little to go on unless you've remembered something since yesterday that could assist us. That's what I've come here to ask.'

I'd shaken my head. 'Nothing, I'm afraid.'

He'd pursed his lips. 'We've searched for fingerprints on the bag but the assailant must have been wearing gloves, probably against the cold. And CCTV from the Cresta Run itself and from nearby buildings shows nothing more than a distant blurry figure on the bridge. So far, we have been unable to find any witnesses or dash-cam footage from the few vehicles that crossed the bridge close to the time. Indeed, it would seem that no one saw anything.'

'How about distinctive footprints in the snow?' I had asked.

Now it had been his turn to shake his head. 'The last fall of fresh snow in St Moritz was nearly two weeks ago and far too many people have walked across that bridge since then for anything useful to be found.'

'So what now?'

'We will continue to appeal for witnesses, but things don't look very promising. If someone hasn't come forward by this stage with all the publicity that's being generated, it is doubtful that they ever will.'

'Do you have any theories?'

'It looks increasingly likely that it may have been a random act of vandalism after all, carried out by someone who perhaps didn't realise the danger they were posing. You were just the unlucky person who was in the wrong place at the wrong time.'

And travelling at eighty miles per hour.

I didn't believe that for a second.

CHAPTER

31

On Friday morning, four days after seeing the psychiatrist at the Royal Berkshire, I went back to riding
the horses, at least at exercise, and it was a huge relief to
finally get out of the house and into the fresh air up on the
Downs.

Not that I was yet able to go where I pleased.

Sabrina had made it very clear that she did not want to
find that I had been sneaking off to the village shop to buy
booze and, to ensure that I didn't, she even came down the
path from the house to the stable yard to watch me leave
in the string of horses, and was waiting there when I got
back. Short of taking my mount on a detour away from the
others, there was no chance.

'You're doing so well,' she said. 'You've hardly had any
alcohol for nearly two weeks. It would be such a shame to
go back to your old habits.'

Would it?

It's our habits that make us happy.

It is how our brains are wired. Our lives are mostly dic-
tated not by threats or ideals, but by our habits. We expect
to do what we have done before, to exist in familiarity,
and habits are the manifestation of mostly unconscious,

involuntary actions. Even if our habits are not always in our best interests, like smoking, or drinking and eating to excess, we do them anyway out of comfort and because it makes our lives easier if we don't have to change, or to stop.

Habits override good intentions. It is why all New Year resolutions that involve an alteration in our behaviour are so hard to keep. Unlearning old habits and relearning new ones is hard—not impossible, just hard—and it needs constant concentration and vigilance, as well as a strong desire. Forget or weaken for just a moment and it is all too easy to find yourself lighting up a cigarette, knocking back some vodka shots, or eating a whole packet of chocolate biscuits. And being happy as a result, at least for a short while, until the self-recrimination sets in.

'I'm only trying to help you get better,' Sabrina said.

'I know,' I replied. 'But it's difficult.'

'But it will be worth it in the end.' She smiled. 'You'll see.'

Jerry, meanwhile, was not as understanding as his wife.

'Bloody waste of money,' he'd mumbled under his breath over breakfast on Thursday. 'Paying good money for no work.'

I presumed he meant my salary as a conditional jockey, but I tactfully didn't ask. Instead I'd suggested that I should start riding out again the following morning, and he'd agreed.

'How about racing?' he had asked.

'That's surely up to you,' I'd replied.

Part of me was keen to get back to race riding but the thought of being a failure once again filled me with huge trepidation.

'Best not to be too hasty,' Sabrina had interjected.

'OK. We'll give it a bit longer. There's not many jump meetings on this week anyway, not with the St Leger meeting on at Doncaster. Just Uttoxeter. And Perth, of course, but I can't be bothered to send any runners all the way up there this time. Not for the meagre prizes they're offering.'

So it was decided that I would ride out for a week and then we'd see how things were, and the first day had gone pretty well as far as I was concerned. I hadn't fallen off or been made to look foolish by being run away with, and even Jerry seemed reasonably satisfied.

At lunchtime, after getting back from the gallops, I went up to my room and phoned Rachel Valentine.

'Hiya,' she said with a wonderful lightness in her tone as if she had been hoping I would call. 'How did the psychiatrist go?'

'OK, I think. I don't feel any different, but he wants to see me again next week.'

'Well, that's good. Recovery from mental health problems is always a slow process, mostly achieved by exploration of events through conversation and dialogue between patient and doctor. That's why it's called the talking cure. There is no such thing as a sticking plaster for the mind.'

I laughed. 'So speaks someone who's training to be a psychiatric nurse. How's that going?'

'Pretty well. I've got some exams coming up in two weeks and, if I pass them, I'll then just have my practical skills to complete and I'll be done with that bit. But it's only the next step. I want to be a clinical psychologist eventually.'

'Do you fancy having your own pet patient to practise on?'

'Are you offering yourself?'

'I certainly am.'

There was a long silence from her end and I wondered if I'd made a huge misjudgement. Had I sounded too eager to her ears, as I had to mine? Far too eager.

'It wouldn't work,' she said eventually. 'I'm in Lincoln and you're in Lambourn. It's too far.'

'We could try and make it work. What are you doing tomorrow afternoon?'

Not that I knew how I could even get there tomorrow afternoon. I was all too aware that trains to and from Lincoln were a nightmare at the weekends, so I'd need to find a car, and I also had my jailer to consider.

I decided that, if necessary, I'd just have to take Sabrina with me.

'I'm meant to be going into the city centre to go shopping with my sister,' Rachel said. 'She's trying to find a birthday present for her husband and he's totally impossible to buy for. I said I'd go with her to help with the kids. Two under-fives are not easy.'

'Can't she leave the kids at home, or buy him something from Amazon?'

'Typical man.' Rachel laughed. 'She can hardly leave the kids at home on their own and her husband will be at the football, as always. And she plans to buy him a cashmere sweater, so she needs to see it first, and she wants my advice.'

'Then can I come and help? I'll be the model.'

'Her husband's six-foot-two and seventeen stone.'

'Ah.'

'But I'll have a word with her.' That sounded more promising. 'I'll call you back.'

And she did, ten minutes later.

'My sister says she can cope without me.'

'That's great,' I said with real joy. 'Where shall we meet? I finish work around ten so could be with you any time after two-thirty.'

I hope. I wasn't sure yet of the logistics but I would make it work somehow. I had to.

'How well do you know Lincoln?'

'I've only ever been to the railway station and the hospital, and then just the once on the night I met you.'

'The station will do. I'll meet you there at two-thirty tomorrow afternoon.'

'Sounds wonderful.'

We disconnected and I went to look for Sabrina. She was in the kitchen.

'Do you know how my car's doing?' I asked her.

'Remarkably well, considering. My friend says that, apart from a few dents on the nearside wing and the broken driver's window, it's perfectly fine.'

'How about the electrics?' I asked.

'Nothing wrong. The bump apparently caused one of the leads to detach from the battery. As soon as his man put it back on again everything worked.'

'Good. I need it tomorrow. I'm going to Lincoln.'

Sabrina wasn't happy. She raised the question with Jerry over supper.

'Lincoln?' he said. 'What's at Lincoln?'

'I'm going to see someone,' I said.

'Who?' he asked.

'A psychotherapist.'

'On a Saturday? Doing overtime, is he?'

'It's a she, actually. She was the person who looked after me that night I had the attack in Newark. She asked me to go back and see her.'

He wasn't to know it was the other way round.

'He wants to drive,' Sabrina said, the disapproval clear in her voice.

'It's his life,' Jerry said, waving a hand. 'But we're not bailing him out of another ditch, that's for sure.'

I turned to Sabrina. 'I've already said that you can come with me if you'd like.'

'I haven't got the time to go gallivanting all over the country with you. It's more than three hours' drive to Lincoln. I know. I went there, remember.'

'We can't watch him every minute for ever,' Jerry said. 'He's a grown man.'

'But it's not safe.'

'It's perfectly safe,' I said. 'I won't do anything you wouldn't approve of.'

We ate in silence.

I didn't like upsetting Sabrina. I knew I needed her. So I thought seriously about saying that I wouldn't go. Perhaps I should just call Rachel and tell her that she should go shopping with her sister after all. But part of me was longing to go because I desperately needed something to raise my mood, and I had this crazy idea that Rachel was the one to do it.

But what if I went all that way, only for her to tell me again that Lincoln to Lambourn was too far, or worse, that she was waiting for me at Lincoln railway station with her boyfriend?

How would I feel then?

But I hadn't detected those sorts of vibes during our telephone call.

If she didn't want to see me, wouldn't she have simply called back and told me that her sister needed her after all?

And she hadn't.

The same questions went round and round in my head and, with them, my confidence diminished by the minute until I didn't know what to think, or do.

'All right,' Sabrina said, finally breaking the silence. 'You can go, but no drinking.' She pointed her fork at me to emphasise the instruction.

'No drinking,' I agreed. 'I promise.'

* * *

I woke early on Saturday morning and was already up and dressed by the time Sabrina arrived to unlock my bedroom door. Her permission to go to Lincoln might have been one thing, but she was still not allowing me overnight access to her drinks trolley.

I had a strange feeling about what lay ahead, a mixture of excitement and dread. Would this be a day to remember for good reasons or for bad? For expectations fulfilled or hopes dashed?

One minute I could imagine this being the first day of the rest of my life, and then, the next minute, the end of everything.

I tried my best not to be too hopeful in fear of grim disappointment, but it did little to reduce my eagerness to get going.

By the time I had ridden three horses for Jerry on the gallops, showered, changed, collected and then set off in my Golf, I was as nervous as on that first day at Duncombe Park point-to-point. And, the closer I got to Lincoln, the more nervous I became.

Thankfully, the weather was fairly typical for early September, with blue skies and warm temperatures, so it was not too onerous having no glass in the driver's door window, although the wind noise was tiresome on the motorway.

I arrived ten minutes early, parked in the pay-and-display station car park, and walked over to the main building not so much with butterflies in my stomach, more like fully grown eagles.

My palms were sweating.

It was almost five weeks since I'd seen her. Would I even recognise her? Wasn't I just being fanciful and stupid?

I could feel myself losing my nerve. Perhaps it would be better to get straight back in the car and drive away now, rather than stay and have my dreams crushed, as I felt they surely would be.

I was on the point of bottling out and leaving when—

'Miles,' she shouted, waving an arm at me from the far side of the car park.

My heart leapt.

'Rachel,' I shouted back, returning her wave.

She ran over towards me and, of course, I recognised her, even though her hair was down and not in the pony-tail as it had been before.

There was an awkward moment when neither of us appeared to know how we should greet each other—shaking hands didn't seem right, but neither did a hug. I held her upper arms and gave her a slight peck on the cheek. It seemed to fulfil the requirement for both of us.

'How lovely to see you again,' I said, while wishing I had brought her something—chocolates or red roses?

'And you,' she said with the smile that I remembered so well.

'What would you like to do?' I asked.

'How about a coffee?'

'Perfect.'

'I know just the place. Come on.'

She took my arm and pulled me after her, back across the car park, over the road and into the pedestrianised high street. After a couple of minutes we came to Stokes High Bridge Café.

'So, where's the high bridge?' I asked, looking at the higgledy-piggledy black-beam and white-plaster Tudor building set tight between Marks and Spencer on one side and a mobile phone shop on the other.

'The building *is* the bridge. The river passes right underneath.'

We sat at a table outside in the sunshine and ordered two coffees.

'Do you want something to eat?' Rachel asked. 'I'm starving.'

So was I, but that was my usual state of affairs.

'Why not?' I said. After all, I didn't have any light-weight rides on the horizon.

So we ordered a late lunch, she choosing scampi and chips while I opted for a ham and cheese toastie.

'I suppose you have to watch what you eat,' Rachel said.

'All the time. It's very boring. I shouldn't really be having cheese—far too many calories—but I love it.'

'I shouldn't be having scampi either, and especially not with chips. What am I thinking of? But Saturdays are always a strange day for me. On Thursdays and Fridays I get back to going to bed at a normal time but then, on Saturdays, I have to start preparing for a night shift on Sunday. I normally try to sleep in late and then stay up until two or three in the morning.'

'Your body clock must be all over the place.'

She sighed. 'You get used to it.'

You can get used to anything, I thought. That's what First World War soldiers in the trenches had said, and the surviving inmates of Auschwitz.

We sat there together in easy companionship, drinking our coffee and eating our food, learning much about each other. I felt she was enjoying it.

Why had I been so worried?

'Have you always lived in Lincoln?' I asked.

'Born and bred,' she said, clearly proud of the fact.

'Is it a good place to live?' I asked.

'The greatest. We have the best-preserved castle in England, after Windsor, and a fabulous cathedral that was the tallest building in the world for over two hundred years.' She smiled that smile at me, and my heart flipped. 'Do you know that there was also a racecourse in Lincoln? It's been closed for donkey's years, but the grandstand's still there.'

'A grandstand but no racecourse. That's novel.'

She playfully punched my arm. 'Don't make fun of me. It's true, I tell you. It's a listed building so they can't pull it down. My grandad is always telling me about going to the races when he was a boy to watch Sir Gordon Richards win the Lincolnshire Handicap. And Lincoln also has one of the only four remaining originals of the Magna Carta. It's on display at the castle.'

'You should be a tour guide.'

She laughed. 'I was. Five years ago. Between leaving school and starting my nursing degree. I did it for a whole summer. American tourists, mostly. If you need to know anything about Lincoln, I'm your man or, rather, your woman.'

'OK,' I said, taking a deep breath for courage. 'Where's the best place in Lincoln to take someone I'm falling in love with?'

32

'I'VE ENTERED GASFITTER in a two-mile handicap hurdle at Worcester next Monday,' Jerry said over supper the following Wednesday evening. 'You'll be riding him. Two miles is a bit short for him but the horse needs to regain his confidence after falling at Newton Abbot.'

He wasn't the only one.

I'd spent that afternoon in a second session with Dr Mitchell, exploring over and over again the childhood relationships I'd had with my parents.

'It was not in my childhood that I had the problem,' I'd said to him with irritation. 'It's now.'

'It has been clearly shown that early-years adversity is a major risk factor in the development of psychological problems later in life,' he'd replied. 'Especially childhood neglect and abuse.'

'I didn't feel neglected and I'm certain I wasn't abused.'

'But you said your father wasn't there for you most of the time.'

'My mother was.'

'Boys need father figures and his absence could be considered as both neglect and abuse.'

I had thought he was taking things a bit too far, but he was the expert.

'And you witnessed your father's death. That must have been very traumatic.'

'But you can hardly claim that that was abuse.'

'I certainly would. Abuse doesn't always have to be intentional and deliberate. The very fact that you were there and saw it abused your young developing mind.'

'That's all well and good,' I'd said. 'But is dragging all these dreadful memories up again and again actually helping me to get better?'

'From your history, I can tell that a major contributor to your present condition is your response to the deaths of both your parents. I believe it is the primary cause of your nightmares and the panic attacks. I know it might seem strange but, to move forward, we need to look back, to reconfigure how the brain deals with former events and emotions in life and, in your case, to expunge the guilt you feel over their deaths.'

I suppose it made some sense, so we had agreed to meet again the following week.

'Worcester, you say.'

Jerry nodded. 'Nice flat track with easy turns. Just what's needed.'

For both horse and rider, I thought.

'Not too light, I hope.'

'The weights won't be announced until tomorrow, but he hasn't moved in this week's ratings after that fall, so he'll be in the mid-range.'

Good. I didn't think I could cope with five days of wasting to get down under ten stone.

'Will you be going?' I asked, half-hoping that I'd be left to Norman again.

'I certainly will,' Jerry replied. 'I like Worcester. I'll give you a lift if you like.'

Jerry shot a glance at Sabrina.

I wasn't sure which was worse—being driven by Jerry, which would involve a journey home with him if—when—things went horribly wrong, or driving myself with all the hang-overs from my trip to Newton Abbot.

'Thanks for the offer. I'll decide closer to the day.'

I went up to my room and bemoaned the fact that I couldn't call Rachel as she would be working the night shift at the hospital.

We'd spoken at length, and often, since my trip to see her on the previous Saturday. Thank goodness for free internet calling or my phone bill would be going through the roof.

That day in Lincoln had been magical and we had spent the afternoon walking through the city centre, hand in hand, there having been no adverse reaction to my audacious declaration of love. Quite the opposite, in fact.

She had shown me both the tall cathedral and the well-preserved castle, and we even drove to see the grandstand with no racecourse.

'What happened to your window?' Rachel asked on the way.

'It's a long story,' I said. 'Suffice to say it isn't a good one.'

She sat there expectantly.

This gave me a dilemma.

Did I tell her and risk putting her off me because I'd been a fool who should have known better than to get drunk, and then drive in that condition? Or did I make up a story and then lose her for ever later on if, and when, she found out that I had lied to her? Or did I say nothing, which might alienate her anyway?

Caught between a rock and two hard places, I weighed up the options and then, with my heart in my mouth, I chose the rock.

I told her the whole truth.

She didn't remonstrate or tell me off, she just put her hand on my arm and stroked it.

'Thank you for telling me,' she said.

How could I not?

Fortunately, at that point, we arrived at the grandstand, which, as she had said, looked at nothing, other than the main A57 road-towards Worksop that ran right across the front of it, with open land beyond where the racecourse had once been laid out.

'I suppose the racecourse was closed to build the road,' I said.

'Oh, no. The road was here all the time. They simply closed it to traffic during the race meetings.'

The old metal number-board frame was also still standing there forlornly, holding adverts rather than the horse numbers and jockeys' names that it once had.

'Seems a shame,' I said. 'Bit like a ghost town.'

But it wasn't alone. Over sixty racecourses in Great Britain had been closed during the twentieth century. That's more than currently remain.

In the early evening, I had taken Rachel back to her sister's place on the eastern edge of the city. We sat outside the house in the car for a long while, talking, neither of us wanting the day to finish.

'You'd better get going,' she said eventually. 'You've a long way to go.'

I felt like saying that we could go and find a hotel to spend a night of passion together, but it was too soon, too forward. And I had promised Sabrina that I would be back in Lambourn at a decent hour, and sober.

I leant over and kissed Rachel. No peck on the cheek this time—full-blooded on the lips, with a return just as eager.

'I'm so sorry I have to go,' I said unnecessarily.

'Then come back again soon,' she said.

I walked her to her sister's front door and we kissed again, hugging our bodies together as if trying to merge our souls.

There were tears in my eyes as I drove away, leaving Rachel standing on the doorstep, waving at me until I finally went out of sight round a corner, still with my right hand out through the broken window to wave back. It was almost as much as I could do not to turn the car round and go back to her.

It really felt like the start of something special, and in more ways than one.

I hadn't touched a drop of alcohol all day, nor wanted to.

* * *

Very reluctantly, I went to the races on Monday in Jerry's car because mine was in the local Lambourn garage having its window fixed.

The racecourse at Worcester is very picturesque, situated as it is on the Pitchcroft, a floodplain meadow next to the River Severn, which runs alongside the western edge.

'Nowadays they only race here in the summer,' Jerry said as we walked the course together. 'They used to lose so many of their winter meetings due to flooding that they don't bother with them any more. There are even photographs in the weighing room of members of the Worcester Rowing Club rowing up the straight past the winning post on the floodwater.' He laughed.

'You'd think they'd move to somewhere a bit drier.'

'No chance,' Jerry said. 'Worcester is one of the oldest racecourses in the country. They've been racing on this particular patch of land for more than three hundred years and probably will for another three hundred.'

The two-mile handicap hurdle was the first race of the afternoon and I was changed, weighed and ready in good time. Gasfitter, while not actually the betting favourite, was well fancied, which hardly helped my state of mind.

This was my first ride in any race since my fall at Newton Abbot more than three weeks before. One of the other jockeys had even asked if I was recovered and I realised that he must have thought my prolonged absence from the changing rooms was due to me having been injured in that fall.

'Fine now, thanks,' I'd replied.

But I was anxious. Not because we had fallen last time out, or even that Gasfitter might fall again this time. I was anxious in case it was me who made a mess of things. So much so, in fact, that my hands were shaking as I waited.

What would I give now for a shot of vodka to calm me down?

'Jockeys out,' came the call, which raised my anxiety level even higher.

I dragged myself unenthusiastically outside to meet Jerry in the parade ring.

'Just remember,' he said. 'This race is only over two miles when he's more used to three, so this is a sprint in jumping terms. The others will be at it straight from the off, so be ready and keep up.'

Was he alluding to my blunder at Market Rasen?

There were ten runners in total and we circled at the two-mile start while the girths were tightened.

'OK, jockeys,' shouted the starter, climbing up onto his rostrum and raising his flag. 'Walk in.'

We were all still some twenty yards back from the tape, jig-jogging forward in a reasonable line, when he dropped his flag, released the tape and shouted, 'Off you go, then.'

And we did, with two of the others taking us towards the first flight of hurdles at a great speed.

'Be ready and keep up,' Jerry had said, so I'd kicked Gasfitter in the belly just as the flag dropped and he responded with a surge forward, enabling us to jump the first hurdle only half a length or so behind the two leaders.

As we passed the winning post for the first time, still with another full circuit to complete, Gasfitter was running in fourth but, at this breakneck pace, he seemed to be making heavy weather of things, and he hit the tops of all three hurdles down the back straight.

'Come on, boy,' I shouted in his ear. 'Pick your bloody feet up.'

As we galloped around the final sweeping bend, we had dropped to sixth and, in the long home straight, over the last three obstacles, we went even further back, finishing a poor eighth out of the ten.

I felt sick, and was hugely worried about what Jerry would say.

Somewhat surprisingly, however, he didn't seem in the least upset when I returned to the also-ran unsaddling area. 'Never mind,' he said philosophically. 'He obviously needed a run after that fall, but the pace today was too fast for him. We'll put him back to three miles next time.'

But some of the local gambling public were not quite so forgiving.

'Pussett,' one of them shouted loudly at me as I walked past him towards the weighing room, 'you're a fucking disgrace. You should be banned for cheating like that. You didn't even try to win.'

I tried to ignore him but other disgruntled punters also took up the chant, such that I had to run their verbal gauntlet all the way back to the weighing room.

And the stewards must have heard them too because, before long, I was invited into their room to explain why Gasfitter had performed so much below his expectations. Jerry was there ahead of me but now they obviously wanted my version.

The chairman looked straight at me. 'Mr Dickinson has told us that your lack of experience may have had a bearing on the result.'

I glanced across at Jerry.

Thanks a lot, I thought. *Drop me in it, why don't you?*

'Well?' said the chairman. "What have you to say for yourself?"

'Nothing, sir,' I replied. 'As far as I am concerned, Gasfitter did his very best today. I gave him every chance but the pace of the race was so strong that he tired down the back straight and had no realistic opportunity of finishing in a higher position.'

'*Humph!*' the chairman exclaimed. 'Some members of our race-going public seem to disagree with you.'

'Then they are mistaken,' I replied calmly.

I didn't say what I really felt, which was that the particular race-going members of the public he was referring to were all interfering simpletons who were just trying to get me into trouble. They clearly wanted someone else to blame for their own stupidity, having lost their money by backing a horse that was running in a race of the wrong distance.

And whose fault was that, I thought, looking at Jerry.

The stewards told us that they noted our explanations and ordered that Gasfitter be routinely dope-tested.

'What did you tell them?' I asked Jerry, as we left the room.

'The truth. Same as you.' But he was smiling as if there was something else he hadn't told them. Or me.

33

I WOKE IN A sweat, breathing hard, with my heart thumping fast and forcefully in my chest.

Where was I?

I reached out and grabbed my phone. The screen lit up, showing me that I was in my room in the Dickinsons' house, and the time readout showed 02:13.

It was only a dream.

A really bad dream. That was all.

I lay back on the pillow in relief and my heart rate began to decrease a little, heading back towards normal.

But it had been so real. I was running between two lines of people and they were all shouting at me, just like at Worcester races. My mother and my father were in the line and they were shouting too: 'Fucking disgrace, you're a fucking disgrace.' When I looked closer, all the people were my mother and father, like clones, and their shouting became louder and louder until . . .

I must have woken up.

Just a nightmare, I told myself, trying to smile in the dark. Nothing to worry about. Go back to sleep.

But the nightmare came again.

My mother and father were there once more, right in front of me, shouting with angry faces: 'Fucking disgrace.' I tried to run but every way I turned, my mother and father would appear to block my escape. 'You're a fucking disgrace, fucking disgrace.' Their chant went on and on, and their arms beat at my head, forcing me down and down into the darkness, and then I was falling, tumbling over and over towards the turf at Newton Abbot, but never getting there.

I suddenly woke up again and I was shaking.

I turned on the bedside light but, even so, I couldn't get the awful images out of my mind, so much so that I was afraid of even turning the light out again, let alone going back to sleep.

What I desperately needed was a drink.

I knew there was no alcohol in my room. I'd searched for hours before now, hoping that Sabrina had missed something.

I kept thinking about the bottles standing to attention on the drinks trolley in the dining room, until it became an obsession.

I got up and went over to my bedroom door.

Surprisingly, it opened. Sabrina must have decided there was no point in locking it any more, not after I had been all the way to Lincoln on my own without any problems.

I crept silently down the stairs in my boxer shorts and bare feet.

Just one, I told myself. Just to help me sleep without these dreadful visions reappearing in my head. Just one.

But *just one* was never enough.

*　　*　　*

Sabrina found me when she came downstairs to make some tea at six o'clock.

I was lying in a pool of my own vomit on the parquet flooring in her hallway.

'I'm so sorry,' I slurred at her as I cried. 'I'm so sorry. So sorry.'

There was no shouting, no histrionics of any kind.

'Come on,' she simply said. 'Let's get you cleaned up.'

She tried to help me up but my legs refused to work.

'Just lie there, then,' Sabrina said dismissively. 'But Jerry will be down in a few minutes. He's in the shower.'

Somehow the thought of my employer finding me in such a desperate state on his hall floor galvanised me into at least crawling on my hands and knees into the kitchen and hauling myself into a vertical position via one of the chairs around the table.

I wobbled a bit as Sabrina wiped me down with a damp towel.

'Do you think you can make it to the dining room?' Sabrina asked.

The dining room had been the epicentre of this particular earthquake, in particular its drinks trolley, which was now much depleted.

'I could try,' I said, trying to focus my eyes on her face.

'Right, let's do it. But, if you throw up onto my carpet, I'll bloody kill you myself.'

I almost laughed.

She took my arm and together we tacked our way back and forth across the hall, avoiding the vomit, into the dining room, and then on into the dark recesses on the far side.

'Sit there,' Sabrina ordered, putting another towel over one of her best dining-room chairs to protect it. She placed a plastic washing-up bowl onto my knees. 'If you're going to be sick again, do it into that. But don't make a sound. I'll clear up the hall and tell Jerry you're not feeling very well and that you'll not be riding out today.'

'I'm so sorry,' I said again.

'Don't just sit there being sorry,' she said sternly. 'Enough is enough. This has got to stop. So let's bloody do something about it.'

* * *

'My name's Miles, and I'm an alcoholic.'

I was in my first group therapy session at the Granby Manor Rehabilitation Centre near the small town of Didcot in Oxfordshire.

'Thank you, Miles,' said the group facilitator. 'Now, can you tell us all something about yourself, and why you are here?'

I looked round at my fellow group members, all men, sitting in a circle on high-backed wooden chairs, just as I was. There were ten of us in total and nine sets of eyes stared expectantly in my direction. I could feel the panic begin to rise in my throat.

The facilitator spotted it. 'We're all friends together here, Miles. Every one of us has his own personal demons. I promise it will help to share them. You will find you are not alone in your distress.'

I looked down at my hands and they were shaking.

I could do with a drink but there was no chance of that, not here.

Drinking was what had brought me here in the first place and that admission—*I'm an alcoholic*—had been the most difficult thing I'd ever said in my whole life.

Even now, part of my brain disagreed.

Don't be daft, it said. Alcoholics are other people, those who lie unwashed in subways or on park benches, with bottles of spirits wrapped in brown paper bags. You just like the odd drink or two, to steady your nerves. What's wrong with that?

'I'm a jockey,' I said. 'A steeplechase jockey.'

'Good,' said the leader. 'And what brings you here?'

'Depression and PTSD,' I said. 'Nightmares.' I paused. 'And drinking.'

Granby Manor was a residential treatment centre, funded by a combination of fees, government grants and charitable giving, which helped men from all levels of society to move on from a substance addiction, whether it be alcohol or some other drug, and also to deal with various aspects of their mental illness.

I'd been here for three days, since the morning after my binge with the Dickinsons' drinks trolley. Sabrina had fixed it. Some of her friends had been residents here and she'd rung round to enlist their help in finding me a place.

But why she had done it for me, I didn't know. I would have given up on me long ago.

*   *   *

On that morning, Jerry had come down to breakfast while I'd sat silently in the dining room, feeling ill, and staring forlornly at the source of my troubles. Then, after he'd gone out to the stable yard to sort the first lot, Sabrina came back and helped me upstairs to my room and then into the shower.

'How did Jerry not smell anything?' I asked her.

She laughed. 'He's always had a dreadful sense of smell. Ever since he broke his nose in a fall point-to-pointing when he was young, before he got too heavy.'

Over mid-morning coffee, Sabrina had suggested Granby Manor and I had agreed. At that point, I was grateful not to have been thrown out on the street, and would have agreed to anything. And, as she had said, it was time to 'bloody do something about it'. But I hadn't realised how long it would take.

'Six months,' the admissions registrar said, when I asked him how long I'd be there. 'That's the length of our basic programme, but many of our residents stay with us for a year, some even longer.'

'But I can't possibly stay that long. I have a job.'

'We don't force you to stay at all. You're not sectioned and we are not a prison. You can leave at any point. But, if you want to get better, six months is the minimum time it will take.'

Six months!

But what choice did I have?

So I'd signed the papers and moved into a room on the ground floor.

The registrar might have said that the place wasn't a prison but the window in my room would open less than two inches. Enough, maybe, for some ventilation but hardly a means of escape.

Not even wide enough to pass in a bottle of vodka.

* * *

Initially, my time at Granby Manor was pretty grim and full of angry outbursts on my part.

After the first few days of withdrawal symptoms, it was getting used to doing little or no physical activity that I found the most difficult—nothing more than the occasional accompanied walk around the gardens. Instead I spent my waking hours in counselling sessions, group discussions and lectures, mostly on the evils of alcohol and other hallucinogens, as well as in other pursuits normally more at home in nursery schools, such as colouring-in and painting by numbers. Anything, it seemed, that would take my mind off its longing for forbidden substances.

I thought the whole process was pointless and I was quite sure it wouldn't work, not for me anyway, and I said so.

'We don't force you to stay here,' the admissions registrar had said when I arrived, but he didn't really mean it.

All the external doors were locked and the emergency exits alarmed. One of my fellow inmates, an ex-City commodities trader who was trying to kick a cocaine habit, joked about forming an escape committee and seemed quite serious about wanting to dig a tunnel through my bathroom floor. He even referred to the staff as 'goons'.

In those first weeks, I found all the restrictions very oppressive and they did nothing to ease my anger and my longing to be rid of the place. But where would I go even if I could get out?

Going back to the Dickinsons' place was hardly an option, so where else?

The thought of having to live again in the same house as my uncle filled me with horror.

Perhaps I could try to find a job with another stable, but I had to be realistic. My form over the previous six months had been so appalling that no one in their right mind would employ me. I certainly wouldn't. My riding career was clearly over and I'd better get used to the idea.

And that made me unbearably miserable too, such that, after a month at the Granby, my mood was as low as it had ever been.

In the distance, I could hear trains passing through Didcot Station on the Great Western line from Paddington to South Wales, and I imagined being on the platform and simply stepping off in front of one. I even looked up the times for trains from Swindon to London that didn't stop, and estimated when they would be passing straight through Didcot at a 125 miles per hour. I'd surely not feel anything. It would just be over.

It wasn't that I had a great yearning to die. I just wanted to end this constant agony of disappointment and failure.

Only the thought of Rachel kept me from killing myself. Not that it would have been an easy task anyway.

Great care had been taken to ensure the whole place was suicide-averse. There were no convenient points from which to hang a ligature and all electrical leads had been cut very short. The curtains were held up by Velcro so that they couldn't be used as a noose, and the towel hooks were attached to the bathroom walls only by magnets. Even the knives we ate with in the canteen were round-ended and blunt, and all the glassware was, in fact, plasticware.

But here, unlike in Stalag Luft III, at least we did have access to the outside world through our mobile telephones, even if we were required to lock them into a special cabinet in the main hall during the therapy sessions and also every night from ten o'clock, so they could not disturb our sleep.

And the staff insisted on having open access to all our phones, and at any time. It seems that, in the past, one of the residents had been discovered using his to order a fix of heroin to be delivered through his narrow window opening. After that, the druggies were all moved to the upper levels while the ground floor was reserved for the drunks.

But, in spite of the limitations, my phone became my lifeline.

I spoke regularly to Rachel, who kept asking when I was next coming to Lincoln.

'Soon,' I replied.

I hadn't told her where I was because I was too embarrassed to admit to her what had happened. Instead, I made up reasons why I was too busy.

'I'll come down and see you, then,' she said, and I had great difficulty putting her off. So much so that she asked if there was some reason why I didn't want to see her. Had she done something wrong?

'Of course not,' I said. 'I'd love to see you, but things are so busy with the horses right now. But I'll come up soon. I promise.'

Six months!

I was terrified that I would lose her, or already had, and that further compounded my depression.

The trains at Didcot station began to look increasingly appealing.

CHAPTER

34

'MILES, YOU HAVE a visitor.'
It was Thursday just after lunch and I was in my room, reading through some of the literature I had been given in a therapy session, when one of the Granby staff put his head round the door.

'Thanks,' I said.

It had to be Sabrina. She and Jerry were the only ones who knew I was here and I didn't for a moment think that Jerry would have bothered.

I walked along to the visitors' sitting room and went in.

It wasn't Sabrina. Nor Jerry.

I wondered if I was dreaming.

'Why didn't you tell me?' Rachel said, coming over and putting her arms round my neck.

'I couldn't,' I muttered, fighting back tears. 'I'm so ashamed.'

She had tears in her eyes too.

'You silly boy. Getting help is nothing to be ashamed of.'

'How did you find out?'

'I was really cross about you having to work so hard that you had no time to see me. So I called Mr Dickinson to complain. I still had his phone number from when I called him before, remember, when you spent the night in my hospital last month. But his wife answered.'

'Sabrina.'

'That's right. Sabrina and I have spoken at some length over the past two days. She's told me everything.'

'Oh.'

'She's very supportive.'

Rachel gave me another hug, snuggling her head into my neck.

'My God,' I said, hugging her back with, this time, tears of joy filling my eyes. 'I can't believe it. How did you get here?'

'By train to Didcot. I left as soon as my shift finished at the hospital.'

I laughed, but I didn't tell her why. The fast trains through Didcot were rapidly fading from my future. Suddenly my life seemed worth living again.

* * *

Over the following months at Granby Manor my alcohol craving diminished and my mental health improved, helped in no small measure by frequent visits from my own personal therapist from Lincoln. Rachel even took a new job to be nearer to me. Having passed her psychiatric nursing exams, she had been accepted for a nurse's position in the Mental Health Centre at Abingdon Community Hospital, just a few miles away.

Not that my night terrors, or the panic attacks, went away completely, although they became very rare, mostly occurring only when something entirely innocent and unconnected would catch me unawares and remind me of my father, like the day a visitor for one of the other residents arrived in a silver Jaguar identical to the one in which my father had died.

I was outside in the gardens at the time and it was as much as I could do to get myself back to my room in order to lie down and perform the breathing exercises I'd been taught.

One day during my fourth month, Sabrina brought a letter that had arrived for Jerry from the British Horseracing Authority advising him that, in the light of my medical condition and my ongoing residential treatment, the authority had suspended my conditional jockey's licence until such time that the BHA Senior Medical Officer was satisfied that I was well enough to resume riding.

I noticed that the letter was dated only a few days after my arrival at Granby Manor. Sabrina had obviously withheld it from my sight until she thought I was well enough to cope with its contents.

'I'm not surprised,' I said calmly. 'Does that mean I've lost my job?'

Not that I'd been doing any work for months. But my salary was still being paid, even if it went directly to the Granby to offset my treatment costs.

'We'll sort all that out when you're finished here,' Sabrina replied.

'I won't be coming back to Lambourn,' I said.

'No, I didn't think you would.'

I had decided that, for the sake of my long-term mental health, horseracing and I had to part company on a permanent basis, and it seemed that Sabrina agreed.

There were simply too many memory triggers out there.

Plans had recently been revealed to erect a statue of my father at Cheltenham Racecourse and there was even a Jim Pussett Bar at Sandown, with photos of my father's many triumphs there displayed on the walls.

And it was never going to be renamed the 'Jim & Miles Pussett Bar'.

Even I could see that.

* * *

It is five o'clock when my flight lands at Gatwick Airport after an uneventful hour-and-a-half hop from Zurich, during which my mind finally sorts out some of the answers to my unspoken questions.

A kind fellow passenger, noticing my right arm in the sling, helps me by lifting my suitcase off the carousel in the luggage hall and I push it on its wheels out into the international arrivals area, not totally sure where I am going to go now. So imagine my delight when someone rushes up to me and throws their arms around my neck.

'Hello, my gorgeous man,' Rachel says, giving me a hug.

'Careful.' I wince at the pain in my shoulder, but that's a minor irritation compared to the joy of her being here. We kiss, long and passionately.

'I've missed you,' she says, taking over the control of my suitcase and holding my left hand in hers as we walk on towards the airport railway station.

'You could have always come with me. I did ask.'

'You know I couldn't,' she wails in mock annoyance.

She is nearing the end of her training as a fully registered clinical psychologist, three years of two-days-a-week lectures at Oxford University alongside her full-time job as a psychiatric nurse, and any prolonged period away from her studies, let alone a whole month, was simply not possible at such a crucial stage.

'How did you get the time off today?' I ask.

'Easy,' she replies. 'I told my tutor I needed to conduct an urgent therapy session with one of my patients, as part of my course practical requirements.'

'And what sort of therapy session for this patient do you have in mind?'

'Dinner followed by some intensive sexual behaviour counselling.'

I smile. 'An excellent choice. Where?'

'Where would you like? You're surely not going straight back to the Isle of Wight?'

There is a distinct undertone to her voice betraying the frustration she has felt with me for isolating myself so far away from her for so long. But it has been the only way I could cope. Being on the Isle of Wight has prevented the panic attacks—no memory triggers—but, maybe, things will be different now.

'Not tonight,' I reply. 'I have something I need to do first.'

'And what is that?'

'Pay back a debt.'

'Who to?'

'Someone in Lambourn. I'll go tomorrow.'

She looks at me and I know she's worried.

Lambourn is perhaps the biggest memory trigger of them all.

'It'll be fine,' I say.

'I hope it's a lot of money for you to have to go there in person.'

I decide not to tell her it is only ten pounds.

We take the Gatwick Express to London and book into a budget hotel near Victoria Station.

'Dinner first, or therapy?' I ask as we go into the room, as if I don't already know the answer.

'Therapy,' she says with certainty. 'Right now. But I have a feeling you might also need a second session later.'

'And who am I to argue with a professional opinion?'

But the therapy isn't as easy as we expect, in spite of our eagerness. Maybe because of it.

A recently dislocated shoulder, even if now back in place, plus a cracked shoulder blade, make for a somewhat awkward and painful experience, with me moaning far more than might be expected. But we also giggle a lot, and finally get everything together or, at least, those things that matter.

'God, I've missed that,' Rachel says as we lie naked side by side afterwards. Then she turns to face me and strokes my bare chest. 'I love you.'

I turn my head and look deeply into her eyes.

'That's lucky,' I reply, smiling. 'Because I love you too.'

It is, perhaps, the first time we have ever expressed our feelings for each other so profoundly, so intently.

She sighs, but it's not one of contentment, more of concern.

'Do you really need to go to Lambourn tomorrow?' she asks.

'I do.'

'Then I shall come with you.'

'Aren't you studying?'

'I'll call in sick.'

'You don't have to. I promise you I'll be perfectly fine.'

'Are you sure?'

'I'm positive.'

We get dressed—me with her help—and then go to eat at Santini Restaurant on the corner. It will make quite a hole in my remaining bank balance, but so what? It isn't every day that someone tells you that they love you.

After a dinner of excellent Italian food—with no wine—we return to the hotel for our second sex-therapy session, more measured this time and less frantic. And altogether more satisfying for both of us.

'I rather like your shoulder predicament,' Rachel says, running her fingers through my hair. 'Because it means I'm always on top.'

* * *

In mid-February, just three weeks before my six-month 'sentence' was complete at Granby Manor, my grandmother died.

I had been looking forward to going up to Yorkshire to see her, just as soon as I was able, and it was therefore a huge blow when I received the brief text message from my uncle early on a Tuesday morning, giving me the bad news.

'Sorry to say that Mum died in the night,' it read. 'Will let you know about the funeral.'

I was greatly saddened by my grandmother's passing but I shouldn't have been surprised. In the last few conversations I'd had with her on the telephone, it had been clear that she was becoming increasingly confused. She had also told me how very lonely she was without my grandfather, and she must have simply given up the fight for life.

I only hoped that the end for her had been peaceful, in her sleep, and she hadn't known anything about it.

Another text message arrived from my uncle at lunchtime informing me that the funeral was set for a week on Friday, at noon, in St Hilda's Church in Ellerburn, the same place we had gathered for my grandfather's funeral, and for my mother's before that.

Did I go? Was there any need?

Would it be too damaging to my mental well being?

My grandmother clearly wouldn't know whether I was there or not. She didn't know anything any more. As far as I was aware, my uncle was the only blood relative I had still living, and I didn't really mind what he might think. There wouldn't be anyone else I'd know, so why bother?

I went to see the director of the Granby, to tell him the news of the death and the funeral arrangements. I was quite hoping that he would forbid me from going but even he wasn't that unkind. Instead, he offered someone from his staff to go with me, for support.

I cynically wondered if the 'support' he had in mind was simply to keep me away from the cheap sherry at her wake, but maybe that was unfair.

I hadn't touched a drop of alcohol now for 161 days—not that I was counting or anything—but that was largely due to a lack of opportunity rather than a lack of desire.

Initially, I had found things very difficult, and had often found myself clenching my teeth together in frustration. As the months had passed, the cravings had become a little easier to manage but there were still times when I would have almost killed for a drink. It made me worry how I would fare when I left this place, for I had no wish, or intention, to go back to dependence.

However, strangely, I also felt that I had lost something very precious to me. My alcohol intake had become a sort of comfort blanket for me, acting as a shield that I could hide behind, but now I was having to learn to live, fully exposed, in the real world.

If there was one thing I had learned from all the lectures, it was that the difference between a problem drinker and an alcoholic is that, while the problem drinker drinks too much alcohol for his own health and wellbeing, the alcoholic simply doesn't have the capacity to stop, because he suffers from a physical addiction.

I thought back to my fateful encounter with the Dickinsons' drink trolley. I had only intended having one small swig of vodka to help me sleep but, once I started, I had been unable to stop myself from consuming the whole bottle, and then some. The only thing that finally halted me on that night had been my inability to stand up and reach for any more.

My name is Miles, and I'm an alcoholic.

35

IN THE END, I did go to my grandmother's funeral, and Rachel came with me.

I tried to put her off coming but she insisted.

'I'd like to see where you once lived,' she said. 'In fact, I'd like to know everything about you.'

Hence, on that Friday morning, we caught an early train from Didcot to London, and then one to Malton via York.

On the way north, Rachel tried to tackle the elephant in the room, which was where I was going to live when I left Granby Manor.

'You could move in with me,' she said, but I knew she only had a small bedsit in a rented house that she shared with other nursing staff at the hospital in Abingdon.

'Let's get today's proceedings out of the way first,' I replied. 'We'll talk about it later. At least I should have some capital coming my way now, and that might help.'

'How much capital?' Rachel asked.

'Half the farm. Certainly not a fortune. It's very small and only viable because it has grazing rights on the high moor for the sheep. But Grannie didn't own that land, of course. I think she paid an annual fee for its use.'

'Even so, a farm's a farm. It must be worth quite a bit. Who gets the other half?'

'My uncle. He lives there and he's been running the place since before my grandfather died.'

'Can you sell your half with him still in it?'

'I want him to buy me out.'

But, of course, that wasn't as simple as I'd hoped.

*　*　*

Rachel and I took a taxi from Malton Station to the now-familiar church in Ellerburn,

If anything, this funeral service was even shorter than that for my grandfather, and with disappointingly fewer people. Indeed, apart from my uncle, Rachel and me, there were only four others present, and one of those was the vicar.

Then it was off to the crematorium in the undertaker's car behind the hearse for a quick committal to the flames. To me, it all seemed to have been done with excessive haste.

Rachel and I, plus my uncle, were taken back to the farm where one of those from the meagre congregation was waiting. He handed us his business card and introduced himself as my grandmother's solicitor, and he was there to read the will. It felt a bit like a scene from some old black-and-white horror movie as the three of us sat around the dining-room table facing him. There was even a grandfather clock ticking menacingly in the corner. It read one forty-five.

After some preamble about my grandfather and uncle being the executors, he got to the meat of the document.

'I leave my entire estate,' read the solicitor, 'to my husband and, if he predeceases me, then my estate shall be split equally between my son and my daughter. Should either or both of them predecease me, then their shares shall be left, *per stirpes*, to their further issue, if any.'

I inwardly sighed. The will was just as I expected, and unchanged from what I had believed.

But my relief was rather premature.

'However,' went on the solicitor, taking another piece of paper from his briefcase, 'there is a codicil.'

'What's a codicil?' Rachel asked.

'It's an addition or supplement to a will. Something that is added at a later date.'

'What date?' I asked with concern.

'The tenth of August last year.'

Just after my grandfather's funeral, when my uncle had first spoken to me about securing the farm for himself.

'And what does this codicil say?' I asked in trepidation.

I could feel a slight tingling in my fingertips and my breath was beginning to shallow. I forced myself to breathe deeper and the moment subsided.

The solicitor looked down at the handwritten paper in his hand. 'Whereas the ownership of the farm will be shared,' he read, 'my son shall have the right to live in the farmhouse and work the land, rent free, until such time as he dies or he alone decides to move away. During this period, no sale or partial sale of the property can be made without his consent.'

He laid the paper down flat on the table and we all sat there in silence.

So I did still inherit half the farm but I couldn't realise my asset. Not for as long as my uncle was alive or wanted to live there. And for no rent.

The solicitor looked across the table at me. 'You will, of course, be entitled to half the profit from the farm.'

I laughed. 'This place hasn't made a profit for years, decades even.'

My grandfather had almost boasted that he had never paid a penny of income tax in his life because he earned so little. In all the years I could remember, neither of my grandparents, nor my uncle for that matter, had ever taken a day off, let alone gone away on holiday.

'Right then,' said my uncle, standing up. 'Would anyone like a sherry?'

*   *   *

The centre of Lambourn village hasn't changed much in the seven years since I was last here. The convenience store on the corner, where I had bought my curry suppers, and the booze, is still there, although the name has changed, and a newsagents has been converted into yet another betting shop.

I travelled down from London on the train to Hungerford and then took a taxi to Lambourn, in exactly the same way I had done so often in years gone by.

I finally convinced Rachel that I would be fine on my own, especially after she admitted that she had an important early lecture to attend and then a course-assessment interview scheduled for the afternoon.

And fine I am, strolling at ease around the village centre. I even walk past the Minster Church of St Michael, where my father's funeral was held, and then out on the Upper Lambourn Road, past the equine hospital, to the house where I'd spent the first fourteen years of my life, with not the slightest flicker of a palpitation nor a fingertip tingle to be found.

I really must be getting better at long last.

Rachel had to catch the 6:50 train from Paddington to get back to Oxford in time for her lecture, so we woke very early to fit in another extensive therapy session before I took her to the station. Hence I'd caught the 7:07, arriving at Hungerford just after eight o'clock.

I stand on the grass verge as a string of horses walk past me, on their way to the gallops, the riders dressed in padded jackets and gloves against the February cold.

'Morning,' one of them shouts to me from his lofty position.

'Morning,' I shout back.

He doesn't recognise me. Why would he? I am just a not particularly successful ex-jockey who used to live here for a while in the distant past.

I watch them go, remembering back to happier times when I would have ached to be among them. But my life has moved on and I now have other tasks to fulfil, so I make my way back into the centre of the village and then down the Wantage Road to the Dickinsons' establishment.

I don't go through the stable-yard entrance but walk a little further on, taking the driveway up to the house and ringing the bell. It is a quarter to nine and I have picked my time with care.

Sabrina answers the door and she is genuinely delighted to see me, at least I think so.

'Hello, stranger,' she says, giving me a huge kiss on the cheek. 'Come on in.'

I step through the front door into the hall, and can't prevent myself from glancing down to see if there's still a mark on the parquet where I'd thrown up.

There isn't.

We go through into the kitchen.

'What happened to your arm?'

'A dislocated shoulder and a busted shoulder blade.'

'Fall off a horse?'

'Something like that. I fell on the ice in St Moritz.'

'Yes, Jerry told me you were there. The place must be jinxed. One of our lads broke his ankle doing just the same thing, and Jerry's got a right shiner too.'

Yes, I thought, *but all for different reasons.*

'I'm afraid he's not here at the moment. He's up on the gallops with the horses.'

I hoped he would be. That's why I've chosen this particular time to arrive. I want to speak to Sabrina first.

'Want a coffee?' she asks. 'And some toast? I was about to make some for myself.'

'That would be lovely, thanks.'

She puts the kettle on the AGA hotplate and pops two slices of bread into the toaster before turning back towards me.

'It's been a long time,' she says. 'How are you, apart from the shoulder?'

'Dry.'

She smiles broadly and claps her hands together. 'I'm so glad.'

'Only thanks to you. I haven't had a drink now in years.'

'No relapses at all?'

'Only once. Soon after I left Granby Manor. I thought I could go back to social drinking but I found I couldn't. Once I started, I couldn't stop.'

She laughs. 'The mark of a true alcoholic.'

'Oh, thanks.'

She laughs again but then stops suddenly.

'Seriously, though,' she says. 'I'm proud of you.'

She pours boiling water into two cups and butters the toast.

'And how are *you* doing?' I ask.

'Much the same,' she replies. 'Struggling on.'

'And Jerry?'

'Jerry's just being Jerry.' She sighs audibly. 'I swear he loves his bloody horses far more than he loves me. Mind you, he always has. I'm surprised he doesn't sleep with them.'

'And your son?'

'Nigel? He's still in New York. He's living with someone now.'

'Do you see much of him?'

'Haven't seen him in over a year. He came over for the Christmas before last. He's asked us to go over there but Jerry never wants to go anywhere unless he can take his beloved horses. And he and Nigel don't really get on.' She sighs again. 'I may go on my own in the summer if I can summon up the courage to fly. Or perhaps I'll take a ship. I might not come back, either.'

'Are things that bad?'

'Not really,' she says. 'But Jerry was sixty-two last birthday and, when I talk about the possibility of him retiring, he goes mad.' She sighs once more. 'We've been here thirty years now. Paid off our mortgage. We could sell this place for a fortune, buy a small house somewhere by the sea, and still have enough left to live on very comfortably, perhaps even take a cruise or two together before we're too old to enjoy them. But Jerry won't hear of it. He says that Mick Easterby trained winners in his nineties so why shouldn't he.' She rolls her eyes in dismay. 'And when he's not actually out with the horses, or at the races, he's sitting in the snug watching the bloody stuff on the television. I want a bit more out of my life.'

'Then leave him.'

She looks at me.

'Don't be bloody silly, Miles. I love the old bugger.'

I laugh but, at that point, the old bugger himself returns, and he is not as happy to see me as his wife is. I can tell that in spite of the 'right shiner' round his left eye, although the redness in the eye itself has decreased considerably since I'd last seen him at the clinic in St Moritz on Sunday evening.

'Hello, Miles,' he says, rather clipped. 'What brings you here?'

'Repaying a debt.'

I take a ten-pound note from my pocket and put it on the kitchen table.

'You needn't have bothered.'

But we both know that I am not here because of a ten-pound debt.

'Let's go and talk in the snug,' he says.

'Man talk, is it?' Sabrina asks with a laugh. 'Over what you naughty boys got up to in Switzerland?'

'Something like that,' Jerry replies, but he isn't laughing with her.

Neither am I.

36

I RESISTED HAVING A glass of cheap sherry at my grand-mother's wake.

To be honest, I was a bit shell-shocked from the reading of the will, and the codicil, so Rachel and I soon made our excuses and left, calling a taxi to take us back to Malton station.

'Why didn't you say something?' Rachel asked when we were on the train to London.

'Like what?'

'That it's so unfair. You need the money from the farm right now, not at some distant time in the future when your uncle dies. He might live to be a hundred for all we know.'

He probably would too, I thought. *Just to spite me.*

'But what good would it do? That solicitor said that the codicil had been properly drawn up and witnessed.'

Rachel threw her hands up in exasperation.

'For God's sake. Why are you so bloody calm about it? You should launch a legal challenge. Fight back. Give your uncle what for.'

Did I really want to take my only living relative to court? Especially as part of me could see the sense of what had happened. The farm had been my uncle's home and workplace all his life. Was I really prepared to have him made homeless?

I suddenly realised that I was, indeed, surprisingly relaxed about it. No anger tantrums at all. My therapy at Granby Manor must be working after all.

'Have you ever heard of *Bleak House*?' I asked.

'Vaguely. Isn't it a book?'

I nodded. 'By Charles Dickens. It's the only thing I studied in my English A level before I dropped out of school.'

'What about it?'

'Much of the story is about opposing factions of the Jarndyce family contesting a will. The arguments go back and forth through the courts for many years until it is found that the whole value of the estate has been consumed by the legal fees and there's nothing left for anyone to inherit anyway.'

'So you think that would happen here?'

'It might. The farm is not worth that much and lawyers are very expensive. It would all go very quickly and then I'd end up with nothing.'

'It's still bloody unfair,' Rachel said with resignation.

'You're right but, this way, I might get something eventually. And, when my uncle dies, I might get all of the farm, unless he leaves his half to the dogs.'

We laughed and then travelled on in silence for a while, holding hands and watching the countryside flash past the train windows.

'You could always hire a hitman to bump him off.'

I laughed again. 'I'm not that desperate.'

How lucky I had been to end up in Lincoln Hospital on that dreadful night after Market Rasen. Meeting Rachel had changed my life. If it hadn't been for her, I'd have dug that tunnel with the ex-City trader and escaped from Granby Manor to a life of drink, drugs, disaster and, no doubt, an early death. As it was, I was looking forward to a future, and one with her in it.

We travelled on again in silence as the rolling hills of South Yorkshire gave way first to the woodlands of Nottinghamshire and then to the flatlands of the Fens near Peterborough.

'So what have you decided to do?' Rachel asked, finally confronting the elephant head on.

'For the time being, I'm going to stay where I am,' I said. 'The director has said he will find me a place on their advanced scheme. I'll have to move out of the main house into one of the self-contained flats in the grounds, but it means I can continue to participate in the therapy sessions.'

Rather than being pleased, as I'd thought she would be, she is clearly concerned.

'How can you afford it without selling your half of the farm?'

I smiled. 'It seems that I'm entitled to housing benefit and that pays for almost everything.'

'What do you mean by almost?'

'Well, the housing benefit pays for the accommodation. I have to find a bit more to cover the cost of food but that's all. And I'll be able to claim the dole once the Dickinsons finally do the paperwork to terminate my job; and, until they do, I'm technically still employed by them.'

And that was all thanks to Sabrina. She had insisted that I remain on the stable payroll during my time in treatment. I could only imagine what Jerry thought of the idea and I knew it couldn't go on for much longer.

'Or I'll just have to find a job,' I said. 'Maybe stacking shelves or something. There's a huge new supermarket opening down the road. They'll be looking for staff.'

'Can you do that?'

'The director is actually very keen on the idea. As a sort of halfway house to getting back to full independence.'

She finally seemed to be satisfied, happy even.

'That's good. You've done so well.'

I thought I could still detect some hesitancy in her voice. Maybe it was because I had not committed to moving in with her but, for some reason, and as much as I loved her, I wasn't yet ready for that. Perhaps it was the strong belief I had inside me that I needed to get away from everything in order to get better and that taking on another responsibility would be too much, at least for a while.

However, with my short-term future now decided, I did need to start planning where I would go and what I would do when I finally made it out of Granby Manor into the wider world.

I'd already done some research online and the only place I could find in England with no connection whatsoever to horseracing was the Isle of Wight. So I resolved to go there, in spite of its remote location and the distance away from Rachel.

'The Isle of Wight!' My ex-City-trader escape-committee friend was horrified when I told him. 'You cannot be serious. It must be the most boring place in the whole world.'

But that was just what I needed. No stress.

'I'm sure it's not that bad,' I said. 'There must be some excitement.'

He looked at me as if I was unhinged, which, of course, I was.

'I suppose you could always ride donkeys on the beach.'

'No,' I said emphatically. 'No animal riding of any sort.'

'But you're always telling me you miss the adrenalin rush of racing.'

'Maybe I do, but I value my mental health more.'

'Tell you what,' he said. 'The most exciting thing I've ever done in my life is go down the Cresta Run. That gives you a massive adrenalin rush.'

'The Cresta Run?'

'It's in Switzerland. You go down head-first on the ice, lying on a glorified tea tray, and there's not a horse in sight. It's scarily dangerous but far more fun than anything else you'll ever do with your clothes on. You should try it.'

'Thanks,' I said. 'I might just do that.'

37

'WELL?' I SAY. 'Speak to me.'

Jerry and I are sitting in his snug with the door closed.

'What about?' he asks.

'You know damn well what about. Why did Clive-den Proposal run at White Turf carrying so much extra weight?'

He stares at me and I think for a moment that he isn't going to answer. But I am wrong.

'Obviously because I didn't want him to win,' he says.

'Why not?'

He sits there again without saying anything.

'Come on,' I urge.

He looks away from me.

'Was it because you bet against him?'

He turns back and stares at me again.

'Did you?' I ask.

'If you say so.'

'I thought that was against the rules.'

'Depends how you do it. I didn't lay the horse on an internet betting exchange site or anything like that. That would have been really stupid because I'd have been found out. I simply backed another horse to win instead.'

'Foscote Boy.'

'Yeah, well, no. I didn't expect him to win either.'

I almost laughed. But not quite.

'But he wasn't carrying any extra weight,' I said. 'I know, because it was me who saddled him. Not unless he also had chain-mail wrapped round his legs.'

'No, he didn't, but I wish he had. I thought the colonel's horse was a shoo-in with Cliveden out of the running.'

'So you bet on that?'

'Big time. It cost me a packet when Foscote Boy won that bloody race. But my share of the purse made up for some of it.'

'But surely that's the point. Doesn't the prize money count?'

'You must be joking. Almost all of it goes to the owner. Less than six per cent comes to the trainer even though I do all the work. That's peanuts. At least that White Turf race had a decent purse. In this country, most jump races are worth less than ten grand, many of them under five, some even under three—you know that. Well, do the maths. I could end up with less than two hundred quid in prize money for training a winner. That doesn't go very far. It hardly pays for the fuel to get the damn horse to the racecourse in the first place. Hence, I bet to survive.'

'But the owners must pay you training fees.'

'Those barely cover my overheads. Do you know how much it costs to train a racehorse? What with staff wages, bedding, feed and hay, to say nothing of ulcer powders, farrier fees, vets' bills and everything else, I make next to nothing to live on. On top of that, it costs me more than a grand every month just to get the bloody muckheap cleared. So, of course I bet.'

'But you were cheating.'

'Don't be so fucking self-righteous. I can't afford the luxury.'

I am taken aback by his dismissive attitude to the Rules of Racing, and to fair play.

'So have you done this before?' I ask.

'Get your phone out.'

'What?'

'You heard. Get your phone out. I want to check that you're not recording this conversation.'

'I'm not,' I assure him—but perhaps I should be.

'I still want to see your phone.'

'Why?'

'Because your phone listens to you even when it's not being used.'

'You're kidding.'

'I am not. How else do you think you get all those appropriate ads? Simply mention around your phone that you are thinking of going on holiday to Japan and, the next thing you know, pop-up ads appear for cheap flights to Tokyo. I tell you, your phone listens to what you say all the time. Unless it's physically switched off. So do that now.'

I remove my phone from my pocket and Jerry takes it from me, switches it off, and then takes it out and leaves it in the hall for good measure, closing the door as he comes back into the snug.

'If the advertising companies can hear you, then you can bet your life that the security services can too, maybe even the BHA. And I'm not taking any chances that just switching it off is enough.' He sits down again. 'Now, where were we?'

'I was asking if you had done this extra-weight thing before. But I have already worked out the answer. Wisden. Runs over and over like a carthorse carrying loads of extra weight to get his handicap down and his odds up. Then

one day he runs at Huntingdon without the weight and
sprints to victory like he has springs in his shoes—when
you had gambled heavily on him to win. And Gasfitter
too, but I cocked that up for you at Market Rasen by missing the start and he gets beaten by a nose. No wonder you
were so cross.'

Jerry says nothing.

'And all those other losers I rode, performing so much
below their expectations. They never had a chance, did
they? And, all the time, I'm thinking it's my fault and you
did nothing to change that. Indeed, you even blamed the
losses on my inexperience.

'Have you any idea what that did to my confidence?
To my self-esteem? To my mental health? To say nothing
of how it destroyed my riding career.'

I'm very angry and he knows it.

'Then, on Monday, on top of all that, you tried to kill me.'

'Don't be bloody ridiculous,' he responds quickly, but
I can tell that he's rattled.

'It was you who dropped a bag of cement onto the
Cresta Run when you knew I would be coming down at
high speed.'

'You're crazy. How could I have possibly known where
you'd be?'

'Because Susi Ashcroft told you when you had breakfast with her at the Kulm earlier that morning.'

'What utter claptrap.'

'It's not claptrap. Susi told me you asked her if she
knew where I was. She must have mentioned the Cresta.
She also said you were particularly insistent that she
remember everything we'd spoken about over dinner on
Sunday night. You wanted to make sure I hadn't mentioned anything to her about the weighted breast girth and
the chain-mail. What would you have done if I had? Try
to kill her too?'

He shifts uneasily on the sofa.

'And, anyway, you've just proved to me that it was you.'

'How?'

I stared across at him.

'You haven't asked me why I'm sitting here with my arm in a sling.'

He stares back, saying nothing.

'That's because you already know why. You're the one who's responsible for it.'

'You're madder than I thought you were.' He starts to stand up. 'I've had enough of this fucking nonsense.' He may be trying to bluster his way out but there are beads of nervous sweat on his forehead.

'Sit down!' I snap. 'I'm not finished with you yet.'

He hesitates but then sits slowly back down. He forces a smile across at me. If bluster won't work, perhaps charm will.

'Miles, my dear fellow, you're wrong. Totally wrong. Why on earth would I do such a thing?'

'To prevent us from having this conversation. You knew that, after what I discovered at White Turf, I would work it all out. I would realise that what you did to Cliveden Proposal last Sunday was exactly what you'd done to all those horses I rode that lost so badly. All of them wearing nice fluffy sheepskin breast girths—the Dickinson trademark. Except that the sheepskin was full of lead weights so we had no chance of winning. And then you allowed the blame for their failures to rest on me. You sat back and did nothing to quell the vindictive and destructive press reports. You simply went on doing it, adding to my mental agony, just so you could cheat the system and win your bets, with absolutely no regard to the damage you were causing.'

He sits there in silence and makes no attempt to deny it.

'You can't prove it,' he says eventually. 'It would simply be your word against mine.'

I laugh. 'I don't need to prove it. All I have to do is go to the newspapers and tell them about Cliveden Proposal running at White Turf with an overweight sheepskin breast girth and chain-mail boots. I took photos of them.'

He stares across at me but I'm still not finished with him.

'And the records of all those other races I rode in still exist. Any journalist worth their salt will find the bookmakers you bet with and match up the dates of your big wins to when your horses exceeded expectations, especially if I point them in the right direction.

'The papers will print it all. Everyone will then understand why your horses sometimes performed so much above their previous form, and why at other times they didn't. And the racecourse stewards will realise that they have been made to look foolish. All those post-race enquiries where they could do nothing more than order the horse to be routinely dope-tested. Of course, the results were negative. No dope test will be positive just because a horse is carrying excess baggage.'

I look across at him and suddenly he appears so much smaller.

'You'll be finished,' I go on. 'Your reputation will be in tatters. Even if you aren't banned from racing for life, your owners will desert you. And then they'll sue you for breach of your duty of care towards them and their horses. You'll lose everything—this house, your stables—the lot.'

He continues to stare back at me. No longer the confident and arrogant trainer in total command of his life. More like an empty shell. And maybe his eyes are not actually focused on me at all but on the dark abyss opening up in front of him.

'And, even if I can't prove in a court of law that you fixed all those races, I *can* prove you tried to kill me.'

'How?' It's barely more than a whisper.

'Your mobile phone—that of which you are so wary. I'm sure you had it with you on Monday—we all carry them with us everywhere. Location-finders can determine where your phone has been to within a few feet, and when. I'm sure the Swiss police will find it most revealing. It will show that you were on that bridge in St Moritz at exactly the moment the bag was thrown onto the ice.'

'I'll dispose of it.'

'It's too late for that. They don't need the phone itself. I only have to give them your number and the digital records will show everything.'

I don't know whether that's true or not but he's not to know it either.

'Then why haven't you told them already?'

It's a good question. Partly because I didn't work it all out until after I had left St Moritz—all that thinking on the train and on the flight home had its uses. But also largely because of what it would do to Sabrina.

I arrived here early today, when I knew Jerry would be on the gallops, to find out. I'd even suggested she leave him but that, it seems, was not an option.

Don't be bloody silly, Miles. I love the old bugger.

So bringing him down would bring her down too. And I couldn't do that. Not after all she had done for me, in spite of it being largely her husband's fault that I'd been so ill in the first place.

I just need Jerry to admit it all, at least to me, and also to stop it happening to any other young conditional jockey he may be responsible for.

'What do you want for your silence?' he asks quietly.

'Silence about what? The fixing of the races or you trying to kill me?'

'Both.'

'So you admit it was you who put the bag of cement on the Cresta Run?'

He is silent for a moment.

'I'm sorry.'

It is as much of an admission as I can hope for. But it's enough.

'So what do you want,' he asks again. 'How much?'

'I don't want your dirty money.'

'What then?'

I think back to what Sabrina had said to me.

'You will retire from racing. Sell this house and the stables. And move somewhere by the sea.'

I TAKE THE TRAIN back to London from Lambourn but instead of going straight back to the hotel from Paddington, I go to St John's Wood, specifically to a quiet residential street just behind Lord's Cricket Ground, which is lined with expensive mansions occupied by multimillionaire rock musicians and captains of industry.

I ring the bell of number 5.

The blue front door is opened by an elderly lady, smartly dressed in a green tweed suit.

'Hello, Brenda,' I say. 'Do you remember me?'

'Of course I do,' Brenda Fenton replies curtly, but she doesn't seem very pleased to see me, and she doesn't invite me in. 'If this is about my grandsons accosting you in the streets of St Moritz, I have nothing to say on the matter.'

'So they told you about that?'

'Of course. Now excuse me, I have other things to do.'

She starts to close the door.

'Did they also tell you about beating up your trainer? They put him in hospital.'

The door opens again, and a slight tightening around her eyes gives me the impression that the boys had left out that part of the story. And I can see her looking closely at my arm in the sling and wondering if that, too, is down to her relations.

'My grandsons can be rather impulsive at times. But I still have nothing to say to you.'

She begins to close the door again.

'Don't you want to know why your horse ran so badly in that race at White Turf? To know why it didn't win?'

Once more the door opens slightly.

'And do you know why?' she asks through the gap.

'I certainly do.'

The door opens fully.

'Then you'd better come in.'

'Are your grandsons at home?'

I have no wish to step into a lions' den with the lions in residence.

'They're out shopping,' Brenda says.

Terrorising someone else, no doubt.

So, with trepidation, I walk through her front door and follow her across the hallway into her kitchen.

'How did you find me?' she asks.

'The internet. Seems you have a bit of a reputation in these parts.'

She laughs. 'Concerning a planning dispute with my next-door neighbour. Bad news travels fast. But what's all this about my horse at White Turf? Tell me why it didn't win.'

I realise that there is a risk in telling her, a chance that Sabrina might be damaged by any investigation, but it is a risk that I calculate is necessary.

Brenda would not have a case without my co-operation, even if she wanted to pursue one, which I doubt. Other than Jerry himself, I am the only witness. I can always refuse to help or claim indecision and confusion if forced to give testimony in court, and I am quite sure Jerry will have disposed of the physical evidence just as soon as I left him, if he hadn't done so before.

So why should I tell her?

Indeed, why have I come here in the first place?

Perhaps I believe that if she takes her considerable string of horses away from the Dickinson stable, it might hasten Jerry's decision to retire from the sport. But have I misjudged the situation?

Time to find out.

'Cliveden Proposal didn't win at White Turf,' I say, 'because he was carrying things he didn't need to.'

I tell her about the weighted breast girth and the chain-mail boots. I even show her the pictures of them on my phone.

She is shocked. 'But that's outrageous. Why?'

'Because Jerry Dickinson didn't want your horse to win.'

'Why ever not?'

'Because he'd bet on another.'

'Susi bloody Ashcroft's,' she says angrily.

'Actually, no. She had absolutely nothing to do with it.'

I explain that Jerry hadn't expected Susi's horse to win either and he'd lost a lot of money as a result.

She laughs again. 'Serves him bloody right. But why are you telling me this? Were you in on it too?'

'No, I was not. The first I knew of it was after the race when I unsaddled your horse and found the extra weight.'

'So why tell me now?'

'I thought you should know.'

'And what do you expect me to do about it? Jerry Dickinson has trained me lots of winners over the past five years. I am certainly not going to complain to the racing authorities, or to the police, if that's what you think,' she says with conviction. 'That would simply make me appear as Jerry's patsy and everyone would laugh at me, as

I suggest you might be doing right now. Is that why you've come here? To have a good laugh at my expense?'

'I assure you that I have never laughed at you, either now or at White Turf. But Jerry Dickinson might have done. He was certainly trying to make a quick buck for himself at your expense. Did he also charge you for my services?'

She nods. 'A hundred quid. He told me he'd add it to my training fees account. He claimed you demanded it from me for looking after my horse after the race.'

What a bastard he is. But I already know that.

'He charged the same amount to Susi Ashcroft. She told me. But it isn't true. I never demanded anything from either of you.'

It seems to me that Jerry's little attempt to swindle her out of a hundred pounds has annoyed her even more than him preventing her horse from winning 400 times that much in the race.

'Jerry's always been on the make,' she says. 'He'll charge me extra for almost everything—I'm surprised he doesn't add a percentage for the air the horses breathe. I know for a fact that he once sent a horse of mine all the way to Scotland to run, not because he thought it would win but just to make a few quid on what he charged me for the transport. And I know that because he did the same to another of his owners who I just happened to meet at a mutual friend's dinner party. Our horses had gone together on the same damn horsebox but that hadn't stopped Jerry charging both of us the full whack, as if each of ours had been on its own. I had words with him about that.'

'And what did he say?'

'He claimed it was an administrative error by one of his staff, but I didn't believe him for a second. He just got undone by a chance encounter between two of his owners.'

'But you stuck with him, nevertheless?'

'Yes, but I told him at the time that he had better not over-charge me again.'

'And now he has.'

She is silent for some time, and then she sighs deeply.

'Maybe it's time for me to get out of this horseracing lark. I'm almost ninety and, if I'm not careful, some of the horses I own now will outlive me. Who in their right mind would take on a dead person's horse? I hate to think of them going to the knackers before their time because no one wants them, and there's no one left to pay the training fees.'

She pauses again for a moment and I just wait for her to continue.

'Racing has cost me a small fortune over the last few years.' She sighs again. 'And a whole lot more besides.'

'A friendship?' I ask.

She looks across at me sharply as if surprised, then she slowly nods again.

'Susi and I used to have so much fun together.' She says it wistfully.

I feel for her. But racing has cost *me* a lot more than that.

Brenda claps her hands together as if making a decision. 'Right. From now on I'll not buy any more horses, and I'll tell Jerry to gradually start selling those I've already got, especially the youngsters. I won't tell him what's prompted my change of heart. He can work that out for himself.'

I am pleased. It is more than I could have hoped for.

But my happiness doesn't last.

I hear the front door being opened.

'We're home, Grandma,' shouts a male voice with a New York accent.

The lions are back.

*   *   *

I think it is safe to say that Ronnie and Reggie are not pleased to see me in their grandmother's kitchen.

In their usual 'act first, think second' manner they both advance on me, grabbing me by the upper arms.

I grimace as my fractured shoulder blade objects.

'Steady, boys,' I say. 'I'm on your side.'

They relax a fraction but don't let go of me. Far from it.

'What do you want?' the one on my right snarls into my ear.

'I was talking to your grandmother about White Turf.'

They tighten their grip and I wince once more.

'Leave him alone,' Brenda orders. 'He's right. He's on our side.'

They finally let go but they don't move away, just in case I'm fooling them.

'In what way, exactly, is he on our side?' Tweedledum on my left asks his grandmother, the doubt heavy in his voice.

'He told me why my horse didn't win at St Moritz.'

'And why was that?' Tweedledee asks, grabbing me again by the right arm and making me jump with pain.

'Will you stop doing that?' I shout at him and, amazingly, he takes a step back.

'Tell my boys what you told me,' says Brenda.

So I do. I tell them everything—the weighted breast girth, the chain-mail boots, Jerry betting heavily on another horse—the lot. I even tell them of Jerry's attempts to keep me quiet by putting a bag of cement on the Cresta Run as I was coming down.

'Is that how you hurt your arm?' Brenda asks.

'It is indeed. The collision caused my right shoulder to dislocate.'

There is obvious relief in her face that it wasn't the doing of her grandsons. I decide not to mention that I'd thought it was, and had said so to the Swiss police.

'So what do we do now, Grandma?' asked Declan or Justin, I don't know which. 'Do we go to the police?'

'No, we certainly do not,' Grandma says.

'Then what?'

'We do nothing.'

'Nothing!'

'This is all our little secret,' Brenda says forcefully. 'You will tell no one, do you understand? No one.'

The two boys eventually nod at her but it is abundantly clear from their demeanour that neither of them likes the idea of doing nothing.

'I think you had better go now,' Brenda says to me. 'But thank you for coming.'

She sees me to the front door and even gives me a peck on the cheek as a parting gesture.

Beyond her, still in the kitchen, I can see her grandsons in a close conspiratorial conversation, as if they are planning to sort this out in their own special way.

And that's what I am banking on.

* * *

But Rachel is cross with me when I tell her of my trip to Lambourn, and my confrontation with Jerry.

'Why didn't you tell me your plan yesterday?' she demands.

We are once more lying naked in bed, side by side on our backs, in our room at the budget hotel near Victoria Station, having indulged in more therapy prior to going out to dinner, but I have just ruined the moment.

'Because you'd have stopped me going.'

'You're bloody right I would. You must go to the police.'

'Why must I?' I ask.

'Because, if this man has tried to kill you once, he may try it again.'

To be fair, the same thought has occurred to me too. That's why I told Jerry that, in the event of something bad happening to me, all the details would be laid before both the British and Swiss police. That's also the reason I'm telling Rachel now, so she knows the whole truth, and what to do with it, if such a situation were to occur.

'Anyway,' she says, propping herself up on one elbow and looking at me, 'don't you *want* to go to the police? Look how much damage that dreadful man has done to you. Surely you want your revenge?'

Do I?

Part of me does, for sure, but it's not that simple.

'Without him causing me mental-health problems, I would never have met you. So perhaps I should be grateful to him.'

She lies back on the pillow with a sigh. 'You're mad.'

I laugh. 'Is that your professional opinion?'

'What did he say when you told him to retire?'

'He said he'd think about it.'

'That'll be a 'no', then,' Rachel says with certainty.

And I'd thought the same when he'd said it. So I'd given him an ultimatum—announce his retirement within a month or I would go to the Swiss police. But I still reckoned he would need some persuading. That's why I'd gone to St John's Wood. 'He might be made to see sense.'

'That's just wishful thinking.'

'Wait and see.'

'Not another half-baked plan.'

I tell her of my visit to see Brenda Fenton, and why I went.

'I was right. You are mad.'

She turns over onto her side and pushes me away.

'Careful,' I say, wincing from a stab of pain from my shoulder.

We lie there in awkward silence for a few minutes.

'But I have made one other half-baked plan you might be interested in.'

She doesn't turn back. 'What's that?'

'I'm finally going to leave the Isle of Wight and return to the real world.'

'Alleluia! And about bloody time too.' She turns back to face me. 'There's a limit to how long a girl will wait, you know.'

'I'm sorry. I just needed space. But now I feel that I've been away long enough.'

'So what's suddenly brought this on?'

'Mostly because I feel I'm better. I'm mentally much stronger. And I am no longer terrified of going backwards.'

She strokes my arm.

'Also, the man that runs the amenities on the beaches on either side of mine has been pestering me for ages to let him take over my pitch and I'll now let him know he can. And he's offered to buy all my equipment.'

'So where will you live?'

'Wherever you are.'

She says nothing but, when I turn my head towards her, she is smiling and there are tears in her eyes.

EPILOGUE

THREE WEEKS LATER, I catch a train from Oxford to London.

I have received an unexpected invitation to have lunch at the Ritz Hotel on Piccadilly.

My shoulder is much improved and I have finally dispensed with the sling, at least for most of the time, even though I tend to wear it in the evenings when my arm still gets sore.

However, that is the least of my worries at the moment.

I am barred from entry to the dining room by the maître d'hôtel.

'Sorry, sir,' he says. 'We have a strict dress code at the Ritz, and you need to be wearing a jacket and tie to come in here.'

'But I've been invited to lunch.'

'Sorry, sir,' he says again. 'You cannot come in dressed like that.' He indicates with disdain towards my open-necked shirt and pullover. 'However, you may borrow a jacket and tie from the cloakroom near the gentleman's lavatories.'

He points back along the Palm Court and I make my embarrassed way to the cloakroom, where there is a whole rack of different-sized jackets waiting, plus a tray full of ties in various colours.

'Please remember to hand them back,' says the attendant with a smile. 'We had a cabinet minister here last week and he took his borrowed tie away with him.' He *tut-tuts* as if it proves that all politicians are untrustworthy.

Now suitably attired, I make my way back to the maître d', who smiles in satisfaction.

'Now, sir,' he says. 'What name?'

'I'm joining Mrs Brenda Fenton.'

'Ah, yes. Her other two guests are here already.'

Other two guests? I had rather hoped the terrible twins wouldn't be with her. I might not have accepted otherwise. As it is, I'm confused as to why I've been invited in the first place—or why I've come.

'This way, sir,' says the maître d', setting off with me following behind.

With its sparkling chandeliers, towering marble columns, exotic drapes and soaring floor-to-ceiling windows overlooking Green Park, the Ritz Hotel restaurant is rightly considered to be one of the most beautiful dining rooms in the world, and I am led to a square table for four at one end, close to a whole wall of mirrors.

Brenda sees me coming and waves but, to my surprise, it is not her grandsons who are sitting with her, it is Susi Ashcroft plus another tall, slim woman with shoulder-length blonde hair, elegantly dressed in a pink suit with a matching printed pink chiffon scarf draped over one shoulder, drop pearl earrings and a double row of pearls tight around her neck.

'Hello, Miles,' Susi says, offering her cheek up for a kiss.

'Hello, Mummy,' I reply, much to her amusement.

Now Brenda and the other woman are the ones confused.

'Well,' I say, sitting down with my back to the mirrors, opposite the lady in pink, 'the world today is certainly full of surprises.'

'What sort of surprises?' Brenda asks.

'For me to be invited here in the first place is one huge surprise, and then to find you two ladies,' I indicate towards Brenda and Susi, 'sitting here happily together at the same table rather than scratching each other's eyes out is another.'

The two women briefly look at each other and smile as if there has been some scheming between them.

'Are you here to act as the referee?' I ask the third one.

'I'm so sorry,' Brenda says. 'How rude of me. Can I introduce Christine St George? Christine, this is Miles Pussett.'

I stand up and reach across the table to shake her offered hand.

'Christine has been a friend of both of ours for years,' Brenda says.

'That must have been difficult,' I say, still smiling at her.

She laughs with a loud, high-pitched guffaw. 'They told me you could be blunt.'

A waiter arrives. 'Would you also like a Ritz Cocktail, sir?'

I glance around the table and the three ladies already each have a large martini glass in front of them containing a yellow liquid.

'What's in it?' I ask.

'Cognac, maraschino and orange triple sec liqueurs, plus a little freshly squeezed lemon juice, all topped up with Champagne.'

The combination sounds absolutely delicious, and how lovely they look with neat twists of orange zest resting on the rims.

'Just sparkling water for me, please,' I say. 'I'm driving.'
Even though I'm not.

I may be getting better, but I'm not yet that well.

'So why am I here?' I ask.

'I wanted to thank you,' Brenda says.

'For what?'

'For opening my eyes to what's important in life.'

I wonder if, in fact, I should be thanking her for opening mine to the same thing.

If her horse, Cliveden Proposal, hadn't run at White Turf, if Susi's horse hadn't won that race, and if Jerry hadn't been trying to cheat the system, I would never have worked out that my own sense of inadequacy and failure, so debilitating over so many years, wasn't as a consequence of my own ability, or the lack of it.

Since my return from St Moritz, I've felt free. Free of the burden I have carried like a millstone for so long. I feel alive once more, no longer suffering from self-doubt and overwhelming guilt. Not forever looking inward at my shortcomings but outward towards a happy future I can enjoy with Rachel. Indeed, we have already moved into a rented flat together in Oxford and we have hopes of soon finding a place to buy.

The deal with my neighbour on the Isle of Wight is done and I have his money in the bank, and half a farm to look forward to . . . maybe all of it.

I haven't yet worked out what I will do for a living, but even that isn't causing me any anxiety. I've decided that, first, I'll spend some time completing my education, getting some qualifications, maybe even going on to university.

I feel the world is now my oyster, with Rachel as its pearl.

Brenda puts her hand on my arm.

'With Christine's help,' she says, smiling at her friend, 'Susi and I have been talking. She is now fully aware of everything that you told me three weeks ago about White Turf. We have decided that, in future, our horses, both hers and mine, shall be owned by us both jointly. So that we can enjoy their success, or otherwise, together, as friends.'

'Yes,' says Susi, 'and we also told Jerry Dickinson last week that we are sending them all to another trainer.'

'Which one?'

'David Maitland-Butler.'

The colonel. The bully.

I laugh. Do they really expect to be treated any differently by him? Probably not, but it's their money, and it is not for me to say anything. Not now.

'Have you seen this?' Brenda asks.

'What is it?'

'A cutting from last Friday's *Racing Post*.'

I haven't. I don't buy that publication any more.

She hands it over.

'DICKINSON TO RETIRE,' states the headline. 'Top trainer Jerry Dickinson made a surprise announcement last night that he will retire from all racing activity at the end of the current jump season in April. Dickinson, 62, who has won almost every major steeplechase honour in the sport, together with many on the flat, told reporters that he had fulfilled all his ambitions and it was now time to take life a little easier and spend more time with his wife. It is our opinion that he will have no difficulty whatsoever in finding someone to take over his highly successful Lambourn training operation.'

I hand it back.

'And that's not all,' Brenda says.

She hands me another cutting, this time from this morning's *Daily Mail*.

'RACEHORSE TRAINER ASSAULTED AGAIN,' reads this headline. 'Jerry Dickinson, who announced only last week that he is retiring from the sport of horseracing, was assaulted in Lambourn late last evening, and for the second time in a month after being previously mugged in Switzerland in mid-February. This time he was attacked by two as-yet unidentified assailants as he walked along the path between his stable yard and his home, in what appears to have been an attempt to steal his mobile phone. In the end, nothing was taken, but Dickinson was badly bruised and he had his right shoulder dislocated during the incident.'

So Jerry had been attacked even after he had announced his retirement.

I smile at Brenda and hand back the cutting.

'Thank you.'

A dislocated shoulder!

Revenge is sweet.

My recovery is now complete, or at least as complete as it ever will be.